NOTHING BUT A RAKEHELL

DEB MARLOWE

To Tammy
for sharing information, laughs and secrets
and for being a quiet, necessary cheerleader

and with many thanks to
Ruth Atkinson, who suggested Poppy's name
and to
Lori Meehan, for her suggestion to name the tavern the Crown and Cock

CHAPTER 1

Colm Newland, Lord Keswick, stood up from the card table—and promptly swayed on his feet.

"Well, damn, Kes, but you've gone bosky." The Earl of Chester frowned up at him.

Keswick blinked.

"Nonsense," Lord Whiddon objected. "He's just a trifle disguised, at best."

Keswick left off staring at his friends and frowned down at the cards he'd left on the table. He'd stood up with a purpose. What had he meant to do?

"I think we're all sunk beneath the mahogany," Mr. Barrett Sterne declared. "But perhaps only a few inches."

"No. Keswick's bosky," Chester insisted. "Completely bosky. Damned if I ain't, too."

"Don't know what else you'd expect," Keswick finally spoke up. "Dayle keeps a damned fine cellar. And he's not too stingy to share it, either."

He frowned—and his stomach rumbled. Oh, yes. That's what he'd meant to do. Pillage the buffet table. A bit of food would be the just the thing to soak up some of Dayle's excellent wine. "I'll bring back enough for the lot of us."

"Be careful out there," warned Sterne. He gestured toward the door, through which music and laughter drifted.

"Aye. I saw the Vernon girl eying you the same way Chester does a fine chop at Lapwell's." Whiddon laughed loudly at his own joke.

"A chop does sound just the thing," Chester mused. "Or perhaps a nice, thick beefsteak."

"Perhaps we should all go with you, Kes," Sterne offered. "The debutantes are thick out there and the wine is sure to have dulled your reflexes."

"Nonsense!" Keswick took offense. "My reflexes are more than—"

He winced as a coin bounced off of his forehead.

"See?" Chester announced in triumph. "Bosky!"

Keswick gathered up the shards of his dignity. He would show them. He turned and made his way out of the card room, growing steadier with each step. Perfectly normal. He turned toward the ballroom—

"Oof!"

He collided full on with someone emerging into the passage from another room. Flailing, he reached out for support and found himself gripping a thin shoulder.

"Lord Keswick!"

It was Miss Vernon's shoulder and her shrill gasp ringing in his ear.

He let go at once, and made his apology, but the girl looked triumphant instead of scandalized. Instantly wary, he bowed and turned to leave. "An accident. Again, I offer my apologies. Please, do excuse me."

But the girl reached out and grasped his arm. "I will forgive you only if you will dance with me, my lord."

Still a little befuddled, Keswick worked desperately to scrape his wits together. He'd seen the predatory look in this girl's eye. Lord knew, it had to be noticeable for Whiddon to have remarked upon it. The last thing he needed was to engage her in this . . . condition.

"Alas, that's a pleasure that must be delayed, Miss Vernon. I am on a mission and cannot indulge myself."

"Surely you can postpone your errand for a short time, sir. Just long enough for a stroll on the patio, perhaps?"

He saw her glance toward the room she'd just left. Following her gaze he saw her particular friend, Miss McNamara, give her a slight nod.

It smacked of conspiracy and sent a surge of clarity up his spine and into his brain. "Alas, it is an urgent matter." Carefully, he disengaged his arm. "Another time, I hope." Stepping away, he moved into the ballroom. A glance over his shoulder showed the two girls whispering and turning to follow him.

Exasperation stiffened his posture. For a moment, he was tempted to scold her for the relentless flirt she was—but he'd had a substantial amount to drink and she was sober and on the prowl. He couldn't risk her and her friend maneuvering him into a compromising position and forcing his hand. He cast about the crowded room, but the only exit he could see was across the dance floor and onto the patio. Too dangerous by half.

He moved through the room, squeezing through the throng. They followed in his wake.

Ah, salvation ahead, in the delectable form of Chester's former mistress. She was a merry widow with notably lax morals and an infamously generous bosom. Keswick bowed low over it and grinned up at her. "Save me, my dear, and I'll owe you a favor?"

She looked over his shoulder, then raised a brow at him. "Don't you already owe me five guineas, Keswick?"

"Waltz me away from the determined virgin and I'll double it," he vowed. He held out his hand and she took it. They both ignored the protest of the gentleman she'd been talking with.

Keswick pulled her closer than was strictly necessary and swept her onto the dance floor. Her bosom bridged the gap between them and rubbed against his waistcoat. She looked down. "I should charge you extra," she told him as the flow of the dance took them around to the other side of the room.

"Worth it," he said with a laugh.

"She's circling around after us," his partner reported. "Gracious, she's a dogged one, isn't she?"

"In the most disagreeably Machiavellian manner," he agreed. "Which is why I am going to abandon you once we reach the next corner. The crowd should prevent her from seeing us clearly."

"I'll expect your payment tomorrow, Keswick," she warned.

"You shall have it." He maneuvered them so that several other couples danced between them and his pursuers, then pulled his partner abruptly off of the dance floor, bent low over her hand, and as she turned away, he used her as cover and slipped behind a thick pedestal set in the corner of the room and surrounded by lush greenery and flowers. Glancing about to be sure no one watched, he ducked down and sat, back propped against the stone, legs tucked up.

Several long moments passed while he breathed deeply. His head still spun a bit. He tipped it back to rest against the pedestal. Behind him, the ball whirled on, but he'd found an oasis of peace. He allowed it to settle into him—until he heard Miss Vernon's sharp whisper.

"Where has he gone? He cannot have disappeared into thin air."

Damnation, they were right behind him.

"Perhaps he went outside and around the house to call his carriage," Miss McNamara suggested with a sigh. "I don't know why you are pursuing him so vigorously, at any rate. My mama says that Lord Keswick is nothing but a rakehell."

"I'd chase him around the house for the sake of that square jaw alone, but despite his rakish ways, he has many desirable qualities."

"Yes. Tens of thousands of them a year, or so I hear. But really, Alice, could you not find someone as rich, but more . . . manageable?"

"Perhaps I could, but you have snapped up the last titled gentleman of the Season who is both doting and doddering," Miss Vernon retorted. "You will be a widow soon enough after you are a bride. If I have to take on a younger man, then I want one who looks like that."

Keswick rolled his eyes.

"You will have to behave," Miss McNamara warned. "At least until you give him an heir."

"Yes, and it would be so with any titled nobleman. I might as well enjoy what I can of it. But once the succession is assured . . ." she let her words trail away.

"Well, Keswick is unlikely to settle down, despite his marriage vows."

He bristled. Really! The pair of brazen hussies assumed too much. He would never don a leg shackle. Once he'd finally aged out of his father's pernicious grip on him, he'd vowed he'd never let anyone hold sway over him again. Particularly not a manipulative jade like this one.

"Of course he won't. His taste for ladies of low virtue is legendary," Miss Vernon declared. "But it will only mean that he'll have no room to reprove me if I have my own . . . fun."

"I suppose not," her friend agreed. "But you'll have to catch him, first."

"Let's slip outside, as well," Miss Vernon suggested. "I have an idea."

The young ladies wandered off and Keswick let his head drop down onto his knees. What a ghastly girl. He must avoid her completely during the rest of the Season.

The thought exhausted him. Truth to tell, he was already tired. *Always* tired, he should say. Tired of the frenzy of the Season, tired of aimless pleasure-seeking that steadily felt less pleasurable, tired of the same faces day in and out. Except for his friends, of course. He never wearied of them and their unfailing loyalty. He was . . . just . . . so . . . tired.

"Keswick!" someone said in a harsh whisper.

He jerked awake, scrambling away from the pedestal. How long had he been asleep?

"There you are." Sterne peered down at him through the foliage.

"Oh, hell and damnation, Sterne. You scared me. I thought you were *her*."

"Her?" Sterne's brow lifted. "Oh. The Vernon girl caught you?"

"Nearly."

"Well, you've been gone an age. We couldn't find you anywhere.

Then I remembered the time we played faro all night—and couldn't find you in the morning. Eventually we found you curled up asleep behind the ferns."

"I had to hide," Keswick told Sterne, taking his hand and rising to his feet. "Too much wine sloshing about in my brainbox—and the girl has set her sights on me. She thinks I'll turn the other way and let her have her *fun* after we marry."

"Good heavens," Sterne grimaced. "That McNamara girl has surely been influencing her. You need to keep away from them both, then. Come on, now, though. The ball is winding down. It should be safe. There's been no sign of her while I've been looking for you."

"Where's the rest of the lot?"

"Gone off to Lapwell's. Chester's had a bee in his bonnet since someone mentioned chops. I said we'd come after them. You brought your carriage tonight, did you not?"

"Aye. I'll ask for it to be brought around."

"You know," Sterne mused as they left the house. "It might be a good idea for you to leave London for a bit. Give that Vernon girl a chance to set her sights elsewhere." They strode down to the street as Keswick's carriage drew closer in the line.

"What? You want me to allow that chit to run me out of Town?" He recoiled, as he always did when he thought of leaving London to return home. "I only need to avoid her. I'll just stay away from the events of the Marriage Mart. There is still plenty else to get up to."

Sterne, sterling friend that he was, understood his reluctance. "No, I don't mean you'd have to go back to Devonshire. Don't forget, Tensford has invited us all to his house party towards the end of the Season. I'd wager he wouldn't mind if you head down early. I've half a mind to go with you."

Keswick was shaking his head as his carriage rolled up. A footman opened the door and Keswick stepped up—and froze, halfway in.

Miss Vernon lolled inside, one shoulder of her gown pulled low. "Lord Keswick," she said with a smile.

He sank back onto the pavement as Sterne peered over his shoulder. "What's the delay?"

The girl's smile faded. "Mr. Sterne." Sitting up, she straightened her frock. "Goodness. Whatever are you gentlemen doing, climbing into Miss McNamara's carriage?"

Wordlessly, Keswick took the door from the gaping footman's hand. He closed it and eyed his family crest with a raised brow, then looked at Sterne.

"Where is Miss McNamara?" the girl asked, her tone growing shrill.

The coachman, craning his neck at the delay, heard her voice come from within and blanched white. "I'm sorry, my lord! I had no idea!"

Keswick stepped away from the carriage. "It's all right, Dobbs. Take the lady home. Berkely Square, I believe." He turned to Sterne. "So, Tensford's place. We are for Gloucestershire, then, are we?"

* * *

Lady Glory Brightley kept a forced smile fixed firmly in place. Her ankle felt as if it were on fire, but she took Mr. Thorpe's right hand and circled with him, keeping time with the music. She winced as she twirled to take his left hand and circle again, in the other direction.

"Relax your features, Miss Brightley," Mr. Thorpe implored. "You must at least give the impression that you are enjoying yourself."

She'd like to see how much he enjoyed dancing while lightning bolts of pain shot up his leg, but she gritted her teeth and continued. All went well for several minutes until, hands joined with Mr. Thorpe and her sister Hope, she moved forward—then forgot to fall back the required steps. Losing her balance, she stepped wrongly with her weak leg and tumbled to the floor.

Her face flamed as her sister and Miss Penelope Munroe, who made the fourth in their set, scrambled to help her up.

"Oh, dear," Mr. Thorpe fretted. "I had so hoped that this dance was the one. Mr. Beveridge's Maggot is slow and stately." He frowned, thinking. "The Shrewsbury Lasses will not do—all of that skipping around! But I thought this might be the dance for you, Miss Brightley."

"It's just the turnings that are difficult, sir. My ankle . . ." She let the words trail away. If there was anything she hated more than showing weakness, it was making excuses.

"Oh, but turning *is* dancing," Mr. Thorpe began.

Hope cut him off. "I think you are quite right about this dance," she told him. "It is stately and less demanding than so many of them." She turned to Glory. "And you made it so far into the dance, darling. With practice, I'm sure you'll improve even further."

Hope gave her a squeeze. "I do think you are quite right and extra-ordinarily brave to take on this challenge. When the gentlemen are flocking to you in London, you'll be glad of the chance to be able to dance at least a little, with the man of your choosing."

"Just think of it as another weapon to add to your arsenal," Miss Munroe said cheerfully. "Although you are altogether well-armed, one more arrow in your quiver won't hurt."

Nodding, Glory moved toward the window. Miss Munroe was a perfectly nice young lady, a girl of good family and fortune from an estate near to this, her sister's new home of Greystone Park. Glory knew that Hope had invited the girl to tea and to share in the dancing lessons in the hopes that Glory would befriend her. They were of similar age and would both likely be making their debuts in London next year.

Glory did, in fact, like the girl. Miss Munroe had been accepting and matter-of-fact about Glory's . . . differences. Not one prying question, mocking remark or pitying glance at her limp. An unusually benign reaction, and one which Glory appreciated. She did like the young lady, truly. But . . .

The breeze from the open window beckoned. The sun shone and Greystone's parks, farms and forests waited to be explored.

"Thank you, both," she said, summoning a smile. "And you, Mr. Thorpe. I hope I will do better tomorrow, but for now, I think I should rest my ankle."

She heard her sister sigh as she exited, but she kept going, and in less than half an hour she was changed into her riding habit and in the stables, allowing a groom to assist her into her specially-constructed saddle. She'd been at Greystone long enough to have won the battle about riding out alone, so she was soon heaving a massive sigh of relief as she cantered away from the house.

She went first past the little experimental field of lavender. The young plants her sister had nourished grew lushly grey-green and healthy. Once past, she headed toward the river, following the established road through the crop lands. They were busy with men tending barley and corn, now that her brother-in-law had money for seed once more. She urged her mare, Poppy, to a run along the familiar path, feeling unfettered and happy and free as she only ever did in the saddle. The pain in her ankle had faded. Her leg, hooked around the modified pommel and supported in the special cradle built into her saddle, no longer ached.

Here she was not slow and awkward. Astride Poppy, she was just like everyone else—the equal of anyone—with a better seat than most.

She breathed a happy sigh and urged the mare onto the fork in the road that led higher, toward the forests.

The woods here were ancient, dark and mysterious. They had nothing so old and untouched in Sussex, at her family's estate. She and Poppy went slowly, exploring the shadows and the sun-dappled open spots, the downed trees lined with moss and the ridges of limestone rising unexpectedly from the forest floor.

They intersected a faint path that Glory recognized. Following it, they emerged onto an irregular field. It was one of her favorite spots. Smaller than most of the fields that bordered the river, Tensford told her that it had been cleared by hand, long ago and carved from the forest by tools more primitive than the ones used now. He'd said that he hadn't planted it this season because he planned to fertilize it, but she rather suspected he'd left it because it was so beautiful.

Covered in high grasses and clumps of wildflowers, it whispered with the music of peace and birdsong and the buzz of insects. Butterflies danced from bloom to bloom and a slight breeze called her. Awed as always, she pulled Poppy to a halt and drank in the loveliness.

Gradually, Poppy began to move down the meadow, cropping the lower grasses at the edge. The border higher up was irregular and forested, but Glory knew at the bottom quarter the boundary transitioned to a thick hedge that separated the field from a swampy drainage area. They were rounding a protruding copse of elms, nearly to the hedge, when Poppy's ears swiveled forward, listening.

Glory paused, and listened as well. Nothing disturbed the peace of the place for several long moments. Then she heard a clear snort and the jingle of harness.

On alert, she urged her mare ahead. Coming around the copse, they found a rider-less horse, reins tangled in the branches of the hedge. It was a chestnut gelding, average of stature and bloodline, she judged with a knowing eye. Not one of Tensford's. A job horse, she would guess. Hired out of an inn or livery. She could see no sign of its rider.

"Is anyone there?" she called.

Nothing.

She waited. Called again. Waited a few minutes longer.

Feeling foolish, she debated what to do, but with a shrug, she loosened the entangled reins and led the horse on down toward the bottom of the field and the path that would lead home.

This time, she and Poppy caught the sound at the same time. A voice. Male.

She paused to listen.

A single voice. No pause for conversation with another, just one man droning on. From the other side of the hedge.

She frowned. She could have sworn there was nothing on the other side of that hedge but a murky, marshy bog, a low place that acted as a natural collection of field drainage.

The droning continued, and so did she, reaching the corner of the field and the worn path. She followed it a bit, still leading the gelding and trying to decide what to do, as the man's monologue grew fainter.

She didn't want to meet anyone out here, after all. She should just go on, return to Greystone and send someone back to investigate.

But then the voice fell suddenly silent and alarm quickened her pulse. Had the man fallen into the water? Passed out? Or just moved on? Curiosity won out over caution and inclination. She looped the gelding's reins over a branch and urged Poppy higher and to the right and into a newly planted barley field. If they wandered back the other way, keeping to the furrows, they could approach the marshy spot from the other side.

She held Poppy back, watching the ground as the cultivation gave way to undergrowth. Advancing slowly, they made their way to the edge of the murky bog. "Is anyone there?"

"Marooned!" The man's voice sounded suddenly loud and it came from *within* the marsh. Moving closer, she scanned the dark water.

"Reefed!"

At last she spotted him. He was so covered in brown muck he was barely discernible, but he was up to his waist in the stuff, a good distance away, nearer to the hedge that separated the spot from the meadow on the other side.

"Yes, I've forgotten to explore the nautical terms. Stranded—no, I've used that already." His eyes were closed and he swayed a bit, but the water was so thick with mud at that spot, it barely rippled around him. "Foundered! Wrecked!"

Glory cleared her throat. "Excuse me?"

His eyes flew open and he turned his head toward her. "Grounded?" he asked.

She pursed her lips and paused a moment. "Swamped," she said wryly.

"Yes!" He smiled in delight and his teeth looked very white against the mud spattering his face. "Perfect!

CHAPTER 2

Keswick stared across the expanse of murky water. From this distance he could only surmise that his savior looked and sounded young. She sat straight in the saddle, certainly, as she waved a hand.

"Now that you have satisfactorily labeled your situation, are you going to come out of it?" she called.

"If it were possible, then so I would," he told her. "But I'm sunk in a good eight inches of sucking mud at the bottom of this. I cannot move my legs forward or backward at all, and if I bend my knee and lift straight up, then the mud grips my boots tighter than my Irish granny squeezes a penny—and that's saying something."

She said nothing, merely waited.

He frowned. "I cannot abandon my boots!" It did not bear thinking of.

"I'm not overly familiar with the local village, but I feel sure it must boast a cobbler's shop."

"These are my *favorite* boots," he explained. "They were made by Hoby himself. They've been re-soled twice already by that same craftsman." He wouldn't budge on this. There were damned few things allowed any permanence in his life. His boots—after his friends —were something for which he allowed himself an attachment.

"Very well, then." She shrugged. "I hope you and your boots are very happy together in your new abode." She gathered up her reins.

"No! Wait! The track that leads to Greystone Park is nearby, is it not? Could you not just ride there and send back help?"

"I'm not sure anyone is getting both you and your boots out," she said skeptically—and then she made a face. "And what are the odds that you won't just fall straight back in?"

"Why would I . . ?" He flushed suddenly. "Oh. You are mistaken. I am not inebriated. I didn't land in here because I've had too much drink."

"Then, *how?*" she asked with another wave of her hand.

"It was my horse, if you must know. I'd taken the long route, through the forest. I've never traveled in this part of the country, you see, and I've never seen wooded areas like this."

"They are magnificent," she conceded.

"As is the meadow on the other side of this hedge. I stopped there." He hesitated to admit that he'd had to stop, to drink in the mystical beauty of the place.

"I know," she said with a nod.

He wiped mud from under one eye, where it had begun to itch. "Well, then, you'll understand why I stayed. I stretched out to enjoy the peace of it, and while my mount was contentedly cropping grass at my side, a bee or a stinging fly must have crawled in under the saddle. When I mounted up and settled in, the horse flinched and jumped—and went wild. After diving and dancing about, he stretched out and raced for the hedge. I'd seen the barley field rising in the distance beyond it and thought I could hold on and make the jump."

She was trying not to grin. He appreciated the effort.

"Your mount balked, I take it? I found him, reins tangled in the hedge."

"He stopped at the hedge, but I went over, only to find it wasn't barley on the other side."

"And once in the bog, you proceeded to recite your mental dictionary of terms describing your predicament." Even from here, he could see her raised brow.

"I did. I knew the path to Greystone lay not far from here. No one passing in normal fashion would think to look for a traveler stuck here—unless they heard him and came to investigate." He returned the raised brow. "And it worked, did it not?"

"I'll give you that."

"Thank you. Now, if you'll just run and fetch some men to pull me out of here? I just need some leverage and a pull. A rope and a couple of strong backs should do it."

"No need." She bent and he couldn't quite see what she was doing, but she came up with a coil of rope in hand.

He stared, confounded.

She tied an end around her pommel and then lifted her chin toward him. "Your hands are free, are they not?"

"They arc."

"Then, catch." She tossed him the other end. A very neat throw it was too, landing in the muck just before him. He grabbed it up.

"Now, hold on. Or better yet, tie it about you."

He did, looping it about his chest.

Bending low, she whispered something to her mount. The horse began to back away.

Keswick held on tight, though he'd lost one of his gloves in the fall and his hand slipped in the mud. Leaning back against the pull of the rope, he used it as leverage and dug his heels in. Pointing the toes of his right foot upward, he leaned back and strained with the muscles of thigh and shin, fighting against the hold of the mud.

Her horse sank back, keeping the rope taut and the pull steady.

There. A bit of wiggle room. He kept it up and after a moment, his booted foot broke free.

"That's one!" he exclaimed.

The second came about rather more awkwardly. He took a closer grip on the rope and leaned even more heavily against it, trying to pull his second foot out without digging the first one back in. It took longer, with more strain and more wiggling, but eventually, it popped out too.

"That's both, then?" she asked as he flailed and fought not to go under.

"Yes. Can your mount back further up and pull me out?"

"Of course."

He let the horse and the rope do most of the work until he drew close to the bank and the bottom firmed up. Clambering out, he bent over his boots, scraping mud away and assessing the damage. It was bad, but salvageable. A good cleaning with water and vinegar, a couple of days to dry and a thorough oiling with his special mix of tallow and neat's foot oil should do the trick.

And then he looked up—and forgot about his boots entirely.

"Thank you . . ." He'd already begun, but the words faded and stalled. "How *old* are you?" he asked suddenly, instead. She looked like a girl—an uncommonly pretty girl with fiery coloring.

"Nineteen years, nearly twenty," she replied as she untied the rope from her pommel and began to coil it up again. She gave him a sharp look. "How old are you?"

Not the polite answer, but the one he deserved, no doubt. "Six and twenty," he answered absently. "You are terrifyingly competent," he said as she tugged at the rope, waiting for him to release it.

More than uncommonly pretty, he thought, as he worked to free himself. And yes, that was the right word to pull from his mental dictionary, as she had worded it. For her looks were not in the common way at all. Her eyes were deeply set and slightly slanted and just the dark, amber color of good, old French cognac. His glance bounced between her other attention-catching features--wide cheek-bones and a pointed chin and rich, auburn hair curling beneath a military styled hat.

"Forgive me," he said, shaking his head in an attempt to clear it. "My manners are inexcusable. But seeing as there is no one to make the introductions and given the bizarre nature of our situation, perhaps you will forgive me." He sketched a bow. "I am Colm Newland, Viscount Keswick."

"Ah, yes," she said with a faint twist of a grin in his direction. She turned to fold back the long edge of her skirt and tuck the rope into an oddly shaped and positioned saddlebag. "I recognize your name. I heard—"

"That I am a rakehell?" he interrupted bitterly. "A dangerous flirt? To be avoided at all costs?" Usually it was a relief when his reputation preceded him. It saved him from having to do something to establish it again. But this time—he felt a surprising stab of disappointment.

"I heard," she said deliberately, "that you were coming early to stay at Greystone Park before the house party."

"Oh." He pushed back a surge of embarrassment. "I apologize. My manners are truly atrocious today."

She shrugged. "Easily forgiven—if you will but promise to do the same for me. I am forever saying the wrong thing or asking the wrong question, so your turn to be gracious will undoubtedly come soon enough."

"You are very kind, Miss . . .?"

"*Lady*," she corrected. "Lady Glory Brightley."

"Ah, sister to Tensford's new wife, then?"

She nodded.

"I'm astonished that they've let you go out riding on your own," he remarked. "Grateful, but astonished. Is that the usual thing for young ladies, these days?"

Her generous, pink lips tightened. "No. It is not."

"Well, then, I must be thankful that you are an unusual young lady. And may I add that I am also grateful for your unusual mare? That was a fine trick, and she's a beauty, besides."

The girl's manner thawed instantly. "Isn't she?" She stroked the high arch of the mare's neck and her whole face softened into a warm expression of affection that made her look utterly . . . likeable. And like he wanted her to look at him in such a way. "Poppy is a wonderful friend. She has many useful skills."

"All of which must have taken a good deal of patient training, if they are of a similar nature. I commend you."

"All gallantries must be given to her. Poppy is willing and eager, which makes everything easier."

"Then you are as lucky in your friend, as I am in my new acquaintance."

"Don't." She'd stiffened up again, sat back and gathered up her reins. "Please."

"Don't . . . what?" he asked, perplexed.

"That. Whatever it is that you do . . . that you are known for. Dangerous flirtation? Is that what you called it? I'm not that sort of girl."

He stilled, suddenly wild with curiosity—and when was the last time anything had made him feel that way? "What sort of girl are you, then?"

"The sort who is leaving." The mare spun around and Lady Glory looked back over her shoulder. "You'll find your mount tethered on the path to Greystone." She gestured with her chin. "Just that way, and past the edge of the field."

"Wait, you will not return to Greystone with me?"

"No." She didn't offer further explanation, just set off, leaving the bog behind and heading up the edge of the field, away from his destination. "Good luck with your boots," she called.

* * *

GLORY RODE ON, flustered by the encounter.

Once she was safely away, she stopped and dismounted. She toyed with her whip a bit, practicing her aim by setting pinecones along a low branch and flicking them off.

She didn't meet many new people. As few as her sister would let her get away with, as a general rule. She'd known things would be different when she came to stay here with Hope. And she was so glad she had made the move. Life at home had changed since her brother, the Earl of Kincade, had married. Matthew was tolerable as elder brothers go, but his wife . . . She sighed. Catherine was pushy, overprotective of her authority and obviously horrified at the idea of sheltering her husband's lame sister for the rest of her life.

Whereas Hope had always been Glory's rock, her support—and also the one to push her out of her comfortable isolation. So she'd known she had to prepare herself for the approaching house party, but she'd thought she had some time, still. She'd already adjusted to Miss Munroe and the dancing lessons. Bad enough. And now, this . . . gentleman . . . had arrived.

But, perhaps this particular gentleman wouldn't be so bad? She rather thought he would turn out to be handsome. There had been signs of it, beneath the mud spatter. His eyes were a piercing blue and that strong, square jaw was nearly a wonder of human architecture. And the outlandish nature of their meeting—it actually gave her the advantage. She had not been the strange one, for once.

Oh.

All of her small hopes abruptly withered. She tucked the whip away again, unable to focus, and leaned into the comfort of her horse.

She'd been lucky. But his absurd situation and the happy coincidence of meeting him while mounted were just that—luck. All of it a mere fluke. In the drawing room, in the ballroom, in *every* other situation, she would be at the disadvantage. She would still be . . . herself.

Poppy, as always, picked up on her mood and began to toss her head. Glory recalled herself and mounted up and urged her mare on. They explored the edges, where the fields met the forest, for a bit, until both of their nerves were somewhat settled. Then she turned them back toward home. She wanted to be safely ensconced in her rooms before Viscount Keswick had time to emerge from his bath.

She made it unobserved, settling Poppy in her stall and stopping to give Grumpet, the heavily pregnant barn cat, her due. Then she snuck in through the servant's entrance, made it to her room and threw herself into a chair to brood.

Terrifyingly competent. That's what he'd called her. A left-handed compliment, to be sure, but she felt like he'd meant it in an admiring way. And yes, he had remarked on her riding alone—but he'd professed to be grateful and he had said kind words about Poppy.

A knock sounded and her sister's maid entered, intent on helping her dress for dinner. Glory sent her off instead, requesting a tray in her room. She didn't want to see Lord Keswick again. Not yet. Until she had to meet him properly, and see pity—or scorn—bloom when he noticed her limp, she could still hold on to the fleeting feeling of his admiration.

The maid must have run straight to her sister, for Hope came bustling in. "What's this? A tray in your room? Did you injure yourself in that fall today?"

Glory slumped further in her chair. "What? No. I'm just . . . a bit tired."

Her sister sat across from her and raised a skeptical brow. "Or perhaps you've heard that we have a new guest?"

Glory scowled.

Hope leaned in. "Are you hesitant to come down because of something you've heard? About Lord Keswick?"

"No. Not at all." She thought of what he'd said. A rakehell, he'd called himself. "Why? Is there something I should know?"

"He has a bit of a reputation. Or, perhaps more than a bit of one." Hope sighed and met Glory's gaze straight on. "I want you to know, though, that the viscount is William's friend. Despite what others say, William swears that he is harmless and promises that he will never do anything to cause the wrong sort of talk or to make you feel uncomfortable."

"Tell Tensford that I appreciate his thinking of me, but that's not why I want to stay in my rooms this evening."

"Well, then?" Hope asked.

Glory didn't answer.

"Fine," Hope sighed again. "But you must meet him sometime." She brightened suddenly. "I know. William is sure to wish to take his friend about the estate tomorrow. He'll want to show off some of the improvements he's working on. Why do we not ride out with them?"

She grinned. "Then you can get to know the viscount in your natural element."

Glory straightened in her chair. "Yes." It was the perfect idea. "That sounds pleasant." She smiled at her sister. "I'll go."

Hope breathed her relief. "Good. Rest tonight. I'll see you at breakfast."

Glory waved her off. It *was* the perfect idea. She'd already met him out riding once—and it had gone tolerably well. If she could see him again, while mounted . . . she could make a good impression. Couldn't she?

She wouldn't go to breakfast. All she would need to do was to contrive to be in the saddle before the rest of them. They could spend the day riding and Lord Keswick would see her at her best. Her heart pounded. Another day—and he wouldn't know.

Nothing would come of it, to be sure. She didn't even want anything to come of it. He was a London fellow. A fixture in Society. A self-confessed rakehell. He would never be interested in a country girl like her. But for just a day, he might look at her, talk to her, and interact with her as if she were just like everyone else.

She wished Hope was still here so she could kiss her. It was a brilliant idea—and perhaps she could even manage to keep it going. In sudden good spirits, she stood and went to ring for the maid again. A bath before dinner would be the just the thing. She could wash her hair and dry it before a fire as she ate.

For the first time in a long time, she looked forward to tomorrow.

CHAPTER 3

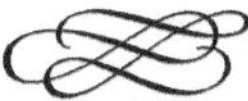

Keswick entered the dining room to find Tensford and his wife there before him. He bid them a good morning and took a seat.

"Good morning, my lord." The countess smiled at him. "Coffee or tea?"

"Tea, please," he said gratefully.

"I hope you slept well?" she asked as she poured.

"I did." Lamentably well. He'd woken more refreshed than he could remember. It had left him with a surfeit of energy and a fervent hope that Tensford could provide something to help dispel it.

Looking around, he wondered if the sister would show herself at last. There was a mystery there, he would guess.

She'd avoided the company last night, keeping to her room. Part of him had felt relieved. He could imagine her telling the story of their meeting with more than a little relish.

Honestly, though, Tensford knew quite a few of the ugly truths of his life—and was still a steadfast friend. Being the butt of the joke would be nothing next to all of that—and he had to admit, he was curious to see the girl again. She was pretty, prickly—and different from any other young lady he'd ever met. She might prove a distraction, though he'd have to tread carefully.

"Our cook has heard of your Irish connections, my lord," Lady Tensford said with a smile. "Since she possesses a few of her own, she thought to plan a surprise for you this morning."

A footman placed a dish before him and drew the cover away with a flourish, revealing his breakfast.

"Thank you," he said reflexively. His stomach rumbled at the sight of the eggs, bacon, mushrooms and . . . "Colcannon!"

He dug into the treat. It had been fried up in patties for breakfast and he bit into the crispy outside and closed his eyes against the familiar taste of creamy potatoes and leafy greens inside. "Mmm . . .Delicious. That does bring back memories. My mother and I used to have special dinners in the nursery—sausages and colcannon and fresh brown bread." He smiled at the countess. "Please pass my compliments and my thanks to your cook."

"She'll be thrilled to have pleased you, sir."

"Eat up, Kes," Tensford ordered. "We have a lot of ground to cover. I have something to show you."

"Let me guess. Fossils? Sterne has already described his fossil hunts with you with great enthusiasm."

"Oh, we'll get to the fossils later, when the rest of the guests arrive. This expedition is more with you in mind. You were always fascinated with pulleys and scaffolding and industrial bits—it will be right up your alley of interest."

His wife tilted her head. "Scaffolding, Lord Keswick?"

He flushed. "Please, call me Kes. All of my friends do."

"Thank you, I will, if you will call me Hope, in return. But what did you find interesting in scaffolding, Kes?"

"He found it useful, more than anything, my dear," Tensford answered, his grin spreading wider. "He grew to be quite skilled at adjusting it for height and configuration—whatever was needed to get him to the window of the girl he was interested in at the time."

"Oh!" Her mouth twisted, though she tried to hide the grin. "How inventive of you, Kes."

"Yes, well. Needs must, my lady."

She laughed outright as she buttered a piece of toast.

"I'm sinking a new coal pit," the earl explained. "I thought you might want a look at it."

His interest perked. That did hold promise. "I would, in fact. I've always heard that much of my mother's family's money came from coal."

Tensford spoke about the new venture and he listened while he ate. After a few minutes the countess broke in.

"My sister and I mean to join you as you ride out today. If you wouldn't mind, that is." The countess smiled. "Glory is an enthusiastic rider."

Now he was even more interested. "By all means." He threw down his napkin.

"I'm not sure why she hasn't come down for breakfast yet. She's usually an early riser."

A footman stepped forward from his spot near the door. "Beg pardon, my lady. Lady Glory set out for the stables some time ago."

"Well, then," Keswick said with enthusiasm. "I thank you for breakfast, Hope. I'm ready to go whenever you two are."

* * *

THE GIRL WASN'T to be found at the stables, either.

"Poppy was feeling her oats this morn, sir," one of the grooms explained. "The young lady took her out to the long field to run some of it off her."

"Very good." Tensford seemed satisfied. "We'll stop for her there. It's on the way, in any case."

Keswick swung up onto his job horse.

"Apologies," his friend said, flushing a bit. "For the lack of depth in our stables. It's one of the things we just haven't had the chance to address, just yet. But no worries for the house party. The local squire is a very good fellow and has agreed to stable a few of his fine steeds here for a couple of weeks. We'll see you properly mounted then."

"This fellow suits me fine, despite our contretemps yesterday. And there's no need to apologize, especially for the knowledgeable grooms in your stables. The poultice your man used appears to have taken all of the sting from this fellow's wound. I can't even tell where he was afflicted, and it doesn't seem to bother him a bit. We'll get along fine, now."

They rode out on the same track he'd come in on yesterday. He held his breath a bit as they passed the spot where the bog lay hidden, but suffered only a quip from Tensford about him bringing the whole thing into the house yesterday. Apparently the girl had not mentioned their meeting. Certainly, he was in no hurry to revisit the story.

They came through a wooded spot to a bridge that deposited them in a large, open area. He could see that the river bent into a wide curve. All of the long space between them and the curve was open field. At the very end of it, looking out over the water, he spotted a figure on horseback.

The earl cupped his hands and called across the distance. The horse and rider turned and at once set out in their direction.

It was her, surely. Who else? He stared as he saw her small figure bend low. The horse responded. They came flying toward them, and he held his breath, unable to look away.

He'd never seen anyone ride like that. The pair of them streamed toward him, moving seamlessly, looking like one creature. Skirt and mane and ribbons and tail trailed as they flew over the earth. Gradually, she sat back and slowed her mount. As they drew closer, he could see her wide, happy grin.

"That was . . ." he stopped, at a loss for further words.

"I know," the countess said smugly.

"She's a magnificent rider," Tensford said with a grin.

It seemed too small a word. "And with a side saddle," he marveled. He watched as she approached.

"Good morning," she called.

She had a marvelous seat. Her mare circled them, blowing slightly, moving with incredible responsiveness to the girl's every movement.

"Show off," her sister said, laughing at her.

"Keswick," the earl said. "I beg leave to present to you, *not* a trick rider from Astley's, if you will believe me, but my sister-in-law, Lady Glory Brightley."

She looked different today. Not as stiff, perhaps. Her hair curled enticingly from beneath a jaunty hat and she wore a stunning riding habit of a dark blue-green that complimented the rich auburn in her hair. He waited to see if she would confess to their first meeting, but she merely sparkled at him, waiting with raised eyebrows.

He suppressed a grin and played along.

"It is a pleasure, indeed, Lady Glory. May I offer you my compliments? That was quite a display the pair of you gave us."

"I'll accept compliments for Poppy all day long, my lord." She tossed a smile toward her sister. "And also for Hope, who was so wonderfully generous as to give her to me."

"I shall endeavor to come up with a full day's worth, then." Looking at the way her skin glowed against the black trim of her coat and her crisp, white linen, he thought he should have no difficulty finding compliments at all.

She laughed. "Not a man to back down from a challenge, then? Excellent! Though I doubt you will have any difficulty, sir. I have it on good authority that you are possessed of a prodigious mental dictionary."

"Glory!" her sister admonished.

"Oh, come now," the girl protested. "It's not as if I asked about his dangerous flirtations."

"Neither did I ask what next display Lady Glory planned for us," he told the countess. "Although I was sorely tempted to suggest riding low and on the side while she collected brass rings. So, you see, we are both on our best behavior."

The minx looked intrigued, not insulted, but her sister threw a hand up. "I give up," she declared. "One of you is as bad as the other."

She urged her mount closer to her husband's. "I'll ride on with William and leave you two to amuse each other as you follow."

"Yes, let's be off," Tensford said. He looked to Lady Glory. "We are going to show Keswick the pit!"

Some of the brightness faded from her expression, but she nodded and urged her mare after the pair of them. Keswick settled his gelding in next to her.

"What's amiss? You don't seem as enthused as Tensford does at the notion of visiting the coal pit."

"No one is as enthusiastic about the coal pit as Tensford," she said wryly. "No, I must correct myself. Mr. Cutler, the new land steward, is also enamored of the project. He says it is a shame that Tensford's father never pursued it. The estate might have been supporting itself for all of these years."

"Ah, but then Tensford might never have come to London last year, in search of a bride." He watched his friend lean, laughing, toward his wife. "He might not have met your sister."

"And that would truly have been a shame," she said softly. "The only thing they love more than plotting or planning some improvement to the estate, is each other."

"Good for them. It doesn't happen often." Or last long, in his experience. But if anyone deserved happiness, it was Tensford. He shook off the darker thoughts trying to barge in. "So, they are passionate about the estate and each other. You are clearly passionate about your lovely mare and . . . anything else, Lady Glory?"

"No. Well, just riding in general, really."

"You are shockingly skilled at it. Is that what makes you love it so?"

"No. Yes." She shrugged. "It's . . . all of it. Flying so fast with the wind in my face. Feeling the perfect three beats when you slide into a canter. A slow, lazy walk on a warm afternoon." She reached down and patted her mare's neck. "It's the freedom, the companionship, the exploration." Glancing askance at him, she asked, "What about you, my lord? You have a decent seat yourself, it seems, despite yesterday's misadventures."

"That could have happened to anyone," he protested.

"True enough. So, why the job horse? You must be the first gentleman of any standing that has not wished to bend my ear, talking of his prime bloodstock."

He laughed.

"Do you not care for horses, then?"

"On the contrary. I love horses—which is why I do not keep my own." She looked like she was going to question him further, so he gave a nod toward the couple ahead. "Grace and good nature—there's a compliment for your sister. She seems to embody both."

"That's an easy one," she scoffed. "Everyone who is around Hope for more than a minute loves her."

"Everyone?"

"Everyone," she said firmly. "It's impossible not to love her. She is wonderful in at least a thousand ways."

"Good," he said with a smile. "Tensford deserves no less. And I look forward to getting to know her." He pursed his lips. "The house party, though. How early have I arrived?"

"More guests should begin to arrive at the end of the week."

She didn't look enthusiastic about that either—not that he blamed her. "Tell me, I haven't seen Tensford's mother about. Is she no longer staying here?"

"No. She and his aunt have a house on the other side of Brockweir." It sounded like there was more to that story that she wasn't telling.

"Will she be attending the party, do you know?"

"She's invited." She hesitated. "Whether or not she will attend has been a matter of debate and speculation, all across the estate."

"And does the dowager countess love your sister, as everyone else does?"

"Not at first." Her tone was dry. "But she quickly became reconciled to the situation."

"Ah, yes. I'll wager it only took an accounting of your sister's dowry."

She glanced at him. "I take it you are acquainted with the dowager?"

"Oh, yes," he said cheerfully. "She quite despises me."

She gave a startled laugh and then a look of commiseration. "She's not so fond of me, either."

"Well, all to the good then. I had a suspicion that we would get along. Now I know it to be true." He looked ahead, where Tensford and his countess were pulling away. "Let's catch them up, shall we?" He urged his horse into a trot. "I might enjoy being on the dowager's bad side, but I wish to stay firmly in your sister's good graces."

* * *

GLORY FOLLOWED in the viscount's wake as the trail they followed grew steeper and more narrow. She bit back a grin. It was working. He thought she was just like everyone else. They'd talked and even laughed and shared teasing bits of banter. She rather thought he might like her.

She drank it in. Not an ounce of pity or concern for her fragility, or worse—outright dismissal. All afternoon she'd tasted not a hint of bitterness at being labeled less than everyone else.

Oh, but why must Tensford take them up to the coal pit? Everyone would dismount and peer down into it and they would probably wish to go down and explore the depths of it.

She sighed. She wasn't ready yet, to see the change in the way Keswick looked at her.

Tensford's men had cut a circuitous roadway around to the crest of the hill. Poppy put her head down and climbed gamely, but Glory held her back, allowing the others to reach the summit ahead of them.

Good. The others were already dismounted when they crested the hill. Hope was standing at the edge of the large excavation, talking to the foreman. Tensford and Keswick stood at the whim, while the earl explained how the horse-driven engine of pulleys and gears ran the buckets down into the pit and back up.

Hope beckoned her over, but Glory kept Poppy to a slow walk. "I think she's picked up a stone," she called. "I'm going to check it out."

Her sister nodded. The men never turned away from their conversation. Perfect. Glory rode to the far end of the hilltop, where a copse of trees provided some shade and a bit of cover. Carefully watching to be sure the viscount was occupied, she used a downed elm to help her dismount and made a show of examining Poppy's hooves.

The men were soon descending into the pit, excited voices echoing back up as they disappeared over the edge. Glory pulled a book from her saddle bag and settled onto the dead tree.

Hope stood at the edge and looked out over the valley for a while, then wandered over and sat next to her in the shade.

"Not going down this time?" Glory asked.

"Once was enough." Hope shuddered. "It took me days to get clean again." She raised a brow. "You've not been down. Are you not tempted to go down with them?"

"Not at all," she said vehemently.

"Prepared, did you?" Her sister glanced at the book.

"Always."

"Well, put it away for a moment and tell me what you think of Lord Keswick."

"Why?" She closed the book. "He is your guest. I should think it matters what you think of him, not me."

"Well, I find I quite like him." Hope sounded surprised.

"He's amusing, I'll give you that. Quick." He'd been quick to change the subject of conversation when he wished, too, she'd noted. She tilted her head at her sister. "You'll never guess who does *not* like him," she teased.

"Who?"

"Tensford's mama."

Hope blinked. "He told you so?"

"Yes—and he thought better of me when I told him I'd earned her disapproval, as well."

"Well, now I know I like him."

They both laughed.

"You seemed comfortable with him," Hope said tentatively. "I was thinking, perhaps we could invite him to the dancing lessons, to—"

"No."

"But, it might give you a chance to practice with a real gentleman—"

"No." She said it flatly. With a tone of utter finality. "If you even tell him about the lessons, I will quit them."

"Glory—"

"No, Hope!" Her skin crawled at the thought of stumbling and lurching around the handsome viscount.

"Very well." Her sister sighed. "I did want to thank you for allowing me to include Miss Munroe, though. The poor girl could use some companionship. Her mother is a bit of a . . . an eccentric, shall we say. She does not like people about. I think the girl is often lonely."

"Miss Munroe seems nice enough," Glory admitted. She straightened as the sound of voices drifted from the pit. "They are coming back up." Standing, she pulled Poppy close and tucked the book away again. Gripping the extra strap that hung from her saddle for support, she stepped up onto the tree where she'd been sitting. She placed her good foot into the stirrup and hopped into the saddle, pulling her right leg up and settling it around the pommel and into the special cradle.

Hope watched, frowning.

"I'm going to walk Poppy for a bit, to be sure her hoof is fine."

Hope only nodded, staring with narrowed eyes, then strode back to greet the men.

Glory took a slow turn around the top of the hill before making her way to the excited group.

"You barely look dusty, my lord," she said, leaning down toward the viscount with a grin. "Did you not lend your shoulder to the efforts below?"

"No, no. The men were at their break. But they were kind enough to share their meat pies and I shared my own supplies." He patted a pocket where she assumed a flask resided.

"A fair trade, and no risk to your boots."

"No risk to mine, nor any to Tensford's, since I am wearing an old pair that he lent me. My own are still in the process of recovery."

Too late, she recalled that she should not know about the condition of his boots—or his attachment to them. Before her sister or Tensford could think more on it, she smiled at the earl. "Where are we off to next, Tensford? You are spoiled for choice if you mean to show off your improvements."

"I thought the new barn, perhaps." He shot a look at Keswick. "You might be interested in the architectural challenges of the thing. We are digging the back end into the hillside. It will help in keeping the dairy cool."

"What? Cows, too?" Keswick asked. "You've gone absolutely native, my friend."

"I'm afraid it is true. I've got a prime herd of Old Gloucesters, now."

Laughing, the pair mounted up and set off. They rode all over the estate and Glory managed to stay mounted for all of it. Keswick spent a great deal of the day at Tensford's side, as was to be expected, but Glory found herself riding next to him as they turned for home.

"Have you really been to Astley's Amphitheatre?" she asked after several minutes of companionable silence.

He nodded. "Many times."

"What is it like?"

He thought about it. "It is . . . an assault on the senses. But in the best way. It's all music, light and sparkle. Trick riders and dancing dogs and massive military reenactments. It's always a spectacle."

"It sounds wonderful," she said wistfully. "At least I will have one thing to look forward to, when they drag me to London."

"You'll be presented next year?"

She nodded glumly.

"I thought all girls were wild to have a London Season?"

"Most are, I suppose. I'd rather just stay here."

He held silent a moment. "Your brother is Lord Kincade, is he not?"

At her nod, he frowned. "I am surprised he and his countess did not bring you out this year. They sponsored your sister last year, didn't they?"

"They did."

"Then, why not you?"

"Because I refused. I would not put the future of a frog from your swampy bog into Lady Kincade's hands, let alone my own."

"It's not *my* bog," he objected.

She laughed. "I know." She shrugged. "It's just that I'm content to wait. Hope is the one who insists my life is incomplete without a debut—I don't want to disappoint her, but I'm happier the longer her duties keep her here."

"Granted, a young lady's experience of London is far tamer than any man's, but there is still plenty to recommend it."

"Tea, calls and balls?" She made a face.

"I'm sure they are exactly what your sister has in mind," he said sympathetically. "Those are the best venues for the sport."

She frowned. "Sport?"

"The hunt."

"Is there hunting available? Outside London?"

He laughed. "You truly are a horse lover. No, Lady Glory, I meant husband hunting. Isn't that the primary reason for a girl's Season?"

She recoiled. "Not for me."

She registered the skepticism and mischief in the blue depths of his eyes and the devilish curve of his mouth—and imagined that quite a few debutantes must want him in their sights. She was certainly affected, though she knew better. But there was something rebellious in him that called to the dark places in her. "Is that what you do during the Season, my lord? Hunt for the perfect wife?"

"Gads, no." He shuddered. "I prefer to live my life without entanglements."

"No one lives completely free of entanglements." She might have scoffed. Just a little.

He eyed her benevolently. "Take my advice and keep them as few as possible. It greatly reduces the—" He stopped himself.

She raised a brow.

"The disappointments."

She sighed. "That sounds like advice that would be far easier to follow, were I a man."

"Well, yes. Everything is easier for a man," he conceded. "And more fun, too. But London does have distractions, even for young ladies."

"Beyond the marriage mart?"

"Definitely. I was thinking of the museums, the parks, the Tower, Vauxhall—and more, depending on your circle of acquaintance."

Her curiosity was peaked now. "But what do the gentlemen get up to without the ladies? Gambling, I suppose," she said, answering her own question. "And lightskirts?"

He made a disapproving noise. "And what do you know of lightskirts?"

"My brother kept one, before his marriage. I heard his valet talk about it to the other servants."

"Listening to servant's gossip? Never a good idea," he admonished.

"I'd never learn any of the really interesting tidbits, did I not. And in any case, I rather hope my brother kept his mistress, if only so that he will have someone to be pleasant to him. Heaven knows his wife is not."

He snorted. "Perhaps you would do better here in the country. Talk like that in Town and they'll be whispering about you."

"Do they whisper about you?"

"Always."

"Then I won't mind. But what do the men do without us? I'd really like to know."

"Oh, gambling to be sure. Betting on cockfights and cards, fencing matches and sparring at Gentleman Jackson's."

"All of the fun, in short," she said darkly.

"Yes. But also politics and scientific lectures. Clubs. Carriage racing, and driving. Riding." He cast an admiring glance across at her. "I'd dearly love to take you riding in Hyde Park, just so you can show the other ladies how it is meant to be done."

"I think I'd dearly love to go to London as a young gentleman instead of a young lady."

He laughed out loud. "Oh, now that would be a prank of epic proportions."

She straightened in her saddle, mind suddenly racing.

"Oh, no," he said, abruptly serious. "Put it from your mind right now."

"You could help," she began.

"No. It is too wicked, even for me. You would ruin yourself and cast your family into disgrace too. Is that how you would like to repay Hope for all of her kindness?"

She slumped. "No."

"Then do not consider such a thing. But I was serious about taking you out to the park. What do you say? Shall we make an agreement? If I am in London when you come up, I'll take you riding—and we'll go to an evening at Astley's. Are we agreed?"

A thrill of pleasure raced up her spine. Triumph made her scalp tingle. For a moment she gloried in it—his casual acceptance and easy friendship. But the feeling faded. She imagined herself in London. The stares. The whispers. The expressions of dismay and distaste as heads turned away.

It was not her world. It never would be.

She imagined Keswick's face when he saw her dragging her leg along, shuddered at the thought of him seeing her attempts at a dance. What if she fell in front of a ballroom crowded with people? He would turn away in embarrassment and disgust, just like so many others.

She couldn't bear the thought of it.

Ahead of them, Tensford paused at a fork in the trail. "I'd like to introduce you to the Beales," he called back to Keswick. "They are tenants and hold one of the largest farms on the estate. Sarah is known for her cider. I'm sure she'll find us a glass or two."

"Cider sounds like just the thing." Keswick followed readily enough, but Glory hesitated.

When they stopped and looked back, she gave them all a wave. "Poppy is beginning to favor that foot. I think I'll take her back."

"There's no sign of it in her gait," Keswick commented.

"I can feel it. All of you go on. I'll see you at the house." She didn't wait for an answer, but she caught Hope's thoughtful look as she rode off.

It was better this way. She could dismount and see to Poppy without Lord Keswick's sharp eyes on her and she could get to her room without Hope's interference.

And just perhaps, she might stay there until the house party was done and Lord Keswick had gone.

CHAPTER 4

On the third full day of his visit, Keswick's restlessness got the better of him. Tensford was heading out to his new barn this morning, to oversee the placement of the trusses, but Keswick declined to go with him. He'd enjoyed seeing his friend so happy and productive, but he needed some distance from it. Very privately, he admitted to a bit of envy. After all, he had little chance of entering a similar state of engagement. At least, not one he could share with anyone. Not for a long while. Not until . . .

Well, not *until*.

Lady Glory might have provided a distraction, but she was in hiding. He didn't know what the issue was, but he could tell that it was upsetting his hostess, and he knew he hadn't seen the girl since they'd all ridden out on that first day.

She was different, that one. Pretty, yes. That auburn hair and those cognac eyes held definite appeal, but more than that, he was drawn to her wit and unexpected conversation. She didn't look at him with either fear or fascination, didn't watch him with wide eyes as if he were nothing but a walking collection of rumor and whispers of a thousand wicked acts. He suspected she had grit. And perhaps a bit of intractability, hidden away beneath the surface—and the disaffected bits of his soul always did like a bit of company.

He'd actually ridden out alone a couple of times, hoping to run into her somewhere on the estate. He was sure she must ride often. He'd never seen someone so comfortable in the saddle. But he never saw her and her mare remained in the stables.

He sighed. It was likely better this way. She was young. Too innocent for the likes of him. She didn't know how to play the game and she would end up getting hurt. Because someone always did—and he'd stopped allowing it to be him, long ago.

He needed something else to distract him. Heaven knew he could not show the least bit of interest or passion in something solid and real. No, even here, away from his father's spies, he would do best to keep his occupations shallow and preferably full of dissipation.

Unfortunately, dissipation was in short supply at Greystone.

So, he went looking for it.

He got up an illicit card game out behind the stables, drawing in the stable hands, a few of the grooms and a local lad or two. They played for pennies, but there was still a feeling of the forbidden about it, and spirits and pleasure ran high. They had a surprisingly good time at it, in fact, until rivalries ran deep as well, and fisticuffs broke out between a stable hand and a stonemason's apprentice who both were sparking after the same kitchen maid.

Keswick had to take his responsibilities as a good guest seriously. Even he couldn't be responsible for more than a broken nose, and assorted scratches and bruises, so the next day found him wandering to the village in search of amusement. He found it at the Crown and Cock.

The offerings began with the sign outside, an artistic and hilarious depiction of a finely feathered rooster, wearing a proud expression and a crooked crown. They continued with the discovery of the tavern's much vaunted honeyed mead, a specialty whose secret had been known only to the tavern keep's family for a hundred years. Mr. Thomkins was grateful for his enthusiasm for the brew, and tolerant of his enthusiasm for Betsy, the serving maid.

The girl was perfectly willing to provide the distraction Keswick was looking for. He let her sit in his lap and run her fingers through his hair as he considered going along upstairs with her. The straight-forward transaction Betsy offered was the only sort he could tolerate in his life right now—and perhaps, ever.

But this was Gloucestershire, not London, and he was Tensford's guest. And truthfully, the thought of a quick tup with a serving wench inspired mostly . . . *ennui*. Gads, but it was a sad state of affairs when an arse like that only made him feel like a world-weary sack.

It had nothing to do with shining amber eyes and the echo of a quick laugh and smart mouth. He told himself so repeatedly, and went back to the tavern the next day to prove it. He even allowed Betsy back on his knee. If she wanted to press her ample bosom against him while she shared the local gossip, he was in no mood to prevent her.

But as the afternoon wore on and the dinner hour approached, he extricated himself. He wanted to be back at Greystone for dinner.

Lady Glory was going to have to come out of her room sometime. He was not going to be so foolish as to miss it.

* * *

GLORY TOOK part in her dancing lesson as usual, but only because she knew Lord Keswick was not in the house or anywhere near to it. He was at the Crown and Cock again—all of the servants were abuzz with the news. He'd spent yesterday there, as well, sampling *all* of the wares available. She'd heard two of the housemaids whispering about it in the corridor, scandalized and delighted.

Their snickers filled Glory with curiosity and more than a little envy. She was so heartily sick of her room that even the Crown and Cock sounded interesting. And was Keswick truly sampling the barmaid's charms, as well as the mead? Was he kissing her with honeyed lips? Her imagination went wild, thinking what it might be like to be kissed by him. To kiss him back. Her fingers could trail along the sharp edge of his jaw, but surely his lips would be soft . . .

Were a man's lips soft? Hope was the only creature she could remember kissing her, since she was small, and those were mere pecks on the cheek. A man's lips couldn't be so different. Could they? She suddenly blazed with indignation that Betsy likely knew how Keswick's lips felt when Glory herself would likely never know a man's kiss.

Men were such irritating creatures. And so were barmaids. And so was she, for that matter, for caring what they got up to.

At least his absence gave her some freedom in the house. She lingered to speak with Hope and Miss Munroe after the lesson, but declined to accompany them upstairs to Hope's stillroom. The squire's daughter wished to select a few of the lavender sachets Hope had been teaching some of the tenant wives to fashion. Having been present for the birth of the idea and the experimentation and design of the things, Glory was already heartily sick of lavender sachets.

"Will you come down to dinner tonight?" her sister asked softly as Miss Munroe headed for the stairs.

Glory shook her head.

Hope sighed. "You'll have to see him out of the saddle at some time," she said before she followed her guest.

She still didn't want to. But she knew Hope was right. It was just sheer stubbornness at this point. She'd restricted herself to quick rides, very early in the morning, and had been spending most of her days upstairs, trying not to go mad. Despite the damage to her leg, she was not used to so much inactivity and confinement. She had endured it, however, because she obstinately refused to risk heavier damage to her pride.

A walk around the ground floor rooms felt better, though, and she ended up in Hope's favorite parlor, where the afternoon sun came in. She stared longingly out into the garden. Could she risk a quick turn through the blossoms, in the fresh air? Pressing her lips together, she decided she shouldn't. In fact, she should go back up—

She paused, listening. What was that?

A faint, soft noise. Again. There, over by the settee. She crossed the room carefully, making sure her steps were quiet and slow. She thought she might know . . .

Another soft mew and yes, her suspicions were confirmed. Holding on to the back and bracing herself on her good knee, she peered behind the settee.

"Oh, Grumpet!" she sighed. "Look at what you've done, you darling girl." The barn cat had obviously snuck into the house. She'd dragged a lap robe into the corner and now reclined upon it like royalty, with four lovely little kittens mewling around her.

"Oh, but why in Hope's parlor?" There was a bit of a mess back there. "I saw the fine bed they set up for you in the stables." But the grooms had warned her that Grumpet liked to sneak off when her time came upon her.

Glory carefully moved the settee just enough so that she could sit and reach down to lift up one of the sweet babies. "And a good day to you, pretty thing." This one was grey and striped and not afraid at all. "Well, I'll send word to the stables and we'll have you and your mama and your siblings settled in a trice." She set the darling down next to his mother. "The dairy has been waiting word of the blessed event, too, Grumpet. They'll send down some lovely cream for you."

They would need a basket large enough for all of the animals and some soft toweling. She added to the list as she stood and set off to find the housekeeper.

"Well, good afternoon." Lord Keswick stood in the doorway. He bowed and grinned. "Here you are at last."

Caught utterly by surprise, Glory froze.

"You are not talking to yourself, Lady Glory, are you? I seem to recall you giving me some grief over the idea when we first met." He peered around inside the room, his dark hair strangely disheveled, but shining where the sun struck it. "You haven't been helping yourself to Tensford's brandy, have you?"

She raised her chin as her heart raced and her mind cast about for a way to escape. "I have not. Nor am I talking to myself."

"Oh?" He looked around again. "To whom are you speaking, then?"

"Grumpet, if you must know." Yes. If she could lure him over to look, then perhaps she could escape without him seeing . . .

"Who, or what, is a Grumpet?"

She gestured back toward the shifted furniture. "The barn cat. She sneaked in here to have her litter. The kittens are darling. Would you care to see?"

"Yes." He straightened, interest flaring. "I have a soft spot for cats. They are so independent. And occasionally disdainful and downright snobbish."

"Just behind the settee," she said, making a careful turn.

He strode by her and she began to walk toward the door, as swiftly as she could. Almost there. She'd done it. She'd made her escape—

"What have you done to your leg?" he asked casually.

She knew the question didn't truly echo through the room like the reverberation of a gong. But she felt the shuddering aftermath of it up and down her spine, nonetheless.

It was an innocent question.

It didn't feel like it.

She had to answer, but her brow had furrowed and her shoulders hunched as if all the pain of the pitying, judgmental or disdainful reactions she'd ever suffered was about to descend upon her.

Suddenly, she straightened. Shook her head and threw her shoulders back. This was not who she was—a girl who cowered and hid. It never had been. If misery came, she would bear it. She was done hiding.

Still, hope squeezed her heart as she turned to face him. "It's an old injury," she said, cursing inwardly at the tightness of her voice. "It happened when I was a child. The damage to my leg is permanent."

He looked up, distracted from the kitten he was holding.

Chin held high, she took a limping step toward him.

His gaze ran down the length of her and then back to the kitten. "Oh. Sorry to hear it. I suppose that explains why you love riding so much, doesn't it?" He sounded perfectly matter of fact. "So much easier to get around—especially with a seat like yours." He glanced up and beckoned her. "Come and sit and enjoy them for a moment before you run off and tattle on poor Grumpet."

Stunned, she went and sat near him.

"Why Grumpet?" he asked.

She blinked, still not sure what had just happened.

Nothing. Nothing had happened.

She had revealed her secret to this large, striking man, with his coat molded across his broad shoulders and his big hands full of purring kitten, and his reaction had been . . . negligible.

"Did you name her?"

"Ah, no. She's a cranky soul. She loves the horses, but despises the stable hands and grooms. Tensford's personal groom is a Scotsman and he's the only one who can get close to her. He scratches her ears and calls her a 'wee grumpet' and the name stuck."

"A good name, then. Though she's not objecting to me."

"No, she isn't." Tiny smile lines appeared at the corners of his eyes as he laughed at the kitten. *And neither am I.*

"Well, she does need to go back to the stable, doesn't she?" He pulled a face as he glanced back into the corner. "Even if only so someone can clean up after her. Do you have a basket large enough to carry them all out? I'll help you get her home."

"I'll fetch one from the housekeeper."

"Fine. I'll wait here." He grinned at her over the kitten's tiny face. "And don't feel as if you need to hurry on my account. I'm perfectly happy right here."

* * *

AN HOUR later they walked back together from the stables. He carried the basket and had shortened his stride to match hers. When they reached the gate that led to Hope's garden, he paused.

"Do we have time to sit a moment, do you think?" he asked.

She flinched. Was this it? Had he merely delayed his reaction until their task was done? Was he going to be one of those who acted over-concerned and coddled her like a babe in swaddling blankets? "If you are asking because you think I need to rest, there's no need."

It came out sharper than she had meant it to.

He raised a brow at her.

She glared back.

He sucked in a breath and blew it out. "I haven't noticed any grooms carrying you about or anyone pushing you in a Merlin chair. I *have* seen you ride. Enough to know that you must do a great deal of it. All of this makes me assume you are quite willing, able and experienced at walking back and forth between the house and the stables." He waved a hand toward the house. "Go on if you like. Your sister's garden is lovely. I just thought I'd like to sit there with a pretty girl for a moment. But you must do as you see fit."

A pretty girl? A flush of pleasure mixed with her embarrassment. "I . . . I am sorry. I shouldn't be so defensive."

Relenting, he offered his arm. "Come, then."

They strolled among the blooms until they came to a bench. She sat and tried to control her pulse as he stretched out next to her, his elbows on the back and his legs sprawled out next to the basket into the garden path.

"How did it happen?" he asked with a nod toward her skirts.

Her mouth twisted. "Trampled by a horse, believe it or not."

His eyes widened. "No! Truly?"

"My father's stallion. He was skittish. Temperamental. I'd been warned a hundred times to leave him be, to never go near him." She shrugged. "I suppose I've always had a willful streak."

"You must have put it to good use, to brave riding again, afterward —and to have mastered it so completely."

"I was determined. But it took me a while to get there. The doctors told my family I'd likely never walk again. I had to fight to prove them wrong about that before I could head back to the stables."

"That stubborn streak must be a mile wide," he said almost admiringly.

She laughed. "You are the first to make it sound like a virtue."

"I suppose you see that sort of reaction often, then? Others trying to treat you like a perpetual invalid?"

"A fair bit. It's frustrating. But I suppose it's far preferable to being looked at with disdain or disgust."

He sat up straighter. "Over a bit of a limp?"

"To be fair, it is more than *bit* of a limp. But I don't know why so many have such difficulty with it. Women are often condescending— as if it is a judgment upon me and I somehow deserve to be lame. Men are more likely to be repulsed. Or to shake their heads in pity. One of my father's friends used to say, 'Such a shameful waste.' every time he saw me, as if my damaged leg somehow negated every other aspect of my person and situation."

He was sitting straight up now and frowning down on her. "The bounder!"

She shrugged. "Yes, well . . ."

"It's ridiculous." He cast a twisted grin sideways at her. "Disdainful and snobbish is only ever acceptable in cats." He shook his head. "We all have wounds and scars." A dark laugh escaped him. "Your leg would have to be attached backwards to match some of the hidden injuries I carry around."

With a sudden start, he twisted on the bench to look at her. "Hold a moment. Is that why you've been in hiding? Because you believed that I would judge you as harshly? That I would react to your injury in such a fashion?"

"I . . ." Her mouth hung open a little. He looked shocked . . . angry . . . and growing more so by the second.

"After we met while I was hip deep in swamp muck? After we spent a pleasant day riding out across the estate? Did I give you reason to suspect that I might act so . . . disrespectfully toward you?"

"No! Of course not."

"Then I must assume you've heard some of the more vile rumors about me—and have chosen to believe them." He stood, his square jaw tight and his expression closed. "I regret if I should have given you reason to do so." He gave a stiff bow. "If you will make my apologies to your sister? I believe I will dine in the village tonight."

"My lord!" She reached out and gripped his arm. "Please, wait."

He leaned down and spoke through his teeth. "I find myself a fool, Lady Glory, for believing you to be different than so many others."

A barbed insult. Sharp too, for she registered the pain of it past her awareness of his looming muscular frame and the bounding of her heart.

He glanced down and sneered. "Your leg is nothing. Perhaps you think it sets you apart, but it is the rest of you that is so sadly similar to everyone else."

She stood but he scooped up the basket and strode off, moving rapidly. "Lord Keswick, please!"

But he didn't turn or even pause. She could never catch him. Slumping back down onto the bench, she covered her face with her hands.

She was an idiot! As the sun sank lower, she cursed herself. He was right to be offended. She'd acted no better than all of those who had misjudged her. She'd expected the worst without giving him a chance to prove her wrong.

Shadows stretched across the garden and the first stars had begun to wink in the sky before Hope finally found her, still on the bench.

"There you are. I hadn't expected you to come down to dinner, but then I heard you weren't in your rooms either. Is something amiss?"

"Only me. Again."

Hope sat down next to her. "Is it Lord Keswick? He . . . saw you?"

"Yes."

"And his reaction?" she asked gingerly.

"Everything one could hope for. He acted as if it were nothing."

Even in the dim light, she saw the relief spread across her sister's face. "Oh, good for him! I had hoped he would." She raised her brows. "You know, perhaps seeing him first out riding was a good idea. He got to know other things about you first."

"Yes, but he deduced that I expected him to act badly. He was insulted."

"Oh." Hope sighed. "Yes. I can see that."

"I owe him an apology, Hope." She raised her brows at her sister. "And I think I know how to deliver it."

CHAPTER 5

K eswick came down late to breakfast the next morning and dined in sulky, solitary splendor. The earl and his countess were off, preparing for further guests and being productive and happy, no doubt. The sister was likely hiding again, or plotting further insult, or perhaps just lurking about thinking evil thoughts about him.

He nursed a cup of coffee and thought about returning to London. He'd lost his taste for the country. Or perhaps, just for country girls. Surely he could avoid Miss Vernon for what was left of the Season?

A footman entered, carrying a small silver tray. He stopped next to Keswick's chair.

"This came in the post for you, sir."

With a nod of thanks, he took the letter. Grinning, he noticed Chester's seal on the back and opened it up.

Kes,

. . .

I DO HOPE Tensford is not boring you past tears with cows, crops and fossils. Strike that—I highly suspect he is—but even so, I dash this note off to tell you that you've done the right thing.

That Vernon Girl is a menace.

The damned chit has got a maggot in her brain that your trip to Gloucestershire is a sham. She believes you are still in London and just attempting to avoid her. She's begun haunting your usual spots, driving past your rooms and club several times a day. She spent an entire afternoon lying in wait outside of Angelo's and I swear, I saw her carriage parked down the street from the gaming hell we left early this morning.

She's hunting you, old boy, and if she catches you, she's going to stick the steel pin of matrimony through your gullet like one of those simpering butterfly collectors and mount you on her wall.

And if she ain't enough to keep you inured in the country, I heard last evening that your father has come to Town.

So, even if farm life has numbed your brainbox and has you thinking of returning—don't do it, man. Better to stay where you are.

Give Tensford a good smack and tell him it's from me . . .

Yrs . . .
Chester

KESWICK DROPPED the letter like it burned. Good heavens, what had he done to deserve the attention of a harpy like Alice Vernon? He winced, then, at the absurdity of the question. What hadn't he done? Nonetheless, he wasn't going to give in to her, no matter how richly he deserved her. And his father? He shuddered. Nothing he'd done, no matter how wicked, could demand a visit with his father to balance the scales.

No, Chester was right. He could far better stay here and tolerate insults and boredom.

Scratch that. Boredom, he discovered as he left the dining room, was not on the menu today.

Lady Glory lay in wait for him. She sat on a bench in the entry hall, a young gentleman standing nearby. The young man held his hat in hand and looked to be attempting a conversation, but she was watching the doorway through which Keswick emerged.

"Lord Keswick," she called, as soon as she spotted him. "Come and meet Mr. Lycett."

He approached and she made the introductions. "Mr. Lycett is the squire's nephew. He's visiting over at Stroud Hall and will be joining us, along with his family, for some of the house party entertainments."

"It is very kind of you to include me," the young man said, watching her closely.

"Not at all. It's all Hope's doing. She'll be so sorry she wasn't here to offer you tea this morning." She smiled, but seemed a bit tense. "Mr. Lycett made a delivery for us this morning." She gave him a nod. "And I do thank you for it, sir. You are very kind to see to it yourself."

"It was my pleasure. In fact, as soon as I heard it was your request, I told my uncle I would fulfill it myself."

"We must thank you for your attention," she answered. "It is very much appreciated."

The man bowed and waited an awkward moment, but she offered no further comment.

"Well, then. I'll be off." Mr. Lycett gave up at last. "A pleasure to meet you, my lord." The young man made his bow and reached for Lady Glory's hand, as if he was going to kiss it. She grasped his hand instead and gave it a good shake. "Good day, sir. And thank you. We will see you soon."

"Good day. I look forward to it."

She waited until he was gone from the hall before she stood and took a step forward. "I owe you an apology, Lord Keswick," she said directly.

She did, by God. His pride still smarted. He waited. And examined the plain but sturdy habit she wore today. It wasn't as bright and pretty as the sprigged muslin she'd worn yesterday, but it looked comfortable—and the dark fawn color brought out the amber in her eyes. It suited her.

"I was wrong to make assumptions about your response to my lameness—and thus to your character. I do offer my sincerest regrets."

He nodded. "Thank you."

"And to prove the depth of my sincerity, I offer a diversion."

"Even better," he said with approval. "What did you have in mind?"

"Ride out with me?" She led him to the door and gestured outside. Mr. Lycett was gone, but her mare waited in front of the house, along with a splendid, sturdy looking chestnut.

"I begged the use of the squire's gelding a tad early," she said. "That's the delivery Mr. Lycett spoke of. He's a prime goer. You'll love him."

"Mr. Lycett? Or the horse?"

"I meant the horse," she laughed up at him. "But Mr. Lycett may be a prime goer, as well. I have no idea."

They walked down to where her mare waited, already saddled.

"Confident, were you?" he asked wryly.

"Hopeful," she corrected. Glancing up at him through her lashes, she said sweetly, "I'll show you one of my favorite spots on the estate, if you'll agree to come out."

The zing of interest that started at the base of his spine and spread up and out had him glancing around for an attendant. "Shouldn't we take a groom with us?"

Her look turned pitying. "Well, I've no need of one, but if you require someone to help you mount or hold your horse or fetch your hat when it blows off . . ."

He rolled his eyes. "I was thinking of the propriety of it all. Perhaps we can catch Mr. Lycett before he sets off for home."

"Oh, we'll see plenty of him soon enough. The place will be overrun with people within a day or so. Let's enjoy the quiet while we can." She laughed. "I solemnly swear not to assault your virtue, my lord. Now, shall we go?"

He hesitated a moment longer. Was this just a more innocent-seeming scheme to get him into a compromising position? Was she playing Miss Vernon's game—only better?

He looked at her, at her bright smile and slightly wistful gaze—and he could not believe it. He shrugged and nodded.

"I had the footman bring your hat and gloves."

"Confident, as I suspected." He took the articles from the man and asked him to inform Lord Tensford of their whereabouts, when the earl returned. Outside, they walked the horses to the stables, and had the chestnut saddled. Once they were ready, he lifted the minx into the saddle and mounted up, following her behind the stables and to an unfamiliar part of the estate.

They entered the woods after a short while. The path was wide enough for them to ride abreast. Fallen leaves and needles lined the way and they made their way in a strange silence.

He had to break it before it became too comfortable.

"You know, it was your reputation that made me ask about a chaperone," he told her. "I'm sure everyone here knows my history. You won't want them connecting you with me."

"Everyone knows the stories about you. They also know of your interest in Betsy at the Crown and Cock."

He scowled. "Listening to servant's gossip again?"

"It's the only way I learn anything interesting. No one tells me anything. They all think of me as a little girl."

"I'm sure they all think of you as the terror that you are—they just won't say so to your face."

She laughed. "In any case, no one is going to think you are interested in me when you have Betsy waiting." She lifted a shoulder. "Besides, everyone knows I carry this." She gestured to the whip coiled and attached to her uniquely configured saddle. "And they know I know how to use it."

"You never use that on Poppy!" he exclaimed.

"Of course not," she answered, all indignation. "But this one is custom made for my height and reach and I have developed a certain skill with it. I can flick a fly off of your ear without touching the skin

—or not, as I so choose."

"A wise strategy," he said. If she was going to ride out alone, at least she had one means to defend herself.

"You know, I truly am sorry if I caused offense." She sighed. "Hiding was not my best notion."

"You couldn't have carried on much longer, in any case, surely."

"Couldn't have? Of course I could have. But I was already miserable."

"There's that stubborn streak again."

She shrugged. "Ever present. But I was only thinking of my own feelings and didn't consider how it might insult you."

"Perhaps I overreacted." He knew he had, suddenly.

"My mother would be disappointed in me, could she see me now," she went on. "She always insisted that I should just allow my lameness to show and let people and their thoughts about it fall where they may."

He scarcely heard her. He had overreacted. He should have been glad that his reputation had spread ahead of him and cleared the way of entanglements or expectations. Why then, did he continue to shy away from the idea of this amber-eyed sprite of a girl thinking badly of him?

It didn't matter why. It wouldn't do.

"You are suddenly wearing a most particular expression. What is it?"

He shook his head. "I was just thinking that my mother would be disappointed in me, as well." And she would have. She would have seen the pain behind Lady Glory's maneuverings and treated her gently. He sighed. "It would hardly be a novel sensation. I think she must be used to looking down and frowning at me from heaven, by now."

"I'm sorry. You lost your mother, too?"

"Long ago." The trail began to narrow and he urged his mount ahead of her instead of letting her pursue that conversation.

"Keep your eyes peeled," she called. "We are going to take a path to the right, just ahead."

He couldn't see anything except for forest and a carpet of thick ferns. Straining, he saw a small break that might perhaps be a faint game trail. He hesitated.

"Yes. There. That's it. Take it now," she called.

"So bossy!" he called back, but he obeyed and the chestnut left the lighter thoroughfare behind, pushing through a belly-high sea of waving fronds and emerging into a dimmer section of forest. The dense canopy overhead blocked all but small dapples of sunlight. The trees were large and many grew at odd angles. Some of the thick trunks were covered with moss, others bore shelves and ridges of fungi. "It's like nothing I've ever seen before," he said, keeping his voice low.

"I know. It scarcely seems real, does it?" She and Poppy kept close behind and they followed the faint path as it led along a limestone ridge.

"It's like another world back here." The thought jarred him. "Wait. You are not taking me to the riverbank where Tensford hunts for fossils, are you? I promised him I would go when he makes an outing of it, with the rest of the house party.

"No!" She sounded shocked. "I would never steal Tensford's thunder in such a fashion. He loves to show off his collection—and the spots where he finds them." He looked back to see her nod in encouragement. "This will be as diverting, though, I promise."

"More diverting than a bunch of oddly shaped rocks? I should hope so."

"Don't let Tensford hear you talk like that!"

He realized they couldn't be going to the river as the path began to climb. Like the path they had followed to the coal pit, it wended its way around and back and forth a bit as the way grew steeper. The dense canopy overhead kept the light dim, though, even as they climbed, and random outcroppings of rock added to the alien feel of the place. But it was quiet, and he drank in the peace and the strange beauty until the path ended at a large tumble of rocks.

"Turn right and climb," Lady Glory directed.

A path of crushed undergrowth led over a crest, down into a dip and then angled over another high spot. When he crested the second hill, Keswick pulled the chestnut to a stop.

"Ohh."

A small glen spread out before them, surrounded by dense growth and backed by a huge tower of rock. A boulder, bigger than a house, lay at the bottom. Some time in the past, something cataclysmic had knocked away a section, leaving a flat ledge, almost like a stage, carved out of the rock. Trees arched gracefully around it and here the sun broke through a bit more. Three large, moss covered logs sat before it, almost as if they'd been placed there for the purpose of seating an audience.

Lady Glory rode up beside him and then swung down. "Tether your mount here," she instructed. "It's safer."

"Safer?"

"You shall see." With that, she fed her mount and his each a carrot from her pocket, then walked down the slope to the stage. Carefully sitting, she swung her legs and mounted the stage. A hand on the boulder helped her climb to her feet and she moved to the center. Standing there, she grinned and raised her arms. "Isn't it amazing?"

"Yes." But he was looking at her, so slim and straight, full of spirit and pleased with herself. She was bespeckled with sunlight and her amber eyes glowed. With her fawn colored habit, she looked as if she'd been born in this glade. He couldn't imagine her hiding away in her rooms, and he suddenly grasped the steely determination—and the depth of fear—that had kept her there.

"It's a veritable fairy theatre," he said, approaching. "Are you going to sing?"

"Heavens, no. And you'll eventually learn what a kindness that is."

He rotated, taking in the entirety of the place. "Surely this has been used. You can see where clearings have been made, in the past. But for what?" He frowned. "Luddites? Revolutionaries?"

"Perhaps they were children."

"So far into Tensford's lands? I doubt it. Does he know about it?"

"I don't know. I haven't wanted to ask. Certainly I've seen no sign of anyone coming here, except for me." She walked the edge of the stage-like span of rock. "Perhaps it was a secret society. How thrilling. I wonder if they wore disguises? Masks and cloaks?"

"Masons, perhaps," he mused.

"Come up and try it," she beckoned.

He hopped up and stood beside her. It was indeed a heady feeling, as if all the forest waited, breath baited, to see what he would offer up.

She felt it too, for she nudged him. "Come on, then, give us something."

He struck a pose.

"There was a young lady from Saul,
*   whose bottom stretched broad as a wall—"*

"No!" She covered her ears, laughing. "Stop! That doesn't fit the feeling of the place, at all."

"That is the extent of my repertoire, I'm afraid. Limericks and bawdy tavern songs are all I've got. It's up to you, then."

She lifted a shoulder. "I don't even have limericks and drinking songs."

"What? I can scarcely believe it. I know your governesses must have forced a speaking piece upon you. Especially if you do not sing. Don't all young ladies have something at the ready, with which to entertain the masses?"

She pulled a face. "You are entirely too perceptive. Yes, I have one. But no, I will not show you."

He cocked his head and threw her own words back at her. "Come on, then, give us something!"

Her expression grew bleak. "I'm sorry. I cannot. I won't ever be so foolish as to perform that piece again." She went to sit on the edge, her skirts dangling over the edge. "Perhaps I'll write a limerick for you, though."

"Now, that would be worth waiting for." Chuckling, he joined her.

"A fairy theatre, I like that," she mused. "My piece was from A

Midsummer Night's Dream." She glanced over at him. "Do you believe in fairies?" she asked suddenly.

The question caught him by surprise. "I don't know. My mother did, certainly."

That caught her interest. "Did she?"

"Every good Irish girl does. At least, that's what she would tell me when she left out offerings of milk or bread on the window ledge."

"Did you ever see one?"

He shook his head. "No. I only ever saw my father's fury if he caught her at it. He forbade such fancy and could not abide superstitious nonsense."

She sighed. "Perhaps it is nonsense. But part of me wants to believe."

"The world needs a bit of magic, I think."

'Yes, but the world makes it difficult to accept that it exists."

"These are the places that make it easier, though."

"There's more," she said. "Help me down."

He slid down and turned to find her holding her arms out in expectation like a child. She was no child, though. He could feel her curves as he lifted her down and set her before him—perhaps closer than was strictly necessary.

Definitely closer.

She smelled of lavender. Tensford's countess was a lover of sachets, he'd discovered. Likely Lady Glory's bureau drawers and wardrobes were full of sachets stuffed with lavender—just as his contained bundles of bay leaves and cloves.

She had a cravat tied around her neck, as was usual with a military styled habit, and it ended with a flounce of lace upon her bosom—although she was in no need of enhancement there, as he could tell, because he still had not let her go.

He was going to. He was going to withdraw his hands from her and stop the press of his fingers along the underside of her more-than-respectable breasts. Right after he'd done examining the small stickpin she wore, tucked in amongst the lace.

"Lady Glory, is that, by chance, an insect?"

"Where?" She raised a hand to brush away an aerial assault.

"In your stickpin."

"Oh, yes." She hadn't withdrawn from him. Her breathing had quickened, though, and her gaze finally broke away to look down. "It's trapped inside a bead of amber."

He tilted his head. "Other ladies wear sapphires or rubies. You wear a bug."

Now she stepped away. "Tensford gave it to me," she said defensively. "He found the amber here, at Greystone. I thought it was fascinating—frozen forever like that. He had the stickpin made for me."

"I didn't say it was a bad thing," he told her. "It's just another interesting bit about you. I must apologize for my comments yesterday. You are, in fact, different from the girls I've met in London."

"Yes. That's me." She moved further away, her limp slowing her. "Different." Crossing to the copse on the far side of the glen, she held a thick branch back and looked over her shoulder at him. "Step carefully and go slowly."

She ducked into the underbrush and disappeared.

He followed. Branches grabbed at him as he pushed through the bracken—and then stepped out into a clear spot.

And stopped, struck speechless.

The whole, towering hill, up which they'd just wound their way— it fell away before him. Just a few feet ahead a ledge crumbled, leaving thin air and an incredible vista. The forest stretched out first, then came the house and main estate buildings of Greystone Park. Beyond lay the fields and the river, more forest, and in the far distance, the rooftops of the village.

Keswick sighed in awe, then glanced back the way they'd come. To go from dim, enclosed mystery to this glorious, brightly lit scene . . .

"The contrast is amazing, is it not?" Lady Glory clearly relished his surprise.

"It is. It's . . ." He waved a hand.

"I know." She edged a bit further out, but did approach the edge. "It's so beautiful." They gazed in silence for a moment. "It all looks so peaceful from up here." She laughed. "I much prefer this vantage."

He thought about her sitting up here alone, gazing down upon her world from a safe spot—and felt a surprising twinge of empathy.

"Lady Glory," he said suddenly. "You do know that Mr. Lycett was being *nice* to you this morning?"

She glanced back at him, frowning. "Of course. He is a nice man." She moved and took a seat on an outcropping of rock. She looked up abruptly, a look of horror crossing her face. "Are you saying I was not? Did I say something wrong? I was sure I thanked him—"

He held up a hand to stop her. "No. You were polite. But he was trying to be *more* than polite. He was trying to . . . make up to you."

"I think you are mistaken."

"No. I am not." He crossed over and sat near her feet, looking up at her. "Believe me, I know what it looks like." He preened a little. "I'm something of an expert."

"Well, I do hate to level a blow at your towering pride, but in this case, you are wrong. Utterly."

"I'm not."

"You are. Why you would even think such a thing is beyond me."

"Why you didn't see what was right before your eyes is beyond me."

She stared at him while a myriad of emotions flowed over face. Scorn won. "Why in the world would Mr. Lycett flirt with me?"

"Why not? You are a lovely young lady of marriageable age."

"Everyone in this countryside thinks of me as an overblown school girl. A spinster in waiting. They don't see me as marriageable."

He held up a hand and started ticking items off with his fingers. "Young. Pretty. More than acceptable bloodlines—good heavens, you are sister to one earl and sister-in-law to another. That alone would put you at the head of the pack in the minds of all the local bachelors." He raised a brow. "I assume you have a decent dowry?"

She flushed.

He nodded. "Right. So, in reality, instead of being incredulous at the thought of Mr. Lycett's flirtation, you should be considering him and deciding that he is not good enough for you."

Her mouth fell open. "Not good enough for me?" She laughed. "For me? The girl with a permanent, pronounced limp? Who cannot dance or climb stairs easily or even take a stroll in the garden or a walk in the park and keep apace? The one who is as clumsy in her manners as in her stride? I cannot flirt. I'm a horror at managing small talk and social niceties." She sighed. "They start to drone on about their health or their relatives whom I've never met and I find them deadly dull—and it invariably shows on my face."

He laughed. "You do have an expressive face. I find it a joy to watch."

"So glad I can amuse you," she said bitterly. "Also, my chin is too pointy and my eyes are a strange color."

"Your eyes are stunning. Your conversation is lively and interesting—when you are not insulting me."

"I notice you did not defend my chin."

He shook his head, charmed and exasperated in equal parts. With a sigh he climbed to his feet and nudged her aside, forcing her to make room for him on the rock.

"Your chin is just pointy enough." It was true. She was a bit of a beauty, especially when she was arguing with him. "Listen, please. The majority of us are naturally inclined to pair up, to choose someone to put our faith into and settle down. I am not one of them, but you are."

"Wait," she interjected. "You are a titled peer of the realm. Marriage and procreation are practically the reason for your existence."

"Spite and my father's ruthless determination are the reason for my existence." He shook his head. "But enough of that. I am jaded and unbending—while the very idea of marriage requires a certain resiliency of spirit and a wide dollop of steady faith—in oneself and in other people. And despite your varied experiences, you still have both."

She tried to protest, but he stopped her. "Pointy chin and all, you are an enchanting conundrum, my dear, and you'll have to face it." And he'd always been drawn to a puzzle, and to the new and interesting. And he'd been right about her having mettle. It all set his inner alarms to screeching, in fact. *Careful. Careful.* But this girl deserved to know the truth.

She didn't care to hear it. "Stop it," she ordered. Her mobile expression had gone flat.

"Stop what?"

"Stop complimenting me."

He threw back his head, chuckling. "Another first for you, Lady Glory. I know no woman has ever given me that particular command." She would make a magnificent partner for some lucky bastard—and he doubted she would be happy until she had. But it was going to take more than words to convince her of the truth—to make her begin to see her own worth.

He leaned in. *Careful.*

He was being careful, damn it. He was kissing her for her sake, not for his own. Not because her aged cognac eyes were intoxicating him. Not because the sun danced like fire amongst her curls. His gaze followed the sun's path down a little and settled on her fine, plump lips. He wasn't kissing her because the thought of being first to taste that smart, funny, lush mouth made his heart race.

That was just a surprising side effect.

He moved closer still. Too close. She lifted a hand and placed it on his chest. She must feel his heart beat. It pounded as if he'd walked up to this height himself.

He moved to distract her with a touch. A delicate brush of his finger across her cheek.

She stared up at him, her gaze dancing lightly across his face. Her lips parted.

"No," she said.

He stopped.

"No?"

"No." She said it firmly.

He sighed. Fine. Words, then.

When he spoke, his tone sounded low and rough. "You are more than just an injured leg, my lady."

He braced himself. Perhaps she would slap him. Or cry.

He probably deserved both.

But she merely shrugged. "Fine. Thank you. But stop . . . that." She waved her hand again as if she was chasing away a pesky insect. "That tone. The flirting. The . . . rest of it. I've already told you, I don't like it."

"Why not?"

"I don't believe in all of that."

He waited.

"Flirtation. Attachment. Romance."

'Of course you *believe* in it," he told her. "Your sister and Tensford have it. In spades. It stares at you across the dinner table every night."

She lifted a conceding shoulder. "Have you ever seen it before? Love? Real love?"

He looked away. "Once. My cousin found it, I once thought. At least, he and his wife appeared to be deliriously happy with each other." The last time he'd seen his the pair of lovebirds, though, they'd been harried and distracted, chasing after their passel of young children. Picking up a pebble, he tossed it over the edge and into the abyss. "But then, everything has always seemed to come easier for him."

"I say the same thing about Hope." They stared out at the expanse. Keswick became absorbed in watching the shadows of the clouds overhead move across the land below."

"It does exist, I suppose," she said at last.

"For some people," he agreed.

"But not for me," they said in unison.

They shared a long look, then. A moment of perfect communion. Something inside of him let loose a long breath, like a relieved sigh—and relaxed.

"I'll tell you a truth, Lady Glory."

"How refreshing."

He chuckled. "I was not excited at the prospect of attending this house party. In general, I prefer London and its amusements and variety of people. But I'm glad I came. I'm glad I met you."

Her color rose, but some of the tightness around her eyes softened. "I'm glad we met, as well."

"I think we should make a pact. You are not looking forward to the onset of this party any more than I am. What say we help each other through it?"

She nodded. Her gaze turned toward the distant estate. "Yes. I suspect I won't be nearly as helpful to you, but I'll do whatever I can." She held out her hand and they shook to seal the bargain. "Here's to both of us making it through this, unscathed."

CHAPTER 6

The first guest for the house party arrived the next morning. Fortunately for Glory, it was only Mr. Barrett Sterne. An old friend of Tensford's, he was already well acquainted with her and her limp—and he always teased her like a little sister. Teased her about everything *but* her limp—and she both appreciated the fact and cringed a bit over it.

Mr. Sterne was good natured and funny—and also a good friend of Lord Keswick's. They all had a grand day while the men caught up and they all set up wickets and netting for lawn games and partook of a dinner *al fresco* on the terrace. The evening shadows grew long as the friends told stories about each other, each more outrageous than the last, while Hope and Glory laughed until their sides hurt.

She'd been right to stop him, she told herself over and over, as the day went on. She'd been right to stop the viscount before he kissed her. Even though her brain kept dragging the images forth, reliving the moment when those blue eyes had held hers, when he'd touched her cheek and leaned in, his wide shoulders blocking the sun. She'd shivered, but it hadn't been from lack of heat. She'd been practically boiling over with conflicting emotions. Longing, curiosity, nerves, and yes, fear. Fear of the unknown, of appearing foolish—and of appearing to be just another besotted girl, like all the rest.

So, she'd stopped him. And they had made a pact. A friendly pact. That's what she and Keswick would be . . . friendly. Real friends, perhaps. That moment when they'd connected . . . They were similar, in some elemental way. She didn't quite understand it, yet, but surely it must be better than being just another girl that he'd kissed.

By the end of the day, she'd convinced herself it was true. They would be friends—and no more. And that would be both different and enough. When they all retired, Glory went to her room with a lighter heart, and the hope that she might survive this party, after all.

Her hopes wavered the next morning, when a mob of guests arrived all at once—all strangers. The courtyard was a buzz of greetings and laughter and servants running to and fro to see to the unpacking. Glory hung back, but Keswick caught her at it. With a stern look, he pulled her forward, right into the thick of the confusion.

Her leg dragged, but nerves danced to life in her wrist, where he gripped her. His touch sent tingles all along her arm. She could feel the heat rising in her face. Surely the newcomers would notice that. She was too busy noticing how lovely Keswick smelled to worry overmuch, however. It was her sister's doing, she told herself sternly—and yet she couldn't help but take another, deeper breath.

The air came sputtering back out when a pair of young ladies noticed her limping gait and exchanged glances. One merely looked startled, the other wore a familiar frown of distaste.

"Lady Glory," Keswick said, pulling her to a stop before them. "Allow me to introduce these lovely ladies, whom I have only just met myself. Miss Parscate and Miss Redsmock, may I make you known to Lady Glory Brightley, who is sister to Lady Tensford?"

Glory dropped a curtsy.

One of the girls flushed. "Actually, my lady, it is Miss Ruddock."

"Oh, do forgive me!" Keswick smiled, all charm. "I will make it up to you by presenting my very dear friend, Mr. Spurn."

His friend rolled his eyes. "Ladies. I am Mr. Barrett Sterne. A pleasure."

"Miss Ruddock," the girl repeated.

"And Miss Parsonbait," Keswick said smoothly.

The second girl laughed right out loud. "It is Parscate, sir. We are delighted to make your acquaintance."

"My pleasure, and do forgive Lord Westlick," Sterne said with a raised brow. "He truly is terrible."

"At names," Keswick prodded.

"That too," Sterne agreed.

They all laughed and went into the house where guests were being sorted into rooms.

"You appear to be injured, Lady Glory," Miss Ruddock said. "I hope you will recover quickly."

Glory gritted her teeth, then smiled. "It was a childhood injury, I fear."

"Oh, I'm so sorry." Miss Ruddock said it with sympathy, but her friend looked horrified.

"I fear Lady Glory has so many sterling qualities, fate felt it necessary to balance the scales in favor of the rest of us," Keswick announced. He bowed over her hand and excused himself. The two girls exchanged glances and followed.

Glory sighed and turned as her sister called her once more.

More guests arrived as the day progressed and Glory was expected to be present and presented. The viscount largely left her alone after that, but he kept true to his word. He and Sterne lingered, separate, but near, and they treated the fact of her limp so casually that everyone else was forced to follow their cue and do the same.

Grateful for their efforts, she stiffened her spine, smiled, exchanged pleasantries, greeted everyone and watched her sister beam at her in approval.

She also kept a close watch on the viscount. No hardship, there. Lord Keswick stood just a tad taller than the other men in the room. The sharp angles in his face gave him the edge in masculine beauty.

That was not why she watched him, of course. She was looking for ways to return the favor, trying to discover how she could help him in turn. She wasn't alone in staring after him, though—and she knew it was more than his title that drew so many female gazes.

Some watched him with caution and disdain. Clearly, his reputation as a rakehell was well established. Several women watched him with wary eyes and tried to keep out of his way. Some watched with a knowing, speculative manner. And quite a few others gazed after him in fascination. Glory could scarcely fault any of them. Keswick gave off the most intriguing aura—danger and allure wrapped in tight smiles and just-slightly-distant charm.

She breathed a sigh of relief when she finally escaped upstairs to change for dinner. She needed peace. She didn't find it, however. Instead she stared at herself in the mirror and wondered how she could have been so wrong. She wasn't similar to Lord Keswick. He wasn't going to need her help. He was entirely at ease in company and able to turn the mood of an entire room. He was everything she was not. Everything Hope and others wished her to be.

The thought exhausted her. But she would not give up so soon. His interventions had made a difference. She'd been treated with the same deference as the other young ladies, for the most part. There was still the odd stare and whisper, but they were less numerous and open than usual.

She allowed Hope's maid to assist with her hair and she wore a new gown of soft green with gold trimmings that darkened her eyes and made them look less . . . odd. She forced herself to join the company again, taking the servant's stairs so that she wouldn't be seen carefully maneuvering her way down.

She timed it perfectly, arriving just as dinner was called—but then she had to fight to keep her shoulders from slumping when she saw she was to be seated at dinner between Miss Myland and Mr. Lycett.

The elderly lady was companion to Tensford's aunt. Glory summoned a smile for her. "How are you enjoying the new arrangements at Brockweir?" she asked.

Miss Myland shrugged. "The food is decent, even if the company is not," she said. She addressed herself to the soup, slurping it with haste.

She finished before Glory had managed more than a couple of spoonfuls, then dropped her chin to her chest and appeared to doze as she awaited the next course.

With a sigh, Glory turned to Mr. Lycett. She knew he was an enthusiastic hunter. She asked him about his mount, thinking they could converse about training.

"I'm not surprised that you ask, my lady. My Apollo is the best-trained horse in the north of England. Such stamina he has—and it is only surpassed by the steadiness of his temperament. I don't think he's ever flinched at a horn at his ear or a hound at his heel."

"That is wonderful in a horse trained for the hunt, I'm sure. My own Poppy is steady and stalwart as well. She—"

But Mr. Lycett was not interested in hearing about her experiences. Instead, she was treated to an enthusiastic monologue about the superiority of his horse, his dogs, the many thrilling hunt days his local club got up to and the time he'd been invited to join the famous Quorn for one of theirs. Her spirits grew lower as he talked over her comments and ignored her attempts to change the subject.

So much for Keswick's theory that the man had been making up to her, she thought acidly. Worse, she could see the viscount over Mr. Lycett's shoulder, seated between Miss Munroe and Miss Ruddock, looking irritatingly handsome and apparently enjoying an amiable conversation with each lady in turn.

When Hope stood and called the ladies to withdraw, Glory was the first out of the door.

She settled in a dark corner and let the women chatter on without her. Blessed silence held in her hideaway and she hid away for nearly a quarter of an hour before Miss Munroe pulled a chair over and took a seat beside her.

"Forgive me for disturbing you," she said with real feeling. "I saw you with my cousin at dinner and felt I owed you an apology. I surmise, from his fervor, that he got started on his favorite topic."

Glory shot her a sour look and the girl laughed.

"Oh, dear. I have tried to convince him that conversation should be a shared endeavor, but the lesson does not seem to take root. I am sorry."

"You should not take on the burden of his crimes."

"Crimes? Was it so bad?"

"It was definitely an assault on both my appetite and my ears."

The girl laughed. "Curse him. He does go on. It drives my mother mad. She's so grateful to have him included in the festivities over here."

"And out of her hair?" Glory asked with a grin.

"Well, yes. I did hope he would behave better in company. But no, it seems he must go overboard, and just when I was hoping to get on your good side."

"My good side? But, why?"

Miss Munroe hesitated and Glory asked, "Is there something I can do for you?"

"You already have, which makes me feel that much more presumptuous. I so appreciated you sharing your dancing lessons." She leaned in. "And thank you for continuing them, although I know you have no real wish to."

"It does seem a waste, when the last thing I would want to do is to get up and dance in front of a crowd. Did you see Lady Tresham's face when I limped in here, in front of everyone else? I delayed her entrance by a brace of seconds and she looked as if I should be taken out back and given the mercy of a bullet."

"No!" Miss Munroe looked outraged.

"That's exactly why I asked that the lessons be moved to so early in the mornings. Mr. Thorpe is less than thrilled, but if we practice early, then there is no chance of being discovered by Lady Tresham or the rest of the late-rising London crowd."

"Ignore her. She's odious. I heard my mother tell my father that she is somewhat of a scandal, and has been turned away from some of the best houses in London."

Surprised, Glory looked over at the lady. "Truly?" The baroness was a widow who had lived near their family estate in Sussex. She'd suddenly shown a renewed interest in their company after news of

Hope's substantial inheritance and her engagement to Lord Tensford became public knowledge.

"Speaking of Town, I know your sister hopes to take you to be presented next spring—and I know that you are not excited about the prospect." She gave a little shrug. "But I do hope you will go. It's purely a selfish notion, you understand, for I'm to make my debut as well. It would be nice to have someone there." She cast a dark look at the knot of giggling girls by the pianoforte. "Someone with sense and the ability to converse about more than balls, beaux and bonnets." She raised a brow. "There is so much more of London that I would like to see."

"It would be easier with a like-minded companion," Glory said, gratified. "And Lord Keswick has already told me about some of the other attractions in Town."

Miss Munroe leaned in. "I confess, I am interested in the natural sciences and so I'm looking forward to the British Museum, and Kew Gardens, and perhaps a lecture or two. Is there something you wish to see?"

Glory hesitated. "Astley's Ampitheatre," she confessed at last, hoping she wouldn't seem like a child.

"Oh, yes, it sounds so exciting. And Vauxhall, as well."

Glory breathed a sigh of relief. "You almost make me excited for the Season." She broke off as the parlor door opened and the gentlemen began to stream in. Keswick, she noticed, was instantly bookended by Miss Ruddock and Miss Parscate.

"Now there is a man who could give my cousin lessons in charming the ladies. How have you found Lord Keswick, since he arrived?"

The speculation—and appreciation—in Miss Munroe's tone put Glory's back up.

"Is he as naughty as the gossips say? Lady Tresham keeps looking at him as if she'd like to find out."

Perhaps this, at last, might be a way she could help the viscount. "I find him quite pleasant. A true gentleman in word and deed."

"They say he does know how to treat a woman. Any woman," Miss

Munroe said with raised brows. "I heard that the tavern maid at the Crown and Cock is quite taken with him."

Glory's straightened. "Where did you hear that?"

"From my maid."

"Well, I am glad I am not the only one listening to servant's gossip. I heard the same thing. And the next time someone chides me for it, I'm going to tell them so."

"How else are we to learn anything?" Miss Munroe asked. "No one wants to tell me anything!"

"Anything interesting," Glory amended wryly.

"Exactly."

They shared a conspiratorial grin.

But she was supposed to be helping. "Perhaps we shouldn't spread that particular bit of knowledge about, though," she mused.

"Well, Lord Keswick tends to spark gossip wherever he goes." Miss Munroe gestured toward the young ladies around him. "I overheard those two wagering over him, between themselves."

Sudden alarm twisted in Glory's belly. "What was the wager?"

"They've made a bet. Each will try to get the viscount to kiss them. First one to succeed is the winner."

Glory's mouth dropped. "They never! What sort of girls has Hope invited to this house party?"

"Naturally curious ones, I should say." Miss Munroe swung around to look. "Just look at him." She sighed. "He's gorgeous. Those eyes! And that jaw line is spectacular. I'm not sure I would refuse him a kiss in the shrubbery, should the chance come up."

Glory felt ill. Hot and flushed and suddenly horribly aware of the buttered prawns she'd eaten.

Hope, passing by, caught a glimpse of her and stopped. "Glory, my dear, are you well?"

"No. I suddenly feel warm."

"Have you overtaxed yourself? I'm so sorry—"

"No. No. It's just—I think something has not agreed with me." She stood and gave Miss Munroe a nod. "Forgive me. I think I need to retire for the evening."

"Of course." Miss Munroe stood, as well, and squeezed her hand. "I do hope you feel better."

She would. Eventually.

When this blasted party was over.

* * *

Tensford had arranged an expedition down into the depths of the coal pit for the male guests this afternoon. Keswick cried off, using his previous descent as his excuse.

"Very well, Kes, but do come join us at the top of the hill afterward. We'll crack a keg when we come up and Hope has packed us a hamper of cheese and sausages to go with it."

"Ah, manly food," he said with a wink at the countess.

She laughed. "Indeed, and I hope you will enjoy it. I'm taking the ladies for a ride down to the village and then we shall enjoy a more delicate tea, here, afterward."

Which was exactly why Keswick was waiting in the stables after they all set off, currying the squire's fine chestnut and feeding him slices of apple.

It was a hunch that paid off when Lady Glory came in, just as he'd hoped.

She wore her more ordinary habit today—and she didn't notice him at first. She went straight to her mare's stall and let herself in. He watched as she stroked Poppy's nose, murmured something, then hugged the mare, leaning into her, as if seeking comfort.

Approaching, he cleared his throat. She started and straightened— and didn't look too happy to find him there.

It didn't deter him. In fact, the arrival of the other guests had only reinforced how differently she reacted to him. It struck him again, now. No cringing or eye-darting avoidance. No gleam of morbid curiosity or challenge. Every time, she met him openly, with sincere emotion.

Which, to be honest, looked like annoyance right now.

Was she annoyed with him? Or had she, perhaps, run into someone who reacted badly to her limp? He'd caught an arse of a young gentleman leaning over the railing, watching her walk through the front hall on her way to breakfast this morning. The lordling had turned back to his friend, jeering and imitating her limp. Keswick's sharp offer to defend the lady's honor if necessary had drained the color from the boy's face and had him offering up apologies—but it left Keswick sick at the thought of her facing this sort of casual cruelty.

"I had an inkling you would avoid the village—and that you'd take the chance to ride out, instead. I thought, perhaps, I might join you?"

He turned it into a question, as her expression had not lightened. For a moment, as she stared at him, assessing, he thought she might deny him. But she let out a breath and gave a curt nod. "Fine, then. But I've promised not to go far. I meant to merely follow the river out to the field at the bend."

He moved away to fetch a saddle. "The destination doesn't matter. It was your company I sought."

She paused in untangling her tack. "Why?"

He glanced up, surprised. "Because you are the most amusing person here, by far."

It was the wrong thing to say, judging by the growing thunder behind her eyes, but she gave him the truth—he felt he owed her no less.

She turned back to Poppy and he watched her ready her mare as he worked with his own mount. She moved carefully, but with the ease of long habit and no impediment from her leg. How could anyone look at her and see only her lameness? Her beauty was unusual—comprised of high cheek bones and pale skin that contrasted beautifully with lovely warm lips and auburn hair . . . Actually, he thought her color was high at the moment, and her lips were pressed together.

"Is anything wrong?" he asked.

"Wrong?" She blinked at him over Poppy's back. "Of course not. What could be wrong?"

Well, clearly something was wrong. The answers would come, he suspected, because they could talk to each other—which was both surprising and . . . a comfort.

Yes. He felt comfortable with her. Spending time with her was like . . . wearing his favorite boots. He looked down at them with affection —and reminded himself never to be so foolish as to say such a thing out loud.

He reminded himself never to be so foolish as to get *too* comfortable, as well. It was all very well to boost her confidence. But he could not raise her hopes. Not for anything beyond a temporary friendship. He'd meant what he said, back on that ledge where they'd gazed down upon the rest of the world. It wasn't too late for her to consider marriage. He still thought he could help her see that. As long as she didn't make the mistake of considering him.

He would be careful. And in the meantime, he kept his mouth shut and lifted her into her saddle, and followed her out of the stable yard.

* * *

Is anything wrong?

Oh, not a thing. Not one thing. Not the agitation that had kept her tossing and turning all night. Not the irritating knowledge that every woman in the county either wanted to hide from him or kiss him. Not the fact that she still kept alternating between both of those.

No, what bothered her was that she couldn't stop wondering if she'd been a fool to pass up her chance. And worse—the icy fear that it had been her one and only chance at being kissed, by anyone, ever.

She kept silent and he followed suit as they rode past the sprouting fields and over the bridge. Once they reached the open pasture,

Keswick looked over and grinned. "Race to the river and back?" he dared.

In answer, she leaned down, whispered to Poppy and sent her hurtling for the water.

"Wait, now!" She heard him shout. But then he was thundering after her. Poppy picked up the spirit of the chase and stretched out and they fairly flew across the field. Glory pulled her into a tight turn and started back just as Keswick arrived. "Not fair!" he shouted.

She only grinned and bent lower, urging Poppy on. But the squire's chestnut was strong and long of leg and clearly possessed a competitive spirit. He gained on them as they raced for the bridge. But her mare dug deep and put on a burst of speed and by the end had left Keswick and his mount more than a length behind.

Laughing, Glory sat up and slowed Poppy to a brisk walk. They circled around and she smiled at Keswick.

"Feel better?" he asked.

"Yes, curse you." She sighed. "I needed that."

He laughed. "Let's let them walk the length of the field and cool down."

They set out, side by side, taking their time.

"I must thank you for your efforts yesterday," she said at last. "They made a difference. This is the most normal I've ever felt at a gathering outside my own family."

"I'm happy to have helped. That's what our pact was for, was it not?"

"I fear I will not be able to return the favor."

"You are doing so, now," he protested. "You've saved me from another dark and dusty descent into the coal pit. And in any case, just wait. This party has only just begun. The worst could happen at any time."

"What would be the worst?" she asked, intrigued.

"Gossip? Scandal? Jellies that won't set up? I can think of several possibilities."

"None of that would dare occur at one of Hope's gatherings," she vowed. They'd reached the water. "I think these two need a bit more cooling down," she said, reaching down to pat Poppy's neck.

They headed along the long sweep of the river. "I don't understand how you prefer London." She shook her head. "I feel overwhelmed with just a houseful of people—and it's only been one day."

"You are not accustomed to it, that is all. It will grow easier." He lifted a shoulder. "And actually, there is an anonymity to be found in a crowded city. A man can blend in. Here, I walk in the village and everyone knows my name and where I am staying and for how long. In London, I'm just another young buck about Town."

She snorted. "I doubt you've ever been anonymous anywhere, ever, a day in your life."

"Well . . ." His expression darkened. "At times it is easier than others." He held silent a moment. "I am fortunate, though. There are times when I need to retreat." Like now. "Luckily, I have the solace of my friends, then. I can always withdraw to their care, should the need arise."

"That is fortune, indeed."

"It truly is. There are very few constants in my life. My friends are the most important."

"And your boots," she teased.

"Exactly."

She reached to caress Poppy once again. "I think they should be fine, now." Dismounting, she led her down the short bank and across the pebbled edge to the river, so she could drink. "Do you count any women amongst your group of friends?"

He looked over the chestnut's back and tilted his head. "Not until now."

She ducked her head, struck again with conflicting reactions to him. Once Poppy had finished, she led her back up the bank and tethered her at a stand of larch trees. Keswick did the same, then sat on the raised bank.

She didn't join him. She just walked along the pebbled strip of shore, picking her way carefully, thinking.

"Have I said something wrong?"

She shook her head.

He said nothing else, just leaned back, waiting. She was grateful. It took her several minutes and several passes back and forth to summon the courage to say what she wished.

"I would consider it an honor, to be counted among your friends." She said it to the waters, rushing by in front of her. "But I've been thinking about that kiss." She looked over her shoulder. "The one we didn't have."

"Oh."

It was all he said. She *had* surprised him.

"It's just that it occurred to me . . . having refused it . . . that I might have refused my only real chance."

He frowned. "Only chance? I don't understand."

She flushed, annoyed that he was going to make her spell it out. "My only chance at being kissed. Ever. In this lifetime."

His eyes widened. "Don't be absurd. We had this conversation, already."

"It's not absurd. You say I am considered marriageable, but I don't have a tremendous dowry like Hope did. Her fortune came from our mother's sister, who left her a great deal of money and instructions to see to my care. Even she didn't think I would find a man who would take me."

"Then she was a fool." He gave a bitter laugh. "You'll have plenty of chances to kiss better men than me."

"Does that mean that you no longer *want* to kiss me?"

He hesitated and her breath caught.

"It's not that. It's just that I think you should consider my opinion further. I have new eyes and an unbiased opinion. Not like the people who see you every day and see what they want or expect."

"Oh." Her heart fell. "You *don't* want to kiss me."

"That's not what I meant."

"Good." She jumped on his response. "Because you couldn't have been more wrong about Mr. Lycett. All he was interested in was talking incessantly about himself."

"If you let him, then he's probably more interested in you than ever," he said wryly. "Give him a chance, he'll work up to kissing you."

"Well I've no wish to wait upon him. If I have one chance at this, I'd prefer to do it with someone I like."

"Flatterer."

"And I want someone who will do it properly."

He opened his mouth to say something, then closed it again.

"I know. I'm acting terribly. Not only showing fast behavior, but it's also horridly rude to ask, after I refused you."

"Not going to let that stop you, though, are you?"

"No." She moved carefully to stand in front of him, just out of reach. "There is one problem."

"There's more than one." He grimaced. "I just don't think it's a good idea."

"It's a logistical problem," she charged on. "Or perhaps just a problem specific to me."

"My lady . . . Glory . . . Whenever, whomever you choose to kiss . . . Your leg is not going to pose a problem."

"Not my leg. It is another failing of mine, though."

"You have another?" he gasped in pretend shock.

"Oh, stuff it," she said with a laugh. And felt somehow more certain, because of it. Who else could make her laugh at herself? Who else sprinkled conversation with wit that reminded her of her first taste of champagne—surprise at the bubbling humor, appreciation of the quality of it—and a longing for more? "The thing is . . . I *hate* being made to feel . . . inadequate. As if I am somehow less than others."

"As you should. For you are not."

"Normally—just like at this house party—all I wish is to be treated like an equal to every other girl. But in this case . . ."

"Yes?"

"It's just that, there are so many women here—in the village, in the neighborhood, staying in the house—a number of them who are all pining for, or imagining, or plotting to convince you to kiss them."

He blinked. "Are there?"

"Yes. And for the first time, I find I don't wish to be counted among the crowd."

"Problem solved. You've already said you didn't want my kiss."

She merely looked at him.

He sighed, exasperated. "Wait. You are confusing me. You don't want to be kissed. Then you do want it, because it might not happen again, but you don't *want* to want it?" He dug both hands into the hair at his temples. "I have no idea what I'm to do here." His hands dropped away suddenly and he gazed at her with suspicion. "Just what is it that you are expecting of me? Are you asking me to kiss you? Or to kiss all the others, leaving you the odd one out?"

"Actually, it occurred to me that if I kept my mouth shut, that last scenario might come about all on its own." She shook her head. "But I find I don't like that idea, either."

Not at all. In fact, she hated it.

"Well then, we are stumped, are we not?"

She hoped that was disappointment in his tone and not relief.

"I think we should just give the idea up."

"No. I'm not stumped." She moved closer. "I realized that there is only one solution. I will let them plot and pine and plan and wait for you to get around to kissing them—but in the meanwhile, I'm going to be the girl who kisses you."

CHAPTER 7

She caught him completely by surprise.

Before he knew what she was about, she'd grasped his shoulders for support and pressed her lips to his.

His body knew what to do. His arms reached out and gathered her in, settled her on his lap. But his head was swaying wildly between flattered pleasure and wild, alarm-but-not-quite-panic.

He was a connoisseur. He'd well and truly earned his branding as a rakehell, and he'd done it with rowdy living and cavorting with countless women. All kinds of women, from wanton to timid and every sort in between. But he knew, with frightening certainty, that he'd never held a treasure like her in his arms.

This one. She was clever and somehow both innocent and wise. Everything about her was unexpected. Delicate. Entirely too good to be throwing herself at a wastrel like him.

His mind knew it—but the rest of him didn't care.

She kissed him softly. Almost chastely. It was a sweet kiss of closed eyes and pursed lips.

He pulled away and she made a sound of protest.

"I thought you wanted a proper kiss?" he rasped, his voice gone husky and his heart leaping at the thought. He threw up metaphorical hands. It was too late now, he might as well do the thing right.

She nodded.

"Then I'll show you *proper.*"

Her amber eyes darkened and she leaned toward him again, but he stopped. "A moment. Let us take our time."

He kissed the corner of her mouth. A gentle, tiny brush of his lips. Then the other. He kissed her upper lip and drew it between his own, then answered the plump beckoning of her lower lip. Slow. Soft.

He gathered her close again and took her mouth, taking possession, luring her down the path of growing sensation, of spreading desire, becoming more demanding by degrees.

She gave him what he asked for, surrendering bit by bit, until he swept her with his tongue and nudged her lips apart.

Her eyes flew open again. Clearly, she hadn't expected it, but she accepted the invasion and entered into the spirit of it, opening wide and moving her fingers up along his neck and into his hair.

He deepened the kiss again, with bold strokes of his tongue and a tightening grip on her. Her bosom pressed into his chest. He raised a hand to stroke the side of her breast, entranced by her curves, frustrated by layers of linen and wool.

She pressed against him, shifting her bottom as the growing ridge of his cock pushed back.

God, but she was sweet. So warm in his arms while the cool wind blew from the water—

He went still, remembered abruptly where they were. Open. Exposed. Vulnerable.

In one smooth move he lifted her away, stood, rotated, and settled her down into the spot he'd just left. Breathing heavily, he turned and walked to the water's edge, where he sucked in air like a bellows and waited for his cockstand to get the message that this was going no further.

Gad, what was he—a green boy? Letting an innocent girl make him forget—their surroundings, her vulnerability, his extreme unsuitability?

He whirled around, intent on making her understand, and found her still looking a little dazed, her breath coming quicker than normal.

His agitation eased a little.

"That didn't feel proper at all," she remarked.

He couldn't help it. He threw back his head and laughed. His anger dissipated, but not his alarm. She had no idea how dangerous she was.

"That, Miss Critical, was exactly what it was—exactly what a kiss should be. And now you've had it. You've been kissed and have no need to worry further."

She started to speak but he held up a hand. "And no reason to discuss it further, either. We've already stretched the limits of our pact quite far enough."

She frowned. "Are there limits on friendship?"

"Of course there are. Especially on this one."

She deflated. "Well, it does seem a shame. I enjoy your company."

He drew a deep breath. "As I enjoy yours. Tremendously." More than he should. More than was safe. He didn't want to hurt her. "I hate to be blunt about it, but I'll be gone in a few days. As I'm a friend rather than a relation, we cannot correspond. It seems our friendship has its own end date."

"You mentioned going about . . . in London . . ."

"Yes! If you come to London I will be happy to ride with you in the park and to take you to Astley's just as we discussed. We might see each other about in Society. But there can be no more than that. I wouldn't dream of subjecting you to more than that."

"*Subjecting* me to more? Is your regard so dire a thing?"

"It often is," he said wearily. "But I cannot say more."

"Because you cannot add another constant to your life?"

Damnation, but she was quick and clever and she actually listened. He must tread carefully. "That is it, exactly."

She waited, a brow raised in expectation, but he'd be damned if he explained further. And he was done—had had more than enough in this lifetime—of wanting something he couldn't have.

"Fine, then." She stood and made her way to her mare. "I thank you for indulging me. And for stretching the boundaries of our pact. I won't ask again, as you've made my position clear—and I understand that it leaves me somewhere below the level of your boots."

He scowled, knowing he should protest, but she sent the horse over the lip of the bank and used the height of it to mount up herself. With a nod, and without another word, she rode back towards the bridge and the road back to the house.

Cursing, but knowing it was better, safer, to bow to inevitability, he watched her go.

* * *

HOPE'S SALON had been opened up by means of a retracting wall. It looked lovely in the evening, with the walls aglow in the candlelight and the whole long room adorned with the swirling colors and sparkle of the entire contingent of guests gathered in their finest.

Tonight the young ladies were going to provide the entertainment. Except for Glory, who acted as assistant to her sister, moving slowly from group to group, gauging tempers and the temperature of the *hors d'oeuvres* and levels of drinks. Everyone seemed sated and happy and content to show off his or her fine clothes and jewels. Even she felt pretty in her favorite gown of blue-green and a short string of pearls. The crowd allowed her to keep her steps short and her limp less pronounced.

After the first performance—Miss Ruddock was something of a prodigy on the violin—Glory felt her duty discharged and took a seat in an empty grouping in the corner. A seat far from the edge of the performance area, where Lord Keswick stood speaking with a group of guests.

After a moment, Hope sank down beside her with a sigh. "Thank you for your help, Glory, dear. I am glad the ladies are carrying the heavy load this evening. I feel like I have barely seen you the last few days." She followed the line of Glory's gaze. "Why are you staring daggers at the back of Lord Keswick's head?"

"I am not! I am merely waiting for Miss Munroe to begin." She shrugged. "If his head is in the way then it is likely because it's been permanently swollen due to the fawning of all the young ladies."

"Well, I daresay he is the most fawn-worthy of all our gentleman guests."

"Hmmph," was all the response Glory felt safe to offer.

"What is it? I thought the pair of you were getting along?"

She lifted a shoulder.

"Well, I did see him make a point of introducing you to Mr. Sommers earlier. I thought he was being quite considerate of your interests, especially as the gentleman stands to inherit his father's stud farm one day."

So very considerate of Lord Keswick, she thought sourly. One kiss and he was trying to fob her off on someone else. And ring the bell for a bonus—because he found one who likes horses!

One kiss. One stunning kiss that began with light landings, here and there, like the flutterings of a butterfly, and ended with tongues tangled and her breast pressing into his hand and her hair and nipples raised and waiting . . . waiting . . . for what would come next.

She longed to know what came next. She'd been floating around on a cloud of all-consuming lust, recalling that kiss and wishing for more. Dreaming, wondering, imagining what might come next.

Only to find that, in Keswick's mind, Mr. Sommers came next.

"Glory?"

She started. "Oh, yes. So considerate," she said flatly. "But did you notice that Mr. Sommers was quite willing to discuss pedigrees and bloodstock with me, but it was Miss Munroe whose comfort he inquired after? And it was she, he invited to stroll to the punch bowl?"

"Yes," Hope sighed. "I noticed." She reached over and squeezed Glory's arm.

"In any case, I believe it is Lord Keswick you should be concerned for." Glory indicated the viscount with a nod of her head. He'd left his group and Lady Tresham had stepped into his path.

"She does have a predatory gleam in her eye," Hope conceded. "But I'm certain Keswick knows how to handle her sort."

"I'm certain he's had plenty of practice. Handling her sort."

And now the baroness stepped closer still. And Keswick didn't seem to mind subjecting *her* to more of him. He leaned in and said something low that had the lady's eyes widening.

"Don't judge him too harshly, I beg you." Hope's expression had softened. "William won't say much, but he has hinted that the viscount has faced more than a few difficulties in his past."

"In what way?" She shouldn't ask, but she could not help herself.

"I'm not sure. I have the impression that it has to do with his family."

Glory mulled that over as she watched him with the widow. Lady Tresham was making her interest plain. Keswick smiled and chatted, but there was a brittle quality to his laugh. And there was no sign of lightness in his brilliant blue eyes.

She stiffened as Lady Tresham laughed and reached out to touch his arm.

His dark head still bent to hers, but a moment later he pulled his arm back and slipped away. Glory felt her shoulders descend—and thought she recognized a similar relief in him as he moved to join Lord Tensford, conversing with another gentleman near the window.

"Glory, you are staring again," Hope said gently.

"Oh. I shouldn't, I know. But have you noticed?" she asked. "Lord Keswick is all affable charm, but I think he wields it like a tool. Or a shield," she mused.

"He does tend to keep people at a distance," Hope admitted.

"He never seems to truly relax unless he's with Tensford. Or Mr. Sterne." Yes, she rather thought she could see from here that tension had left his expression and his stance looked looser.

"They share a very close friendship," Hope admitted. "They are more like brothers than friends, I believe, and the relationship extends to a couple of other school friends. They are all very close." She straightened. "Oh, here we go, now. Miss Munroe is ready to begin."

Glory listened politely as her friend sang. She had a nice voice, with just a hint of a fuzzy edge that had all the males paying attention. But Glory was thinking about what Hope had just said. A close group of friends must be a blessing, a good thing. So why was Tensford open to adding a marriage and true closeness with Hope to his life, but Keswick appeared to be closed to the idea of growing emotionally intimate with anyone else? Trying to be discreet, she glanced over to see if the viscount was as enthralled with Miss Munroe's performance as so many of the other gentlemen.

Apparently not. He was frowning and gazing around the room, as if he were looking for something. Or someone.

Glory joined in the applause as her friend's song ended. Mr. Sterne stood to escort her from the open stage area. He brought her over to their corner and they both took seats.

"That was lovely, my dear," Hope said.

Glory echoed her compliments. "You should sing us a Scots ballad next time," she encouraged. "One of the ones your grandmother taught you." She smiled at the others. "I've heard a few of her songs and they are lovely."

"I wasn't sure they would be well received in such company," Miss Munroe glanced at Hope.

"I don't see why not. You can sing anything you choose, my dear, and we'll all be enthralled."

"Have you traveled to Scotland?" Mr. Sterne asked.

"Oh, aye," she replied with a smile. "Have ye?"

He looked charmed. "No, but I would like to. I am interested in conducting research on some of the plants local to the northern areas."

Hope looked over at Glory, slightly worried. Glory shrugged. It was not the usual drawing room conversation, but Miss Munroe seemed to find this a perfectly rational reason to travel. In moments, they were off in a discussion about the use of heather to cure digestive ailments and its superiority as a stuffing in mattresses.

Hope watched them, bemused, but Glory merely raised her brows. "Who is entertaining us next?"

"It looks to be Miss Parscate. I believe she is to play the pianoforte."

Any response Glory meant to make died away as Keswick suddenly appeared before them, a gentleman in tow. Suddenly her brain ceased working and her lungs labored to draw in the air that had turned effervescent with sparkling potential—until she remembered that all of the potential was for discouragement and dismissal.

"Good evening, gentlemen," her sister said. "Lord Keswick, have you tried the *hors d'oeuvres*? The salmon mousse cups have been well received."

"They are delicious, my lady," he said with a twinkle. "Although they are not, of course, colcannon and brown bread."

She laughed. "Perhaps at our next gathering."

"Lady Tensford," he said in a scolding tone. "Sir Blackwell has not yet been introduced to your sister."

"Well, that will not do. Glory, if I may present Sir Blackwell? Sir, my sister, Lady Glory Brightley."

She managed a nod. "How do you do?"

Sir Blackwell was a man approaching middle age. He had contrived to find a suit of clothing that exactly matched the brown shade of his thinning hair and bushy brows. Everything was of fine quality but with his slender build, the overall effect reminded one of a walking stick. He gave a perfectly correct bow, but his eyes—also brown—darted toward her skirts as he rose. The relief on his face at not seeing any direct evidence of her . . . deformity . . . was plain.

Keswick saw it too, if the tightening of his magnificent jaw was any indication.

"Your home is near Castleton, is it not, Sir Blackwell?" Hope tried to smooth the moment over.

"It is, madam."

"Sir Blackwell enjoys a friendship with the Prince Regent." Keswick said, clearly trying to recover from that glance.

Sir Blackwell grimaced. "Perhaps friendship is too strong a word," he hedged.

"He knighted you for your friendship and service? Did I not hear you say as much to the squire?"

"Fascinating. What sort of service do you provide for the Prince?" Hope sounded genuinely interested.

Glory was interested in the color rising in Sir Blackwell's face—and the puzzlement in Keswick's.

"Well, I . . ." The gentleman sighed in defeat. "The Prince Regent brought a party to our area. They spent some time enjoying the scenery and the air and the local ale and uh, other attractions. It seemed he ran up quite a number of large expenses, but found it was not so easy to make restitution, away from London and his banks . . . In any case, I helped him out of the situation."

Keswick looked disgusted.

Hope was trying not to laugh. "How kind of you."

Mr. Sterne suddenly looked over from his conversation with Miss Munroe. "He *knighted* you for that? It must have been quite a debt."

Sir Blackwell cleared his throat. "I understand it was quite a party."

"You didn't even get to attend?" Glory asked, indignant for him. "What a shame."

"Sir Blackwell's estate is in the Peak District," Keswick announced. "His properties encompass some of the most beautiful scenic views in England." He glanced significantly at her. "Lady Glory also enjoys beautiful scenery."

Hope blinked. "Do you, Glory?"

"Of course I do," she answered. "Who does not?"

Sir Blackwell cleared his throat. "Perhaps I can make up for the missed revelries during the next Season in London. Lord Keswick has extolled the virtues of spending spring in Town. It's such a busy time of year on the estate, but the rewards of investing a few months might last a lifetime."

"Lady Tensford intends to introduce Lady Glory in Town next year," Keswick interjected helpfully.

Glory wanted to sink into the floor. Was he a notorious rakehell or a matchmaking mama at Almack's?

"What a treat for you," Sir Blackwell told her warmly. "Your sister is very kind." He glanced across the room to where the young ladies were gathered. "Lady Tensford, would you know if Miss Ruddock spent the spring in London this year?"

"I don't believe she did, sir."

"Do you know if her family intends to present her next year?"

Hope blinked. "I'm sure I do not, but her mother is just over there, should you like to inquire."

"Yes. It might be the thing, to make my interest known early." Pursing his lips, he nodded. "Would you be willing to favor me with an introduction to the family, my lady?"

"Oh!" Hope looked startled, but she rose from her seat. "Yes, of course."

Sir Blackwell bowed. "Lovely to meet you, Lady Glory." He gave Keswick a nod. "Sir."

They departed and Mr. Sterne turned back to enticing Miss Munroe with talk of the glowworms that thrived in nearby Gorsty Knoll. Glory looked over at Keswick's astonished expression—and burst out laughing.

Because honestly, it was better to laugh than to cry.

Keswick sank down into a chair.

"What in the name of every patroness of Almack's are you doing?" she hissed at him. "Next you'll be passing out tepid lemonade and extolling the virtues of my family tree."

"I'm trying to prove my point!"

"I rather think you are proving mine, instead. You will cease this matchmaking at once," she ordered ferociously. "You are making me look ridiculous."

"It's not you, it's them!" He slumped back in his chair and narrowed his eyes at her. "Isn't it? Perhaps you should open your countenance a bit? Speak up a bit more? Show them who you really are? I know they will be entranced."

She glared. "I tried that route already. It was a spectacular failure."

"Truly? With who?"

Sighing, she closed her eyes and shook her head.

"Oh." He sank back into his chair. "You cannot count me. I'm not like all of these other fellows."

Exactly. Wasn't that why she liked him? But she could never say so, not now.

He sighed. "Have you ever played with a ball made of Indian rubber?"

Frowning at the change of subject, she shook her head.

"They are marvelous. Full of spring and bounce. You toss it as hard as you can and it flies so high—high above your head. That used to be me. I could take a hit, a loss, and bounce right back. But no longer. I've grown hard and brittle." He shrugged. "No bounce left."

Her heart twisted as she realized it was pain as much as people that vaunted charm protected him against. She felt a wave of protectiveness—

"No." His tone was pointed and urgent. "Whatever it is that has your eyes widening like a doe's—forget it. I don't need anything," he said, suddenly harsh. "Not from you or anyone else."

She opened her mouth to argue—but Hope returned at that moment and took the seat next to Keswick.

"Well, that might have actually worked in Sir Blackwell's favor," she said briskly. "Now, what are we discussing over here?"

"We were deciphering how it could be that so many of the gentlemen here could be such nodcocks," Keswick said easily.

"I may have inadvertently invited a number of nodcocks," Hope told him, "but I am happy not to count you among their number."

Miss Ruddock called for the room's attention and introduced her friend and her choice of music. Everyone stilled to listen, but Glory heard not a note. Keswick's sharp tone still rang in her ears.

When Miss Parscate had finished, Keswick leaned in and said to Hope, "You certainly made no mistakes in inviting the young ladies. They are all of the highest caliber."

Glory was still smarting. "If rumor is to be believed, they are certainly a different caliber than you pursue in Town."

He regarded her steadily. "Fortunately, I know you are too sensible to lend credence to rumor."

"I am sensible enough to recognize what I see with my own eyes." She let her gaze wander over to the corner of the room, where Lady Tresham stood listening to a group of ladies—and watching their group avidly.

"Oh, but you cannot chastise him for that," Hope interjected. "Going in pursuit and being pursued are two very different matters."

The truth of that struck her hard and Glory paled. "You are right," she whispered. She stared at Keswick and he gave as good as he got, returning her measure with unblinking blue eyes. And she flushed, suddenly and horribly aware that from his perspective, *she* might be seen as pursuing him. "I'm sorry," she blurted out.

He shot her a twist of a grin. "There's nothing to be sorry about. Don't waste a moment on regret." And now his smile definitely reached his eyes. "I certainly do not."

In desperation, Glory turned her attention to where the next young lady was making preparations at the pianoforte, but she felt the charged weight of his gaze upon her. It felt considerably heavier than the butterfly touch of those opening kisses.

"So much talent," Keswick mused. He leaned toward Hope. "I admit, though, that I long to see Lady Glory's theatrical piece. If you asked her, do you think she would change her mind and perform it for us?"

"No. I don't." Hope turned to her, blinking. "You *told* him about it?"

"I told him only that it happened. Once. And never again," she said firmly.

"Ah, well. I had to try." Keswick stood and bowed to them both. He took Glory's hand. "Never say never, Lady Glory."

He left them, heading back toward where Tensford still held court near the windows.

Mr. Sterne and Miss Munroe were still huddled and were discussing different types of larvae. Hope just sat and looked at her, brows raised.

Glory held silent.

"Very well. I believe I shall make the rounds and play hostess once more." She leaned in so that her voice would not carry. "But do you know, I believe that Lord Keswick also relaxes in *your* presence, Glory darling?"

Glory stilled, barely noticing Hope's departure. Her sister's words rang in her head like a bell, mixing with Keswick's and starting off a chain reaction in her brain. Quips and confessions, smiles and darted looks, frowns and touches experienced in the last few days were blowing apart and remaking themselves . . . into an idea.

A dramatic, risky idea.

A thrilling idea.

An idea that would be difficult to bring to fruition.

She stood, determined and brimming with excitement. She'd never let that stop her before.

CHAPTER 8

"I t's a relief to see Tensford happy at last," Keswick said in an aside to Sterne.

His friend grinned. "I am beyond glad to see his difficulties behind him. And I'm glad for Hope, as well. I don't think I've ever met a more deserving couple."

The company—consisting of most of the house party guests—was gathered along the riverbank, where a wide, stone-covered strip of shore left the water and led up to a cliff of varying heights. They had gathered around their host—except for Lady Glory. Keswick kept glancing back at her, where she sat on a camp stool in the shade of several large boulders and the woods that had encroached on the area beyond them.

"Step carefully, all of you," Tensford called. "Leave no stone unturned. The rapid erosion at this spot means that there is always something new to find." He held up a rock that wasn't quite a rock. "This is an ammonite. It's the most commonly found specimen at this spot. Note the coiled, spiral design and watch for that. That's not to say you couldn't find other types of fossilized remains. We've seen bones, plants and even some fish scales. Keep your eyes sharp and call out if you need help identifying anything!"

The guests scattered, some examining the scree covering the beach and others approaching the cliff face.

"Be careful of falling slabs, there," Tensford called. He grinned as he approached and slapped Sterne on the back. "It's not as quiet as it usually is when you join me, Sterne, but who knows, with so many eyes, maybe we'll find a serious specimen, yet."

Sterne looked doubtful. "I don't know, Tensford. As often as we've looked, it seems as if we would have found it by now. And you came out here often with your father while he lived, did you not?"

"Many, many times."

"And did you not once think you'd found a significant specimen? When you were younger?" Sterne frowned, trying to remember.

"A partial specimen," Tensford said, sighing at the memory. "I swear I did find it. Just over on that cliff face. It was the back end of some kind of large fish. The tail fin was over twelve inches high. I've often wondered what the rest of the thing must have looked like."

"Do you not have it in your workshop?" Keswick asked.

"No. I was young, only ten years, at the time. I went running back to the house to tell my father. I had to wait, as he was closeted with Mr. Stillwater, one of the neighbors."

"Wait, isn't that the name of the elderly gentleman, over there? Sterne introduced me."

"Indeed, that is he. He's an enthusiast, too. He's made some decent discoveries on his own land. I invited him because he doesn't get out much these days, and I knew he would enjoy it."

"Well, what happened to your fish tail?"

"That's the joke, isn't it? I was wild with impatience by the time the men had finished their business. I was practically jumping out of my skin, wanting my father to come and see it. Stillwater looked at me as if he'd slap me sideways if I was his son, but Father was tolerant. He finished their business and made me wait while he briefed the land agent, then we went to the kitchens and collected a basket to bring with us and we came down to inspect it." He sighed. "It was gone. As if it had never been there. But I swear, I did see it. Father used to tease me and call it my Fish Tale. We never found a sign of it, not crumbled pieces, not the rest of the creature, nothing."

He sighed again. "I came down even more often after Father died." He gave Keswick a sheepish look. "When I discovered the true extent of the condition of the estate and the worse shape of the account books, I used to come out here, hoping and praying to find something spectacular. I dreamed of a new type of creature or at least a whole, intact one. If sold to the right buyer, it could have brought a lump of cash that might have meant seed for a field or a winter's grain or a new roof for some of my tenants. Now, thanks to Hope, I don't have to look for those reasons, but I still enjoy it."

"You didn't know your treasure was awaiting you in London," Sterne laughed.

"I send up thanks for her every day," Tensford said. "And I don't mean for the money. I would be still be happy, even if she had come with only the small dowry I thought she had."

"You wouldn't be throwing a house party," Keswick said wryly. "And I don't know whether to be thankful for that or not."

A cry of surprise and triumph rang out. "I think I've found one, my lord!" Miss Ruddock waved her fist in the air.

"Let us see it, then," he called and set out for her.

"He's in his element," Sterne said. "I'm going to investigate the cliff. You?"

Keswick shrugged. "I'll stay here and look. You go on."

He was definitely not in his element.

Circling, he tried not to look toward Lady Glory. She'd done something to him, that wicked girl. He couldn't settle. He, a man of appetites, found them all dried up. He wasn't hungry. Tensford's best cheroots held no appeal. He wasn't even drinking. Last night he'd taken a tumbler of brandy in the billiards room and stared at it for hours instead of tossing it back. He'd barely slept last night, waking again and again, feeling hot and on edge while his blood pounded for . . . what he wouldn't give it.

And he cursed her through it all, for he was supposed to be done with feeling such things, and with longing for things that could not be his.

And she? Lady Cool as a Cucumber Glory hadn't glanced his way all morning. He'd thought she might stay back at the house with her sister and with those who could not summon up enthusiasm for Tensford's hobby, but no. Here she sat, talking contentedly with Miss Munroe while he moved among the searchers and tried to avoid Lady Tresham, who trailed after him like a cat on the hunt.

He could scarcely believe he was the only one sneaking looks at Lady Glory. Surely not every man here was a blind fool? The sunlight swam in auburn eddies amongst her curls and she practically glowed in a simple white gown, covered with an overdress of spring-green linen.

He dragged his eyes away and thought he should go and join Tensford as both protection and distraction, but paused when he heard his name.

Narrowing his eyes, he moved toward the cliff. Mr. Lycett stood there with another gentleman, and it was he who had spoken.

Keswick bent down, as if examining and following a vein of rock, and listened.

"He'll never offer for her." Lycett was faced away from Glory, speaking to his friend, but he looked over his shoulder and Keswick quickly reached out to pull at a ridge of rock.

Just another fool prowling among the rocks. Nothing to see here.

"She's pretty enough," Lycett admitted. "And her portion is reputed to be quite respectable. But I don't know. They say she can ride. Yet she doesn't dance at all."

"Yes, such a disaster," his friend agreed in a tone of exaggeration. "Because so many men I know are always pining to dance with their wives."

"She would never be able to chase after the children."

"That's what nursemaids are for."

"In all honesty, a thought keeps running through my head." Lycett lowered his tone and Keswick had to strain to hear him. "If a horse had suffered such an injury, it would have been shot. I'm not sure I can keep that from running about my mind."

Keswick straightened. He turned, outrage flaring high and running hot through all of his limbs, but Sterne was passing the pair and heading straight for him. He tried to step around his friend, but Sterne clamped a hand on his shoulder.

"Did you hear what that worm just said?" he demanded.

"Yes," his friend said tightly. "But drawing attention to it will not help the lady." He held up a bucket he'd picked up. "Let's take a big scoop of this debris over to Lady Glory," he said clearly.

"I'd like to dump a bucket over that arse's head," he grumbled.

"Come along, she's alone now. Let's be sure she doesn't stay that way."

"You go." Keswick turned away. "It's better if I stay away."

"Why?"

He just looked at his friend.

"Surely not," Sterne scoffed. "You're a legend, Kes. I've seen you juggle three women in one evening. What could this slip of a girl do to you?"

"None of them were like this slip of a girl," he growled.

"True enough." But Sterne still looked skeptical.

"It's complicated."

"Ah." Sterne's expression cleared and nodded in unexpected approval. "Good. I think it's time you tried complicated."

"No. No, it's not time. There never will be a time. That's the last thing I need—and you know it." Keswick groaned. "Perhaps I should just go back to Town. I could always hole up in some dive down by the docks."

"You could avoid the Vernon chit that way, but I know you've heard your father is in Town. How long do you think you could hide from him?"

He slumped. "Chester wrote you, too?"

"Whiddon did. Your father cornered him at the club and grilled him about your women, your habits, and why you came to the country."

Keswick paled and cursed under his breath, long and with feeling.

"You know Whiddon wouldn't tell him anything."

"Which will only make him more determined. Hell and damnation, what's set the old man off, this time?"

"I haven't the faintest notion—but you are better off here. So, let's go make nice with Lady Glory. At least we can be of use to her while we are here."

He'd already done more than he should with regard to Lady Glory, but he looked over Sterne's shoulder and saw the worry in her face as she watched Lycett and his friends watching her. He stiffened. "Fine. Damn it all."

She focused on the pair of them as they approached. "Good afternoon, gentlemen."

Sterne bowed and held up his offering. "We did not wish you to miss the fossil frenzy."

She smiled her thanks. "Don't worry about me. I sometimes come out here with Tensford. I can navigate the shore line if I am careful, but I thought it best to steer clear of all of the activity today." She held up her hands. Her lap was full of long vines and small wildflowers. "But as you can see, Miss Munroe has set me a task, and I am keeping occupied."

Sterne poured the debris next to her stool. Overturning the bucket, he perched upon it. "I'll sort it, then."

Keswick settled on the ground before her. "What are you making?"

"Oh, just a couple of flower garlands. Miss Munroe and I might wear them in our hair tonight. Or I might just send them along to the children in the nursery."

He imagined the tiny white flowers sprinkled amongst her curls. "You should wear them."

"We'll see how they turn out."

"You seem deft enough at it," Sterne remarked. He was tossing rocks away, toward the water.

"I should be. I had plenty of practice making garlands last Christmas."

"Did you spend it here?" Sterne looked up.

"Yes. It was our first, here in Gloucestershire. Hope's and mine, I mean. It was lovely, too. Even the holidays have been somber at our home in Sussex for the last few years, but it was quite an exuberant celebration here. I swear, I must have woven together miles of greenery. It was all over Greystone."

She had piqued Sterne's interest. "Did you learn of any local or unusual traditions? It's an area of interest for me," he explained.

She tilted her head to think about it. Her lips pursed and Keswick felt it, a hook and a tug at the base of his spine, pulling him nearer.

"There was the greenery and the Christmas pudding. A yule log. But the wassailing was the thing that was mostly different."

"In what way?" Sterne asked.

"The farmers were very serious about it. It was lovely, too. You could tell they had practiced. They visited everywhere and then ended by going out to the orchards to sing to the fruit trees. They believe it wakes them and ensures a good harvest."

"Fascinating." Sterne was staring down at the stone in his hand. "Oh, I say, you're the expert in this group. Is this what we're looking for?"

"Let me see." She leaned down to take the rock and Keswick froze. This was by far the lowest décolletage he'd seen her wear, and it strained as she bent over. "Oh, yes. It's a partial ammonite, I believe." She handed it back and straightened, and Keswick heaved a great breath of relief.

It caught her attention. "What about you, my lord? Your mother was Irish, you said. Did she introduce any interesting and different traditions to your holidays?"

He didn't answer. She had bent down again and was searching among the greens piled at her feet. The green over-gown dipped low to cup her breasts. The pretty little gold clasps that held the bodice together labored to contain her.

Could Lycett see her from his vantage point? Was Sterne watching her bosom swell over, too? His blood rose to an instant boil at the thought, and he turned to his friend—to find him staring at him, not her.

"Kes?"

"What? Yes?"

"Irish holiday traditions?" Lady Glory prompted.

"Oh. Yes." He tried to pull his thoughts together. He had to look away from the bounty before him. "Yes, my mother was a great one for placing candles in all of the windows on the eve before Christmas. She insisted that the weary travelers must know they had a welcome, should they need one."

"That is very sweet." She sat up. "You know, Mr. Sterne, there is another tradition I heard about, in this part of the country. It takes place in the spring, though, not at the Christmas holidays. At the church in St. Briavels, I believe." Frowning, she searched the crowd beyond them. "It has something to do with tossing and catching bread and cheese. The morsels become . . . lucky talismans, perhaps? You should ask Miss Munroe about it. She is likely to know all of the particulars."

"Is she?" Sterne stood. "Well, I've searched through all of these, in any case. I'll go and ask her."

Keswick climbed to his feet, as well. "No, you stay and I'll go and fetch her."

"I'm already up," Sterne said with a devilish grin. "Lady Glory, I leave you in Keswick's capable hands. Don't hesitate to make him fetch and carry for you."

Sterne strode off, the traitor. Keswick looked down at the chit watching him thoughtfully, her cognac-tinted eyes shining. "Don't look so worried, Keswick. I'm not going to send you on a forced march."

* * *

GLORY STARED UP AT KESWICK, his big, wide-shouldered form framed by the bright sky and sparkling water, and she felt a little thrill. Several little thrills, actually.

The foremost one, oddly, was of gratitude. Of all the men to stir up a whirlwind of chaos inside of her—she was glad it was this one. He shifted, fidgeting and frowning. He was clearly agitated. Distracted. Likely annoyed with her, still. But he did not become ill-mannered, short or dismissive. He did seem uncommonly focused on her, though.

And that led straight to all of those other thrills. All the little tremors currently knocking about her interior, waking up heretofore sleeping bits of her and setting them all aflame.

"You should," he said.

She blinked. She'd let herself become distracted by the sheer, sharp-edged bulk of him. "Should what?"

"You should send me marching out of here. In fact, I volunteer. I'll quick step back to the house to fetch you" . . . he circled his hand around his chest . . . "one of those filmy, lacy things."

She watched his hand, frowning. "Filmy . . . a fichu, do you mean? Why?" She looked down. "Have I spoiled my gown?"

"You've forgotten a section of it, rather."

She scowled up at him. "Are you criticizing my gown?"

"No. I'm only informing you that there is not enough of it." This time he pointed to her chest and made that circling motion. "Right about there."

Her heart pounded. How could he be so irritating and . . . stimulating, at the same time? "The neckline of this gown is perfectly in line with fashion—and with those worn by other ladies here."

"Are you sure?" He sounded dubious.

"Perfectly." She decided to be encouraged by his interest. Perhaps it bided well for her plan. "In fact, this décolletage is more modest than some others right here in this gathering."

"Is this bucket taken?" Lady Tresham appeared and sank down upon Sterne's abandoned, makeshift seat.

"And so my point is made," Glory said with a wave. The baroness's neckline was noticeably lower than her own—and her bosom swelled above her bodice—which was the point, after all.

"It's not the same," Keswick answered.

"It is entirely the same!"

"How wise you were to bring a seat along," Lady Tresham told Glory. "Now, what are you two bickering about? You sound like school children."

"We were just discussing necklines and local traditions," Glory answered.

"Necklines?" The baroness waved a hand before her own. "You should lower yours, my dear, and then perhaps you would not be sitting here alone."

"She is not alone," Keswick said curtly.

"Not now," the woman agreed.

"And I've had enough talk of fashion," he grumped.

"Traditions it is!" Glory agreed. "Do you have any personal favorites, Lady Tresham?"

"I do enjoy a nice brandy before dinner." She cast a sultry glance at Keswick. "And I am a great proponent of exercise before sleep."

It took a valiant effort, but Glory did not roll her eyes. "We were speaking more of family and holiday traditions."

The baroness wrinkled her nose. "It's not my sort of interest."

"Not interested? In Maypoles or harvest fairs or Christmas puddings?"

"No. I daresay Lord Keswick is not, either."

"I don't know," he hedged. "I have enjoyed the sight of young ladies dancing around the Maypole, in my younger days."

"And no one can object to birthdays," Glory declared. "Surely birthday celebrations are counted as family traditions."

"I do enjoy presents." Lady Tresham glanced up, making sure Keswick was listening. "But I do not care to restrict them to a single day of the year."

"Everyone likes presents." Glory raised a brow. "What has been your favorite birthday present thus far, my lady?"

Her hand caressed her throat. "A necklace of diamonds and rubies.

My late husband gave it to me, on my first birthday after we were married."

"It sounds lovely." Glory looked at the viscount. "Poppy was a birthday present, did you know? Hope gifted her to me."

"She could not have chosen better," he said gruffly.

"No, and I doubt she'll ever surpass the perfection of that particular gift." She sighed. "But come, we've shared. What has been your favorite birthday present, sir?"

"I can scarcely recall."

"An Indian rubber ball, perhaps?" she asked with a twist of a grin.

He grunted in acknowledgement of her hit. "Very likely. And as it was one of the last I received, I'll call it my favorite, as well."

Her heart pinched. "Do I mistake you? That was your last birthday gift? How old were you?"

"Seven."

"And not a birthday present since?"

"My mother died before I turned eight. My father does not remark upon such things."

"Remark upon? Are you saying you've had no birthday celebration since you were seven?"

He shrugged.

"Not a dinner, a cake, a drink? Not even a heartfelt birthday wish?"

"No. And I've scarcely felt the lack," he said with a lift of a shoulder.

She looked at him for a long moment. "What did you get for your seventh birthday?"

He closed his eyes. "A pony. He was a dashing, high-spirited prince of a fellow. He was grey, with a dappled flank and a white blaze and the heart of a Trojan."

He opened his eyes again and they shared a flash of understanding.

"Unfortunately, perhaps, I had a growth spurt during that year. By my eighth birthday I was really too big for him."

"And you were hoping for another mount that year?"

He lifted a shoulder.

Lady Tresham leaned toward her, which just happened to push her bosom even higher. "Lady Glory, you should take care not to show too much enthusiasm about such things. I'm sure you've no wish to appear childish."

"Of course not." Glory looked away from Keswick to regard her evenly. Was this how this was going to play out? She was heartily tired of being belittled. "But I do not believe enthusiasm should ever be frowned upon, so long as the object is harmless. What is life without enthusiasm? No, we should not allow such narrow judgments to stand. What if others decided to follow the logic of it in the opposite direction? They might decide that your antipathy towards birthdays comes from having seen too many. And we wouldn't want that."

Keswick abruptly sat down again. A little silence reigned in their shady spot. Lady Tresham watched Glory with hostility—mixed with a new tinge of respect. "No," she said. "We would not." She looked around. "It is pretty here, is it not? But I confess, I do begin to miss Town life. What of you, Lord Keswick? Are you pining for London's excitements?"

"I do miss the company of my friends," he admitted.

"The large variety of company is one of the highlights of the city, and the Season," the baroness agreed. She turned an eye on Glory. "Oh, but you have not yet made your debut. Have you been to London?"

"No."

"Don't worry. You will adjust. And some day you might have a larger acquaintance in Town."

"Were the two of you acquainted in Town? Did you meet often?" Glory asked.

"No, we were introduced here, by your sister," Keswick answered.

"Do allow me to advise you a little, my dear," Lady Tresham broke in. "Convince your sister to take you to her modiste in London—and make them dress you in the pastels that are allowed for the young debutantes." She ran an evaluating eye over her. "White so often washes a fair complexion out."

Glory cleared her throat. She knew people discussed her behind her back. Her limp made her a topic of gossip, and there was nothing to be done about it. Lady Tresham knew better than to bring up her lameness to her face, but Glory would be damned if she let the baroness use her youth, her coloring, or anything else, against her. What sort of woman tried to knock another one down to lift herself up? "Thank you, Lady Gresham. I'll let Hope handle all of that. She always knows what is pleasing . . . and what is inappropriate."

Before another silence could stretch out, she held up her garland. "I must get this finished before people tire of the hunt." She smiled at both of the others. "At least we know one thing this house party has accomplished. Now we are all friends and as you say, I will possess some acquaintances if I ever make it to London. Perhaps next spring we will all be together in London and looking back on this day with fondness."

Lady Tresham gave an indulgent laugh. "Don't count upon it, dear. However lax the rules are in the country, they are very stringent in Town. You will scarcely be allowed near Lord Keswick."

"Why ever not?"

"He is a young buck of the Town. He occupies a different plane altogether. London is a very different place for debutantes."

"Lord Keswick has already assured me that there are many activities worth pursuing."

"There are—but you will not be granted access to many of them. The young girls on the marriage mart are coddled and corralled. They might be trotted out at Almack's and at tepid balls, but they are not allowed at the places a man like Keswick frequents."

Glory's hackles began to rise. "A man like Lord Keswick?" she asked dangerously.

Lady Tresham, warming to her subject, did not recognize the danger. She cast an amused glance at Keswick. "Dear, the viscount is a man of diverse tastes and experiences. He spends his time in the clubs, the haunts, hells and back streets of a London you will scarcely see."

She frowned. "You paint an unfairly dark picture, I am sure."

"No, dear. Lord Keswick spends his time with other gentlemen of sophistication, in pursuits that are whispered about in polite society.

He searches out the dark and twisted places that echo the hidden parts of his soul."

Keswick's expression tightened, but otherwise, he made no objection to being described in such a manner. Glory, however, braced herself and carefully stood upright. She could feel the color rising in her face. It curled up from the fire of anger and indignation suddenly alight in her gut. "Lady Tresham, I think you forget yourself, speaking so about one of my sister's guests—and in his very presence! You feel free to say such things about a man who you have only just met? I believe you have paid heed to too much gossip and allowed it to fuel your overheated imagination."

Keswick had scrambled to his feet when she stood. Glory gestured toward him. "Lord Keswick is a gentleman."

He started to interject, but she cut him off. "He is a *fine* gentleman who has demonstrated nothing but friendship, kindness and honor to both me and my family."

Keswick stared at her as if she was a specimen he'd never seen before.

The baroness whipped her head between them. "Silly child! I meant no insult. Lord Keswick doubtless understands and knows just what I mean."

"I am neither silly nor a child. Nor do I believe anyone should have to withstand being labeled dark and twisted with equanimity." She reached out a peremptory hand toward the viscount. "Sir, you promised Mr. Sterne that you would be my aide. I find I need a few more vines to finish my project. Will you please help me gather them?" She nodded toward the faint path that led to the trees beyond the boulders. "There should be plenty just there." She gave the woman a frosty nod. "Good day, Lady Tresham."

And she pulled Keswick along with her to the cover of the trees.

CHAPTER 9

Lady Glory was angry. Though they'd gone a little ways into the trees, her lips were pressed together and she held her chin high. Her step was brisk, her limp more pronounced and she allowed herself to lean on his arm for support—a sure sign of her agitation.

As for him, his head was a churning study in contradiction—a state that he was beginning to become used to, in her company.

"There's no need for this fuss," he said at last. "Nothing she said is untrue."

Lady Glory gave a scoffing sniff.

"I do frequent low places and worse company. I drink and gamble and carouse with my friends." His lifestyle served its purpose. It thwarted his father and caused most women in Society to give him a wide berth. Occasionally, a thrill-seeker like Lady Tresham came around, but they were easily evaded. Or, sometimes, he let them stay.

Why did this girl turn everything upside down?

He usually appreciated it when his reputation cleared the path before him, but he'd been furious when she had expected the worse from him and hidden her affliction.

Now she defended him and his honor. It was not well done of Lady Tresham to speak about such things in front of an innocent. The usual sort of girl would have been flustered and dismayed. But not Lady Glory. She didn't withdraw or back down. She didn't let the idea of his reckless behavior push her away. Instead she'd chided the baroness and spoken of him in glowing terms.

Of *him.*

It left him feeling hot and bothered. Uncomfortable. And frighteningly intrigued.

No. No, he was a fool, that's all. And she was only more stubborn than most.

"Lady Tresham is a widow," he announced belligerently. "She knows how these games are played. I am free to dally with her as I wish."

She pulled her arm from his and took a few steps away. With one hand braced on a birch tree, she waved the other. "Then by all means, go back."

He glared at her. But he didn't leave. "I've entertained widows before. I've had *affaires* with them."

She repeated the gesture. "Dally away."

He held his ground.

"Do you want to take up with Lady Tresham?" she asked.

He winced. "No."

"Of course you don't. She is vain, shallow and self-serving."

"She's also right. About me. I like the back ways and alleys. I do spend a good deal of time there. Everyone wants to put a hand in your pocket or a knife in your heart, but at least it is all up front. You scorned me for my association with Betsy at the Crown and Cock, you would cringe at some of these places."

Her eyes blazed. "I didn't scorn you. You scorned me because I knew about it. Because I learned about it through the servant's grapevine."

Damn. She was right. He gave a nasty laugh. "Betsy is a queen compared to the sort of women whose company I usually keep."

She sucked in a breath and threw back her head. "Yes, yes. You like women without strings or attachments. I understand!" Pushing away from the tree, she took a step, then made a fist and thumped it against her thigh. "My leg is lame. My eyes and ears are fine. My head and my heart function just as they should. I see. I hear. I understand." She paced a bit further and stopped. Bracing herself again against a thick elm, she speared him with a sharp look. "Do you abuse these low women and widows whose company you keep?"

"What? No."

"Do you cheat them? Beat them? Verbally berate them? Break their hearts?"

"Don't be ridiculous."

"Sterne is your friend, as is Tensford. I know you all have others, too, a group you are close to." She put a hand on her hip. "Your friends gamble with you, drink with you, spend time in the same places, do they not?"

He nodded.

"Would you stand by and allow Tensford to be called dark and twisted? Or Sterne?"

"Of course not."

"Why?"

"It's not true."

"It's not true of you, either."

He looked away.

Silence held sway for a moment. Only the breeze rustling in the leaves and the distant sound of the river could be heard. One of the searchers called out, but it sounded so far away.

"I know about the stable boy, Keswick."

His heart rate spiked, but he didn't allow it to show. He let nothing show.

"I know you met the young man playing cards and that you learned he was courting a kitchen maid. He wished to marry her, but he didn't have enough of a living to support a wife."

"The path of love never did run smoothly," he said flippantly.

"No. Not until you leased the old Roudley farm and sent the stable boy out there to begin raising fence and repairing the cottage."

"Yes, well, the pastures there are perfect for raising good bloodstock. And the boy has the touch—the horses are putty in his hands.

All I have to do is set him up. He'll do the hard work and I'll make a fortune selling carriage horses to all of my friends."

"And he'll have a fine position and the wherewithal to marry."

"Don't tell your sister," he cautioned. "I don't want her to blame me for the loss of her kitchen maid."

"You don't want anyone to know you've done something good and kind. Why?"

He shook his head. "Just please, don't mention it."

An expression of vexed determination settled over her. "You are a good man, Keswick, and I do not know why you don't wish people to know it, but the fact that you can let talk like Lady Tresham's stand, even if it is useful to you, convinces me that my plan is sound."

He stood, suddenly unmoving. "Plan?"

"Yes." Her chin lifted. "I've decided we should renegotiate our pact."

Alarm crawled up his spin. "No. That is a very bad idea."

"It is a necessary idea. Only the smallest kiss strained the old one, in your eyes. And now, I feel confident offering up something worthwhile, something you need, as my part of the bargain."

"I don't need anything," he said flatly. "I've told you so, already."

"Well, you are wrong. And don't look so frightened. It's only *me* I'm offering up."

"That is exactly what I am afraid of."

She heaved a sigh. "Clearly you don't listen, even though I've proved that I do. I'm not asking for anything you are not prepared to give. No entanglements."

He did not believe a word of it.

"Well, except for the bond of friendship," she clarified. "I truly believe you could use another friend in your life, Keswick. I've seen you. You are too often alone. Even when you are in a crowd, you are alone. Perhaps, especially in a crowd."

The distress in his spine put out feelers and began to invade his gut. Hell and damnation. She truly did see, more than he could be easy with.

"You need another friend. Someone you can rely on and talk

honestly with. Someone with a feminine point of view. Someone who will tell you the truth, even when you don't wish to hear it. Someone you can trust."

"Trust cannot be had just for the asking," he objected.

She nodded. "I know. But we've a good foundation already, do we not? We can talk and laugh together. You've come to my aid and I've come to yours. I believe that we are friends already—and that I have more to offer in such a role."

"It's what I think you are offering that is worrying me."

She flushed and his dread flared higher. And so did the roiling heat and the damned longing that he kept trying to stuff back in the hole where it belonged.

"I don't think you will object so very much to my request."

Oh, he was in trouble. So much trouble.

"No." He turned to go.

"Keswick, stop! At least hear me out."

He didn't want to. He didn't want to see her pink blushes or the plea in her amber eyes, or recall the feel of her lips under his or the beat of her heart beneath his hand.

He kept going.

"Stop, damn you!" she called. "It isn't fair! I want to know!"

He paused. That wasn't what he'd been expecting. "Know what?" he asked over his shoulder.

She slumped back against the tree. "I saw what happened earlier." She glanced away. "I saw Lycett and his friend. They were watching me. Discussing me. And you were near enough to hear. I saw your anger." She sighed. "I know they weren't saying anything kind. I tried to tell you. Most men are just not willing to take on someone . . . damaged."

He turned back. He had to. But he kept his distance. "Not all men are such idiots. There will be someone, someday, who sees all of the glory of you."

It was small, but it was a smile, and it made his neck prickle the way it did when he sensed a footpad following him in the streets.

Danger.

"Most of it, I don't mind," she said with a sigh. "I don't want to marry any of these men. I cannot even imagine such a thing. I don't mourn the idea of a husband, but . . ."

He took a step back again.

"I've never truly enjoyed the company of a gentleman. Not until you. And I keep thinking about that kiss."

Panic ratcheted high. It tightened around his throat so that he couldn't even croak out a denial.

"No! Don't you dare run! I'm not asking for anything beyond friendship, as I said. Except—"

"Except?" It was the only word that escaped, even though there was a flood of *No, Never* and *Damn it all to Hells* behind it.

"Except—as it becomes clear that I likely will never marry . . . I hate the idea of not knowing . . . what comes after the kissing. It isn't fair!" She struck the tree. "I want to know what I'm giving up. I despise the idea of being forever left in the dark, of never knowing the true, full extent of . . . the physical side of it all."

His heart wanted to explode out of his chest. Every instinct told him to turn and march out of there—but he could not reject her so soundly. Not when she'd been brave enough to make herself so vulnerable.

"That's all I'm asking for," she rushed to reassure him.

Ha. She had no idea what she was asking. He knew how women worked. How emotions tangled with everything and made the simplest transactions fraught with danger. He didn't want to hurt her. It was the last thing he would wish. But that kiss had been bad enough. He had finally reached an equilibrium, had carefully shaped his days, his world, so that he would never have to feel . . . wrong. So he wouldn't have to risk giving away anything and losing everything.

But if she got her way, he suspected things would get out of control quickly. He couldn't see either of them getting out unscathed.

"It's just . . . lessons. I have a dancing instructor, after all. It would be like that, nothing more. You are an expert, or so I have been assured by all and sundry. You would just . . . instruct me."

She turned her liquid, hopeful gaze upon him and waited.

* * *

HE WAS GOING TO BOLT. She could see it. But he closed his eyes and gathered himself.

"You honor me," he said patiently.

Which of course, made her utterly impatient.

"Truly. I do understand the sort of trust that such a request requires."

He was going to refuse her. She couldn't let him. She started to move toward him, stepping carefully over the detritus on the forest floor. "Keswick, I do not want this to be yet another thing I am left out of."

Some of the granite inflexibility melted from his expression. A very small amount.

"How? How did you become so brave?" He asked it as she stepped closer. "Where does this tenacity come from?"

He couldn't hide the marvel in his tone and it gave her courage.

"I think I was born with it," she answered a little breathlessly. "It must have been a blessing." She had to keep him here, where the quiet was full of quivering expectation. Where desire tinged the air between them.

"More like a curse." He said it on a moan, but he didn't back up when she moved closer.

Good heavens, but he was warm. She could feel it from here. And see the quick rise and fall of his chest.

It matched her own.

Another step. He smelled of crushed bay and the faintest whiff of pipe tobacco. She was so near and he was so large. The expanse of his chest filled her vision—until she looked up at the awe-inspiring angle of his jaw. She placed a finger there and ran it along the edge.

Smooth. Warm. Not sharp against her skin, like she'd half expected it to be.

She had to kiss him. Tempt him to stay, to accept her bargain. She had to use the weapons she had. The pulse in the air between them, the tightening of his skin—for surely it was the same for him? The memory of that last kiss, how they had lingered, how they had tasted, together.

She steeled herself, balanced carefully—

And he swept down, grabbed her up and covered her mouth with his. He kissed her with lusty demand, even as he scooped her into his arms and carried her back, to the wide elm where she'd stood earlier. He took her around to the other side, still holding her mouth captive, and set her down where they would not be seen, should someone come along the same path.

He settled her carefully, and after a quick glance to be sure she was steady, he swooped down again, his kiss growing even more ardent. No butterfly kisses this time. He nipped and pressed and coaxed and nibbled until her mouth opened and the kiss deepened.

His hands were moving on her. Fingers trailed up and along her arms, sending shivers throughout her frame. He caressed the curve of her neck and all of her small hairs stood at attention. A single finger ran along the edge of her bodice.

He broke the kiss. Stared down at her. She thought he would say something, but he buried his face in her neck instead, spreading hot kisses along her nape. His hand cupped her breast.

Sweet heaven. Her knees felt weak and she was so glad of the elm's support. She opened her eyes and stared up through the canopy of leaves and branches—giving thanks for him and for this feeling. She'd known she was right to ask him. He was so *good* at this—and he made her feel alive. Even better, he made her feel beautiful and desirable and whole.

The golden fastenings of her overdress gave way beneath his nimble fingers and the two halves sagged away. Now his fingers were busy in the back of her gown. She felt the tapes come undone even as her bodice loosened.

Now there was only her stays and chemise left. He drew back and met her gaze directly as he worked at the laces of the stays. Almost immediately they'd gone loose enough for him to slide his hand in.

"Beautiful," he whispered.

He squeezed her breast and rubbed his palm across her taut nipple. When he pinched it, she gasped. When he rolled it between his fingers, his breath rasped against her ear, and her head fell back. Leaning down, he followed and captured her mouth again.

The passion, the want, it swept her up. She didn't recognize her body anymore. It was alight, charged with a desire that arched back and forth between his fingers and her womb.

"Yes. Feel it," he ordered. He kissed her fiercely before drawing back. "This is what you were made for, Glory." He took her hand and pressed it against the engorged length of his cock. "This is what you do to me. It's a kind of power. It's yours and you should treasure it."

She let her fingers roam and explore the expanse of him. He groaned and pushed into her hold. "You are missing *nothing*, do you hear me? You are whole. Complete. Utterly lovely. Someday you will wield this power again, on a man who will fall on his knees before you and offer you the world." He sucked in a breath. "But it will not be me."

He let her go and stepped away, but she reached out and grasped his arms. "Why not, Keswick?" she asked desperately. "Why not you?"

His face had gone bleak. Color and warmth were draining away. "Will you make me say it out loud? Fine, damn you." He looked away. "Because I have nothing to give. I have a title and an income—and nothing else." He held a fist to his chest. "Everything that makes a man worthwhile is in here. But I'm just . . . empty. A husk."

"No! Keswick—"

But he'd stilled—and the look of horror blooming over him came not from her words, but from the sound of someone calling her name.

"Lady Glory?" A moment's silence, then, "Lord Keswick?"

"Hurry!" He stepped close again and yanked her stay lacings tight. She pulled up her bodice and while he reached around to fasten her gown, she tried to reconnect the two halves of her overdress.

"Here. Let me." He got her fastened and then straightened her skirts.

"Lady Glory?"

"It's Miss Munroe." She patted her hair. "How do I look?"

He shook his head and gave a little laugh. "Guilty."

She didn't join in.

"Come on." He offered up his hand, but she pushed it away. "We'll probably get away with this—and that is all the better for you. But let's go out and meet her."

He could smile about it because he thought he'd made his escape. She stepped carefully out from behind the tree and back to the faint path. He was wrong. This was far from over.

CHAPTER 10

It was, indeed, Miss Munroe calling for them. They met her as they made their careful way back out the way they had come. Keswick watched her closely for signs of censure, but saw none. She didn't appear to be looking for clues as to what they'd been up to. In fact, judging by her darting gaze and wringing hands, he guessed she was caught up in some distress of her own.

"Oh, there you both are," she said with relief. "I'm so glad I caught you. I . . . I have something to tell you." She cast him an uncertain glance. "You, especially, Lord Keswick."

He didn't want to hear it. Now that he knew they were in no danger of being called out for impropriety, his only thought was to escape.

He needed distance. Space to be alone and think about what had just happened—how she had nearly tempted him into crumbling up and throwing away every foundation stone he'd built his life upon.

Damn the girl. She was courageous and loyal. Smart. Amusing. And oh, so very tempting. Curse her, she made him want things again, dredged up the old feelings of longing that he'd hacked off and buried long ago.

But the longing didn't come alone. It dragged along memories—

bad memories of pain and betrayal and the forlorn, certain knowledge of his inadequacies.

No. That was his past. He might have a future. Perhaps. Someday. But for now, his path led only through this barren wasteland.

"Can we speak privately?" Miss Munroe asked. "It's just, we've had an unexpected family visit and I wanted to discuss it with you."

The wood was thinning. The shore lay just ahead.

"Would you mind if I returned to my chair, first?" Glory grimaced. "It is set apart from the crowd and should lend us some privacy."

"Oh, of course! Your leg must grow tired. All of this activity on top of our dancing this morning. Let's get you settled."

"Dancing?" Keswick asked.

He caught the warning look Glory shot the girl.

"It was nothing," she said quickly. "Just a sort of . . . experiment we've been working on."

"Be careful through here, Lady Glory." Miss Munroe stepped closer to her and Keswick fell back, out of the way. "Those boulders must have rolled all the way from the cliff face. There are bits and pieces all along here."

Glory slowed her pace. Keswick let the two of them pull ahead. He hoped Miss Munroe would keep her conversation short. He wanted to get away, back to the house. Or perhaps he would take a page from Glory's book and ride out alone. He peered out, across the stretch of shoreline. Party guests were still scattered along the riverside, but a group had gathered around Tensford at the cliff.

"My lady! Careful!"

He snatched his attention back. Glory had stumbled. She teetered, struggling to keep her balance. Miss Munroe had a hold of one of her arms and was trying to pull her upright. She had reached with her other hand and grabbed onto a boulder, her fingers dug into a cleft in the stone.

He hurried forward and went to support Glory's other side. "I've got her," he told Miss Munroe. You can let go—"

Just like that, the stone gave way. Thrown off balance, Miss Munroe cried out and pitched forward. She sent Glory crashing into him. He felt the shifting of the loose gravel beneath his feet and all three of them abruptly went down in a tangle.

He took the brunt of it, thank God. Glory lay stretched out along his chest and Miss Munroe sprawled across both sets of their legs.

"Are you all right? Both of you?" He struggled up onto his elbows, sharp stone biting into his skin.

"I'm fine. I'm so sorry." Glory sounded mortified.

"No, no, it was my fault. I had no idea the boulder wouldn't hold our weight." Miss Munroe shifted to a sitting position.

The other guests arrived to assist them. Mr. Lycett helped Miss Munroe to her feet and then Sterne lifted Glory away. Keswick saw Lycett exchange a glance with the friend he'd been gossiping with. He bristled. He would give the man the drubbing he deserved—

"By God." Tensford said it in a hushed tone. "By all that is holy."

The earl stood behind him. He didn't take note as Keswick got to his feet and brushed himself off. The chatter of questions and reassurances around them all died away as their host stepped past him, his eyes transfixed, his expression changing from concern to elation.

"By God," he repeated. "Keswick! Glory! Miss Munroe!"

"Yes, yes. We are all fine," Keswick said irritably. "It was an accident, nothing more."

"The most fortunate accident! Look! You've done it!"

He pointed and everyone turned. Keswick started.

A whole section of rock had peeled away from the boulder. There, highlighted in the newly exposed stone, was a . . . creature. A fish of some sort, easily four feet long. It stood out, clear as day. Scales, fins and all.

"Are those spines? Or teeth?" someone asked.

"What is it?" Miss Ruddock breathed.

"It is a fossil," Tensford answered.

"It doesn't look like the one I found."

"No, it does not. Nor does it look like any I have found." Joy was growing in Tensford and infusing his voice. "This is a *find*. A magnificent specimen—just exactly what I've been looking for, all of these years!"

* * *

TENSFORD WAS IN ALT. Everyone else got caught up in the thrill of the discovery, too. Hope came down from the house, with the rest of the guests who had skipped the outing. Servants brought cold tea and lemonade and biscuits and an impromptu celebration took place, right there at the riverside. Miss Ruddock sketched the scene, and everyone involved in the discovery.

Except for Keswick, who had disappeared quickly, in the initial frenzy after the revelation. Glory refused to fret over it. She'd spooked him, but she doubted he'd run all the way back to London. He would be back, and she would have to tread carefully. In the meantime, she wanted some answers.

Mr. Lycett became interested when he heard that the specimen might be worth some significant money. He hung around, asking questions, but he and the other guests quickly lost interest once Tensford and Sterne began the painstaking, slow process of digging the specimen out from the boulder. It took meticulous work. They explored, hammered, cut and chiseled and everyone else had returned to the house by the time they fully separated a six-foot slab of rock.

Sterne then returned to the company for dinner, but Tensford stayed out to supervise the transfer of his prize to the small workshop he'd set up long ago, adjacent to the stables.

When the ladies removed to the parlor after the meal, Glory excused herself and went to check on Tensford and his fossil.

He had the tiny space brightly lit. She found him bent over his treasure, poring over it with fingers caked with dirt and covered in dozens of small cuts.

"It looks like you'll need newer, better gloves," she said from the doorway.

"I ruined mine." He smiled up at her. "I've never had to cut so much stone in one day."

Dozens of small fossils lined the room. In his years of searching and collecting, Tensford had previously found several types of specimens, both plant and animal. They were all immaculately cleaned and displayed in cabinets. The new, larger discovery had been laid out on a table in the center of the room.

"I'll have to clean and trim it. Perhaps build a frame," Tensford mused.

Glory stopped next to a table that held small blades, picks and brushes. Gritty dust covered them, most surfaces and the floor. "You've done it at last, Tensford. I'm so happy for you."

"Oh, no. You've done it. You and Kes and Miss Munroe. I'll make sure that you all get full credit for it."

"At least something good has come from this cursed leg," she said with a sigh, moving slowly around the workshop, examining his displays.

He watched her with sympathy. "Hope has told me that the gentlemen seem to be . . . overlooking you." Reaching out, he gripped her hand with his dirty, dusty one—and she didn't mind in the least. "It won't always be that way, Glory. Trust me. You know how it was with me. No young woman wanted to come near Lord Terror—and then they laughed behind their fans at Lord Tender. I thought I would carry my burdens alone, forever. For a while, I feared I would have to marry and yet would still find myself alone—you know what I mean." He smiled. "And then your sister and I both went after the last lobster patty at the buffet at the Loxton ball—and nothing has ever been the same."

"Thank heavens for that lone lobster patty," she said with a laugh.

"I give thanks for it every day. And it will be that way with you, with someone, someday. I know it."

"The house party hasn't been a complete loss," she said carefully. "Some of the guests are perfectly nice—and they will be familiar faces in London if we attend the Season next year."

"If? Your sister has given me to understand that there is very little choice in the matter."

Glory sighed. "I know. She's already begun bullying me about it, as well." She bent over and ran a finger along the curve of an ammonite. Watching from the corner of her eye, she said, "It has been pleasant getting to know Lord Keswick as well. It will be nice to have a real friend in Town."

Tensford stilled a moment, and then went on with his work.

"You've been close with him a long time, I understand," she ventured.

"Yes."

"Tensford, I have . . . questions."

With a sigh, he set down his tools. "Glory, you need to be careful. No, you need to just put whatever thoughts you are having about Kes right out of your mind. I'm telling you this because I care for both of you, and because I know him." He gave her a frank look. "I have loyalty to both of you, my dear, but I've known Kes far longer."

"I understand. And I promise, I'm not going to pry into his deepest, darkest secrets."

"Good."

She moved on to the next cabinet, thinking about how to approach this. "Tensford, can you at least tell me why Keswick doesn't keep his own horses?"

Her brother-in-law shrugged. "He spends most of his time in Town."

"Other peers keep mounts in London. Hope keeps telling me I can ride in Hyde Park and there might be riding excursions to Richmond or elsewhere. Miss Munroe said her father takes his mount because it helps him get through all the traffic in quicker fashion."

"Yes, well, the squire must have a house with a mews, as we do. Kes lives in bachelor rooms. Maybe he just doesn't care for the expense of boarding horseflesh in London."

"Maybe. He rides well. He cares for the chestnut you've loaned him. You know what I mean—he checks him for soundness and takes care of his hooves, he brushes him out himself and gives him little treats. He acts like a man who loves horses, not someone who has never had a mount of his own."

"He's definitely had a mount of his own. At least once. A sorrel chestnut that he loved." Tensford paused in his work. "When we were just boys, I recall him saying he saved up his money and bought the animal himself. He called her Saoirse, because it means freedom in Irish, or something like that." He grinned at her. "Kes is a bruising rider, you know. Perhaps not up to your standard, but very fine. He loved that horse. Our first year in school, he talked about her all the time. Couldn't wait to get back to her on holiday." Straightening, he frowned.

"What is it?"

"I never realized, never thought of it . . . but Kes didn't talk about Saoirse after that first summer holiday. I do know he never went home again, either. He stayed in Windsor over holidays, or sometimes he went home with one of us."

She cleared her throat. "When I asked him, he said that he loves horses—and that is why he doesn't keep them."

Tensford said nothing.

"What do you think happened?"

"I couldn't say, with any certainty." He sighed. "I love Kes like a brother, but there are things he keeps to himself. He has . . . moods, occasionally. And sometimes he goes off and no one sees him for a few weeks at a time."

Her brother in law set down his blade. He left his fossil and went to look out of the open door. Glory held her silence. Tensford looked out over the stable yard for several long minutes, then turned back to regard her with solemnity, his lips pursed. "Glory, I'm going to tell you something I likely should not."

She nodded and sank down onto a stool.

"I just want you to understand . . . and not to get any of the wrong sort of ideas. And I want you to promise not to share the tale, or tell anyone I've told it to you."

"I promise."

Tensford heaved a sigh and sat back down at his worktable, his fingers moving idly over his prize. "In our third year, a set of vile rumors spread about school."

"About Keswick?"

"Yes. They seemed almost . . . designed . . . to goad us, his closest friends, into despising him. To break our confidence in him." His gaze looked beyond her, as if into the past. "Even as young as we were, we felt the wrongness of it. Not one of us believed the lies. We stuck by him. And we worked together to track down the whoreson who was spilling such filth."

"Who was it?"

"A young man none of us knew, not beyond sight. He was in the year ahead of us. We beat the truth out of him, but still, all he could reveal was that he'd been paid to do it—and told exactly what to say." Tensford shook his head. "The whole incident eventually blew over, but now, looking back as an adult . . ."

He blinked and looked at her, his expression still shadowed. "The next year, our last year, we returned from summer holiday as usual. Kes had spent the time with Chester, I believe, and they showed up in the house just as the rest of us did. But Kes was called in to the headmaster. One of the Fellows was there as well. They informed him that he was no longer enrolled. His father had declined to pay the tuition for his last year."

"What? Why?"

Tensford shrugged. "Back at the house, there was a letter waiting. It informed him he could transfer to another school—one we'd never even heard of—or he could leave school altogether and come home."

"Which did he choose?"

"Neither. We all pooled our resources. We used allowances, called in debts and begged or borrowed everything we could. We paid for his last two halves ourselves."

Both hands covered her mouth. "How wonderful you all were. How kind. And how lucky Keswick is to have you all."

He hunched a shoulder. "You know how it was with me. You can imagine I did not have much to give, but my sister had only just married. I borrowed a sum from her new husband to contribute."

She knew how hard it must have been for him—and how much Keswick must have meant to him for him to even consider such a thing.

"Kes paid us all back, of course, as soon as he was able." He sighed. "There was no reason for it. Nothing financial. No family trouble. No reason at all, that we could discern. It seemed like such random cruelty. We couldn't let it stand."

"Of course not."

"And as you can imagine, we all grew that much closer. Our bond has only tightened and it still stands to this day, but . . . Kes does not trust easily."

Suddenly Keswick's words were ringing in her head. "He told me that he had no more room for constants in his life."

"Then you should believe him," Tensford said earnestly. "Be kind to him. He deserves that much. Treat him well, if only for my sake. But don't make the mistake of expecting anything . . . substantial from him. He won't allow himself to give it to you. You'll only be disappointed." He gave her a sad smile. "I wouldn't see you hurt, Glory."

She wouldn't care for it either. "Thank you, Tensford. I'll keep your confidence, you may rely upon it. And you have given me much to think upon."

She left the workshop behind and made her slow way back to the house. Entering through the servant's entrance, she passed by the merry-making and headed to her rooms for a good, long brood.

CHAPTER 11

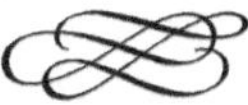

The next day, tables and chairs had been set up in the shade of the house for the afternoon, right near the croquet course and the netting that Glory had helped set up days earlier. Pretty canopies provided shade and groupings for an afternoon outdoors.

She'd come upon the party after her ride, and joined them, still in her riding habit. She sat with Hope and Miss Myland as the guests enjoyed a light nuncheon, finished off with a wonderful confection of blackberries and syllabub. The elderly lady finished off two helpings of the sweet, slightly alcoholic dessert, then promptly began to doze. Hope was called away—and that left Glory alone.

A game of croquet was currently in play. Glory got up and went to fetch a mallet. She returned with it to her chair and turned her seat to face the field. Croquet was a game she enjoyed and could easily participate in. She could maneuver through the course at her own pace and the entire field here was level. Past the last stake, an incline began. It grew steeper and dropped down over a hill. There was a staircase there, and the netting for battledore had been set up in the pretty, green spot at the bottom, but there should be no need for her to go so far.

Just a few feet away, Mr. Lycett stood with Miss Ruddock. They watched the play, talking low together. Both held mallets as well, and they were clearly waiting for their turn to play.

"Those two saw you take a mallet. They know you wish to play, but they'll leave you out of it, if they can."

Glory stiffened. Turning, she found Miss Myland still slumped back in her chair with her hands folded in front of her, but her eyes were narrowly open and watching Glory. "Don't let them push you out," she admonished.

"Oh, surely they will not—"

"They will." The elderly lady's tone held utter certainty. "The girl's mother slipped back to the house for something. The pair of them will be trying to get alone out there on the course. Don't let them exclude you, girl. It will start to become a habit. You need to nip it in the bud, right from the start."

"I cannot be rude," she objected. "They are my sister's guests—"

"That's right! They are your sister's guests, and not yours, so you've no responsibility and no need to coddle them." Miss Myland pushed herself up straight and leaned toward Glory, speaking in earnest. "I've been watching you, girl, and I speak to you now with the voice of experience. You need to step out more, stop letting them turn away from you, stop fading willingly into the background. Get out there into the light and claim your due."

Glory couldn't ever recall seeing the older woman quite so . . . awake. She was intrigued, and a little embarrassed. "How do I know what is my due?" she whispered.

"Bah!" Miss Myland scoffed. "If you see it, and you want it, step out and chase it. Get yourself into that croquet match. It's the first step. You'll need a partner. Find that blue-eyed viscount with the jaw like a game trap and that fine, Roman nose."

Glory blinked.

"I always did like a fine nose," the older lady said with a sigh. She pointed a finger straight at Glory's chest. "I've seen you looking at the man—and guess what, girl? He looks the same way back at you, whenever he thinks you cannot see. You stop hiding in the shadows and snatch him up. If you don't, before you know it, you'll be a drudge in your sister-in-law's household, fetching and carrying, and taking on every unpleasant task. Your only moment to yourself will be when she takes a tray in her room at meals because she cannot abide to hear anyone chew."

"Oh, dear, is that why she's insisting on eating in her rooms at every meal?"

"Never mind!" Miss Myland waved a hand in the air. "It's only her latest fancy. She'll leave it behind and find another, soon enough." She sighed. "I look forward to the day she stops insisting she needs me to sleep near her, in case she needs something in the night. If I must endure such a crescendo of snoring, I'd much rather it come from a husband." She wiggled her fingers. "It's too late for me, but not for you. So, quit dallying. If you like that lantern-jawed viscount, then make him yours."

"I'm not so sure he wishes to be mine," she admitted.

"Ha! There's scarcely a man alive who knows what he wants or needs. You decide for yourself, and grab him if you think he'll suit you. He'll be damned lucky to have you, if you do."

"Thank you." Who would have thought the older woman would be a font of good advice? But Miss Myland was right. She'd pointed out the real question. What did she want? It was time to admit, she'd been lying, just a little. To both Keswick and herself. Yes, she did despise the idea of being left out of the physical side of love—especially after everything they'd done to each other yesterday. She blushed just thinking of it, of the joy and heat of his kiss, of the spark that had blazed through her when he touched her bare breast . . .

She shook her head and reined in her wayward thoughts. Yes, he was the best—the only—candidate she could contemplate asking to teach her such things, outside the bonds of marriage. But also, yes, she had been secretly hoping it would all lead to more.

But now? Now, she had doubts. Tensford had planted them, but Keswick had laid down enough fertile soil for them to grow. He said he was empty. She knew it for nonsense. But something made him retreat from her. He definitely bore unseen, unexplained scars. She might never understand them. But the real question was—would they allow him to feel a real, abiding connection? And if so, would he allow himself to acknowledge it?

Which Keswick was the real man? The distant, cynical rake, fond of gambling and dissipation, low places and women? Or the man who easily looked past her most prominent flaw—and most of her other weaknesses, too? Who told her the truth and treated her with kindness? The same man who leased a farm, ostensibly to enrich his pocketbook, but also to enrich a young couple's life?

She didn't know, but she had to find out. She couldn't make a decision that would affect the rest of her life until she knew.

"Well, girl, here comes your chance to knock two birds with one stone."

Miss Myland hitched her chin in the other direction and Glory turned to see Tensford and Keswick come around the corner of the house. They were talking and they kept to the path instead of venturing out onto the grass where the party was gathered.

"I doubt he'll stop. Tensford is busy and Keswick is avoiding me."

Miss Myland laughed. "Good, that just means you've got to him. And we'll see what we can do about it." She sat straight up and raised a hand. "I say, Lord Tensford!" she called. "Come over here, lad!"

Tensford looked over and she beckoned imperiously. The earl nodded and started to move toward them. As he was talking to Keswick, the viscount had no choice but to follow.

"Good afternoon, ladies." Tensford bowed. "I hope you are enjoying your luncheon *al fresco*."

"Yes, yes. The day is perfect for it and the syllabub is divine. You might tell your countess to use a bit more wine in the receipt, but perhaps that is just my taste. She is a credit to you, my boy. But I do wish to discuss your aunt with you, and there is no time like the present—while the old girl is still inside."

Tensford glanced at Keswick. "Oh, well, I—"

"Come, come! I know you just want to scurry off and muck about with your great, stone fish, but this is important." She glanced at Keswick. "You sir! You may make yourself useful in the meantime.

Lady Glory needs a partner if she is to join the croquet match those two are starting up."

The first game had finished at last. Miss Ruddock and Mr. Lycett were collecting balls from the players.

Keswick looked startled. "Oh, I had planned—"

"Go on, sir. Take the girl over there before she's left out again."

Keswick's expression tightened.

Coming to a decision, Glory stood. She needed to learn more, to get a deeper measure of the man without forcing him to run off or to reject her completely. "Thank you, Keswick. I was hoping to play. With only four of us paired off, the game should go quickly." She listed off balance, just a bit, but it was nothing to do with her leg and everything to do with how close he stood and how the smell of bay was taking her back to that wooded path.

Swallowing, she gave him an even, slight smile. "The mallets are here." She led the way, grateful that she still wore her habit. The color suited her and gave her confidence, even as the heavier fabric did the best job of hiding her limp.

It was a chance. They would be apart from most of the others, but still on display. Paired off with their opponents, but perhaps with a few moments alone. Squaring her shoulders, she vowed to take Miss Myland's advice and work to get what she wanted—as soon as she decided just what that was.

* * *

KESWICK GAVE his friend a look of resignation and followed Glory. He'd successfully avoided her for just over twenty-four hours—which was likely the limit for an event like this one.

He didn't know how to act. He'd never dallied with an innocent before—and he was beginning to see the wisdom of it. She looked so vibrant in her stylish habit, so proper and sweet, as if she'd just been pushed out of the finishing school door. But yesterday he'd held her against a tree and kissed her until they were both nearly senseless. He'd pinched her nipple and made her gasp. He'd pressed his erection into her hand. And now he was supposed to walk tamely beside her and play croquet? When all he wanted to do was grab her up, lay her out on the grass and nip and lick and rip and plunge until they both cried out in completion?

Damn it all to hell.

He dragged a hand through his hair and forced his mind to tamer ground.

"I'm first to go!" Miss Ruddock held up her blue ball and frolicked to her starting point. She made her first hoop and the rest of them followed, using her ball to their own advantage and moving ahead.

"Oh, dear, the gentlemen have already outstripped us, Lady Glory." Miss Ruddock practically skipped up to her ball. He wondered if she was deliberately trying to set herself apart from Glory's slow and careful movements. The girl took her turn, but still found herself behind, after she took aim at Glory's ball and missed.

"Oh, this is going to quickly turn into the most boring of routs if we don't do something to distract the men," she said with a pout.

Lycett had moved so far ahead he had to come back to take part in the conversation. "Perhaps you should show a little ankle," he suggested.

Keswick's heart started to beat faster at the image that rose—Glory sliding her skirts just up, just a teasing inch or two—and then he froze as he realized—and looked to find her rising color was from defiant embarrassment instead of titillation. Damn that Lycett!

"Do not let my mother hear you suggest such a thing, sir!" Miss Ruddock's giggle ruined her attempt to appear shocked. "I know! Let's play the question game as we go along!"

"I don't know that game," Glory admitted.

Keswick rather thought Miss Ruddock had only just made it up.

"It's easy for everyone! I'll ask a question—a *suitable* question—and everyone answers. If you cannot or will not, then you must choose the next question—and it's harder than it seems to come up with them!"

"Perfect!" Lycett declared. "I shall wiggle out all of your secrets, Miss Ruddock."

Keswick had to fight to keep his last meal from wiggling out onto the course.

"Very well then. First, we shall all share our favorite color." She nodded toward her ball. "I'm well known for my propensity for blue!"

"Hazel!" Lycett declared. "Just the exact color of your eyes, Miss Ruddock."

"Chestnut," Glory declared and Keswick had to laugh out loud at that.

They all turned to him.

He blanched. "I'm not sure I've ever thought about it."

"Choose one or offer up the next question," Miss Ruddock said in a singsong tone.

He stared at Glory.

Are you furious with me and too polite to show it?

Do you recall the feel of my hand on your naked breast?

Is your belly churning with the desire to start it all again—and take it further, higher, still?

"Green," he said quickly. "Green like the grass of my mother's home in Ireland."

They played on and reached the first stake, at the far end of the course. A great plane tree stood nearby, double-trunked and spreading out over the incline that led to the hill and the plateau below. A gorgeous, stone staircase led down to the green, which had been set up with a net for battledore.

Miss Ruddock, having asked after their favorite artists and number of siblings, called for their attention. "Now, you must tell me what was the last game you played, before this one. The last one that was *not* cards or billiards," she said pointedly to Lycett.

"Spillikens," he said promptly. "With my nephew."

"Chess," said Glory.

"Mine was lawn bowling," Miss Ruddock said with a sigh. "I enjoy that so much more than croquet."

Again, they all looked to Keswick and he strained to think, to find an answer before his brainbox headed down dangerous roads again. When was the last time he'd played anything other than a hand of cards? Ah. Yes. "Street Sweepstakes," he announced.

They all continued to look, wearing identical blank expressions.

"Well, now you must explain," Miss Ruddock declared.

Glory watched him thoughtfully. "Yes, please do."

"It's nothing. Just a made-up lark." He shrugged. "I bet a young street sweeper that I could finish my corner quicker and cleaner than hers."

Lycett looked slightly scandalized. "What did she have to do when she lost?"

"Nothing. She won. I gave her a crown. That was the bet."

"That doesn't sound at all enjoyable," Miss Ruddock declared.

Glory said nothing, but she watched him very closely. He stared back, fighting to show no emotion at all.

"Oh, dear, look what I've done," Lycett said suddenly. They all turned to see two balls rolling down the incline. "How unfortunate. I've knocked both your ball, Miss Ruddock, and my own, a bit too hard." As they watched, the balls picked up speed and went over the edge of the hill.

Miss Ruddock's eyes grew huge with distress. "Oh, no! How could you have done so?" She turned on him in reprimand. "Will we have to cancel the game?"

"No, no. We shall just have to go down there and look for them."

"Oh!" Sudden understanding dawned on the girl's face. She looked around to see if her mother had returned. "We cannot leave them lost, can we? Lady Glory, I'm sure your leg will not tolerate that sharp incline very well. Why don't you and Lord Keswick stay here while we search? We'll be right back, I'm sure."

"Perhaps not," Lycett corrected her cheerfully. "Who knows where the balls might be hiding underneath all of that ground cover?"

"We'd better begin, then!"

Keswick snorted as the pair of them scampered down the stairs. "And we are meant to act as guards, I suppose. And after Lycett has acted such an ass. We should fetch her mama and fill her ears.

T'would serve him right to be caught out." He sighed. "Come, a couple of those branches are low enough for you to perch upon."

But Glory merely moved closer to him, her eyes watching his face closely. He caught the first teasing tendril of her scent—lavender again, and fragrant tea and the slightest whiff of horse—and he had to fight the urge to lean in and fill his lungs.

"What happened to the girl, Keswick?"

"Nothing yet," he said, moving away to peer down the hill. "Though she might ruin her hems, mucking about in there."

"Not that girl. The other one."

He didn't turn to face her. He didn't want to look upon her fresh beauty, or stand too close to it. Not when he couldn't lay claim to it. "I don't know what you mean."

"Yes, you do know. But you don't want to tell me. Why not?"

He merely shook his head.

"Where is she?"

"Who?"

"The street sweeper. You gave her a crown. And then what? Where is she now?"

He looked away. And then he lied. "In the bowels of Seven Dials? How should I know?"

"You are not telling the truth."

She stepped nearer and he turned away.

"Why won't you tell me?"

He followed the line of a low branch and peered again over the hill. The pair down there stood close together. Were they holding hands? He hoped so. He hoped they did something scandalous to keep his attention diverted and to prevent Glory from pursuing this line of questioning. "There is nothing to tell."

"I don't believe you."

He gritted his teeth against a surge of frustration. "I don't know what you want from me."

"The truth, for a start. Answers, too."

He turned to her finally. "What are you doing, Glory? I thought I made it clear—"

"Oh, you did! You made it clear that I'm to leave you alone. I should listen, I know. The problem is, it's the very last thing I want to do. I don't know why. I didn't expect this to happen. I don't know how you make me feel so easy . . . and so restless at the same time. But you do. You stir me up and make me feel things I never expected to. And if I'm to ignore them, or pretend that they don't exist, then I want to understand why, at the very least. So, tell me about the girl."

She made him feel every empty spot in his soul. Worse, seeing her pain, hearing her put his own thwarted feelings into words, it was as if she crawled inside of him and scraped them more hollow, still.

"No," he rasped. "It won't help."

"It will help me."

She was wrong. Baring his soul never helped anyone.

She glanced behind her to the other luncheon guests, still seated or roving among the seats and then she took the step that would place the plane tree between them.

He glanced down, but Lycett and Miss Ruddock had gone all the way to the green and were partially hidden by the stone balustrade of the stairs.

Glory moved closer still. They were entirely hidden for the moment, from everyone. And he was tempted. So very tempted. He wasn't used to denying himself, after all. The whole point of his lifestyle was to prevent it.

Perhaps he didn't have to.

It was the wicked whisper of the small part of his soul. The hungry part. The part that didn't care if he'd be left alone and wanting at the end of this folly, should he embark upon it.

"You said you would not ask for what I could not give," he said roughly.

"It's just a simple question. Not so very difficult."

She didn't know. It was difficult—and he was hard. He let his gaze roam over her. Creamy skin and pink lips, plump on the bottom at just the right spot for kissing, and so often quirked in wry humor or keen observation. Why? Why did her quick wit and earnest gazes hold him riveted? She roused him in ways that the harlots and barmaids he normally indulged in did not, despite their round arses and bosoms on display.

Glory made him laugh. She made him forget. She made him talk. She woke protective instincts inside of him, urges that he'd thought had died with his mother. And then she turned around and protected him. He ached for more and now he knew how she tasted and how her breast filled his hand and he burned with the urge to discover the rest.

He could tell her.

The evil imp whispered again in his ear.

He could. He could take what she offered, take her at her word. Teach her the ways of men and women. He nearly groaned at the thought. She'd given her word, after all. Friends. And she wouldn't expect more.

Except—she would. He knew why she asked after the street girl. He knew the story she was spinning in her head. She meant to make a hero of him.

"It doesn't matter. It doesn't change anything."

You cannot make a purse from a sow's ear. And not even she could fashion a decent man from a broken, bitter wreck.

"You've changed me." She reached out and took his hand. She held it sandwiched between her own, small, cool palms. He could feel her bounding pulse with a fingertip and wondered if she could feel his.

"I went down to the dining room this morning and the buzzing talk stopped when I stepped in," she said in almost a whisper. "It was early. Not everyone was up. Neither Tensford nor Hope had yet come down. I stood on the threshold and looked at their faces, either quietly averted or deliberately blank, and I went and gathered up pockets full of muffins and apples. I went straight to the stables. As I left, the talking started up again." She looked up at him and smiled. "I didn't care. It wasn't nearly as painful as it once would have been—because of this." She squeezed his hand. "Because I know you see me. And you feel something for me—even if you don't want to."

Oh, bloody, sodding hell. She was going to kill him—or at least make him wish she had. He closed his hand around hers and tugged her closer. Their gazes met and held. His hand rose to touch her cheek. She sighed and leaned in and he lowered his mouth toward hers—

"Miss Ruddock? Lady Glory?"

He closed his eyes. For the second day in a row, Miss Munroe rescued him from folly. He should probably put her on retainer—she could keep saving him from himself until he could get back to London.

He dropped Glory's hand and she stepped back.

Miss Munroe ducked under a branch and stepped around the first, widest trunk of the tree. "There you are." She looked past Glory to him, wearing an odd expression. "We were looking for you."

"We?" Glory asked.

Another young lady followed in her footsteps. She straightened and met his gaze with a wide, challenging smile.

Bloody. Damned. Hell. Fate, the gods, destiny, what have you—they'd all apparently upped the ante in this game masquerading as his life. He didn't even have to break the rules to be punished. Apparently, all he had to do was contemplate it—and they smacked him down with a leveling blow.

"Keswick!" Miss Vernon said his name with possessive delight. "There you are, at last!"

CHAPTER 12

Glory bristled a little as the new arrival focused intently on Keswick and ignored her existence.

"Who would have thought that we'd be together again, and so soon?" the other girl said almost triumphantly.

"Not I, and that is a certainty," Keswick replied. He didn't seem very enthusiastic about seeing the girl again, despite her excitement.

"And in such rustic surroundings!" The other woman looked about her with just the slightest hint of disdain.

There was nothing rustic about her, to be sure. Tall and thin and all sharp angles, she was dressed in an elegant walking dress and striped pelisse, far more fashionable than anything else that had been worn at the house party so far. Her nose was her most striking feature, long and also elegant and pointed. Glory spent a moment wondering what Miss Myland would think of it.

"When I heard that two of my cousins were having a visit together up here in Gloucestershire, we decided we had to come." She cast a smile on Miss Munroe. "Family is so important, is it not? And when was the last time we were all together? You and I and dear Cousin James?"

"Never, in my memory," Miss Munroe said shortly. "Although my mama recalls a time when we were all in the nursery together, when we were very small."

"Exactly! It has been too, too long." She grinned up at Keswick. "And besides, all of the really interesting people had already left London."

Miss Munroe looked as if she might debate the first part of that statement, but she turned to Glory. "Forgive my manners, Lady Glory. If I may present Miss Alice Vernon? She is a distant cousin and has arrived for a visit. Your sister very kindly included her in today's luncheon."

Glory curtsied. "How do you do?"

"Very well, thank you, now that I am here." She turned back to Keswick. "And just in time too! Never fear, Lord Keswick, I am here to rescue you from such bucolic pursuits."

Keswick glanced at Glory. "No one is in need of rescue. In fact, I've discovered the country has unexpected appeal."

Now Glory had the young lady's attention—and the full weight of her displeasure. Miss Vernon shot her a haughty glance and then simpered up at the viscount. "I am so glad to hear it. Now I will have to press you into service and ask that you convince me."

"But you were so determined to come over at once to see Cousin James. After all, family is so important to you! I am sure you must wish to greet him before doing anything else," Miss Munroe said firmly. She said to Glory, "He spent the night at the village with his friends instead of at our home, so Alice has yet to see him. Where is he, by the way? We thought he was out here, playing croquet with you."

"Mr. Lycett hit a couple of balls with too much enthusiasm. He and Miss Ruddock have gone over the hill to retrieve them," Glory told her.

"Well, then." Miss Munroe marched over to the edge of the staircase. The rest of them trailed after her while she cupped her hands and called out. "Come up! You have a visitor, James!"

"It seems our game has come to a premature end, Lady Glory."

Keswick spoke up from behind her. "If you give me your mallet, I will return it for you."

"No, no, you shall not get away again so easily," Miss Vernon admonished him. "Just allow me to greet my cousin and then I shall ask you to convert me to appreciation of the countryside."

"What's this?" Mr. Lycett helped Miss Ruddock up the final steps to join them. "Fresh blood to join our party?"

Miss Munroe made the introductions.

"Cousin?" Mr. Lycett said jovially. "It must be a distant relationship indeed, for me to be unaware of a connection with so fine a young lady."

Miss Vernon preened. "It is lovely to see you again, after so long."

Mr. Lycett looked surprised. "Have we met before, then?"

"Once, when we were all in nappies," Miss Munroe said wryly.

"We shall just have to make up for lost time," Miss Vernon declared, but then she grimaced. "Although the next reunion we plan, do let us meet up in London? The setting, the entertainments, the company, the fashions." She ran an eye over Glory. "Everything is better in London. You must agree."

"I must not," Miss Munroe declared. "Some of us prefer the peace of a country life. And seeing as we didn't plan a reunion, but merely a visit between two families, we have been content right here. And as Lady Tensford has been kind enough to add you to her party, perhaps you should experience one of her entertainments before you disparage them."

"Oh, la! Pray, do not take offense! I have agreed to allow Lord Keswick to prove me wrong." She laughed. "Although it is too amusing to think of you as a country man, my lord, when I am so used to seeing you amidst the glitter and shine of Town."

"Not so very used to it, I should think," Keswick said with a frown. "We travel in very different circles, for the most part."

"Well, now is our chance to fix that. Providence has given us this opportunity, we must not waste it." She slipped her hand through his arm. "Dear me, this is a very pretty staircase. It leads . . . where?"

"To the green below, which has been set up for battledore," Glory answered.

"I've never played," Miss Vernon told Keswick. "But I should be glad if you would explain the game and perhaps give me a demonstration."

Glory saw his scowl, and thought for a moment that he would refuse the girl outright and rebuff her obvious machinations. But he glanced around and then toward the tables and tents, and his expression changed to one of pained resignation.

She pursed her lips. After a moment's hesitation, she stepped forward.

"I am very sorry, Miss Vernon," Glory said firmly. "But I must claim Lord Keswick, as we have a prior commitment." She turned to the viscount. "In fact, my lord, I am sure we are due at the stables very soon. I know we meant to stay until the end of the game, but it appears it is over already." She looked to Mr. Lycett and Miss Ruddock, who had come up the stairs empty handed.

"Yes, we'll have to set the servants to searching the undergrowth," Mr. Lycett said with shrug.

Glory turned back to the newcomer. "I'm sure we would not wish to interrupt your family reunion, in any case. After all, you've traveled such a long way to engineer it."

"Of course." Miss Vernon shot her a look full of venom. "How . . . thoughtful."

"So nice to have met you," Glory said with a smile as Keswick extricated himself from the girl's grasp. "Shall we go, Keswick?"

"We shall," he said with irony. He bowed to the others. "I must not fail to honor a prior commitment."

Miss Vernon caught his eye. "I am sure we'll have a chance to spend time together later, my lord."

He inclined his head and Glory turned away. She did not take his arm as they walked back across the field. She smiled and spoke as they passed through the guests still gathered at table and tent, but her mind was very busy. Was this the sort of thing Keswick faced often? She flushed, hoping that he hadn't placed her behavior in the same category as that young lady's. Desperately, she reviewed her own conduct as they walked in silence along the graveled path.

As they reached the clearing where the stable yard and outbuildings stood, she looked up into his face. "I am very sorry if I have made you uncomfortable, Keswick."

He looked down at her and after a moment his puzzled expression gave way. "No." He took her hand and bent over it. "No. Do not think to compare yourself to that harpy. I do thank you for your intervention, but I think I should go to Tensford." He placed a kiss on her gloved hand.

They stayed, frozen in that position, for several heartbeats too long.

His breath warmed the leather and sent heated currents flowing up her arm and on to all the peaks and crevices inside her. The space between them felt alive with the spark and clash of gathering forces. She could not have pulled away, even if she wanted to.

He broke the contact, eventually. "Good day, Glory." Looking more than a little dazed, he turned to leave.

She watched him go, her mind racing. He disappeared into Tensford's workshop and she clutched her arm tight to her chest. "Good day," she whispered.

* * *

DINNER THAT EVENING FELT INTERMINABLE. Miss Vernon had clearly altered the seating arrangements so that she was seated next to him, which had visibly flustered both the countess and her footmen. Little good it did the chit. Keswick couldn't focus. He could barely summon the energy to answer her myriad questions. He spoke absently and shot an occasional furtive glance down the table, where Glory and Mr. Sommers were talking of equine bloodlines. He ate little, said less and partook of the wine freely.

After the last course had been cleared, Keswick allowed the footman to pour him another glass of port. He tossed this one back as quickly as he had the first and nodded when the servant silently offered again.

Around him, the gentlemen talked and laughed around the dining room table. The women had gone through, and the men enjoyed their masculine solidarity with rich wine and expensive cigars, but Keswick's mind wandered elsewhere.

"Are you all right, old man?" asked Sterne.

"You do look rather . . . distracted," Lycett remarked from his seat nearby. "Something on your mind, Keswick?" He sniggered. "Or someone?"

"Someone, yes."

"Oh, ho!" Lycett crowed. "Shall we take guesses as to who it is?"

"The tavern wench at the Crown and Cock does go on about him," Sir Blackwell said wryly.

Keswick ignored him. "You might guess, but it would be of no use," he told Lycett. "I was thinking of an old gypsy woman."

"Why?" Lycett frowned. "Is there an encampment nearby?"

"Not that I know of. No, I was recalling a night in Covent Garden."

"Tell us," Sterne urged.

He looked around at the men at this end of the table. Several were looking the other way, toward Tensford, asking about the next day's plans, but a few waited expectantly for him to speak. He sighed. "It was late, but things were still in full swing in the Garden, as is often the case. Walking through, I saw an old gypsy woman in a decrepit stall. I don't know which looked older or more worn, but she and her stall were both draped in colorful cloths. The wood of the structure looked wormy, as if only habit and the dust of the place kept it upright." He paused and took a drink. "The strange thing was, I'd been in that part of the Garden a hundred times, and I'd never noticed her there before."

"Odd," said Sterne.

"Yes. She sat outside the place, smoking a pipe. She called out to me as I passed and invited me in. She said she would tell me of my past lives. If I untangled the troubles I'd been through already, they would lend clarity to the path I walked now."

"Past lives?" Sterne mused. "That Eastern belief that we are born again and again, a new person each time?"

"Such balderdash," Lycett scoffed. "It doesn't sound very English to me."

He said it as if there could be no greater insult.

"Nor did it sound so to me," Keswick admitted. "I walked on and went on my way. Yet, I had the strangest dreams that night and I could not get her out of my mind."

"You went back?" Sterne asked.

"The very next night. But there was no sign of her or her stall."

"What nonsense," Lycett snorted. "If you want to occupy your mind, you should do better to think about what spot you'd like for tomorrow's shooting." He turned away. "Tensford, I'd like to lay claim to the blind near the bend in the river where the sand stretches out into the water."

"I don't believe there is a blind located there," Tensford replied with a frown.

"Surely there must be. I gather you've invited Mr. Stillwater to shoot with us?"

"He invited himself, rather," Tensford admitted. "But he was a friend of my father's, so I indulged him. How did you know of it?"

"I ran into him in the village, and he mentioned it. He had a great many questions about where we would be shooting and about that spot near the river in particular."

The conversation turned to the next day's sport, but Sterne ignored it. "It's an interesting idea, isn't it?" he asked, leaning in. "Past lives?"

"Yes. Frightening, too."

"Frightening?"

"Yes, when I imagine what a bounder I must have been, to deserve some of this life's trials."

Sterne looked as if he would like to debate the point, but someone called his name, and soon, he too was drawn into the debate over the best spot to shoot from.

It left Keswick alone with his drink again, wishing he'd gone into that tent, long ago.

The old gypsy woman might have given him some advice that could have him avoiding the current mess he found himself in. Or perhaps—she might have told him of the many sins he'd committed before—and he would know for certain that this quagmire was the punishment he deserved.

That Vernon girl. She was reproof in human form, if ever there was one. Who would have thought that she would get herself to Gloucestershire and find a way to insinuate herself into this house party? She was tenacious, he'd give her that, but it was too damned difficult to find any other qualities to admire in her.

Glory, on the other hand, possessed so many appealing qualities a man would need an abacus to number them—and yet she failed to see them for herself.

It was that vulnerability that had dropped the first stone into the calm and placid waters he'd finally achieved. The ripples had spread, however. Her lively humor and charming wit, the entirely familiar way she could care for others and still remain wary of them, the way she could stand toe to toe, challenging him with a smile, her inner strength, and outer loveliness, they were all great boulders she tossed at him, stirring up foam and swells and waves within him.

Stirring up feelings.

Bloody hell, but she'd defended him once more. Well, extricated him, rather. And heaven knew, he'd needed it. Appreciated it. Felt knocked quite askew by it—by her perception and her willingness to step in on his behalf.

On his behalf.

It made him wild. It made him want to weep a little.

He'd felt affection before. Want and need and longing. He'd experienced them all in familial and romantic directions. He'd spun adrift in their currents, and they had all led to loss. Pain. Grief.

A sharp bark of laughter made him look up.

"Still lost in Covent Garden, Keswick?" Lycett laughed loudly at his own joke. "Come back, man, and give us a lark." The man shook his head. "I don't mind telling you, I've been waiting. We heard all manner of things about your reputation when you first arrived. We've expecting a dust-up out of you, but you've disappointed us so far."

At the head of the table, Tensford straightened in his chair and put aside his cigar. "On the contrary, Mr. Lycett, Keswick has been an exemplary guest in my house. If you are disappointed in any aspect of our party, you must lay the blame at my door."

"No, no, that's not what I meant." Lycett threw up a hand. "No offense meant, sir, to either of you. It's just we'd heard the stories, you must understand. We'd heard of women and gambling and drinking and racing and all the fun you get up to." He looked around the table. "It's just, we've been waiting to see a sign of it."

Keswick stood. "You are right, sir."

For the last several years he'd been all tumult and shambles on the outside, while remaining calm, ordered and untouched on the inside. Somehow, since coming to Greystone Park, he'd got turned inside out.

He gazed at Lycett. The man seemed very far away. They all seemed . . . distant.

"Are you going to get us up a lark, then?" Lycett asked eagerly.

"No, but I do thank you."

"For what?"

"For reminding me of who I am."

He was going to snag a bottle of brandy and walk down to the village. He was going to buy rounds of honeyed mead at the Crown and Cock. He might get in a fight and he rather thought he should take Betsy upstairs and give her the swiving she'd offered up his first evening there.

Turning, he stalked out the door.

He was going to get back to himself.

CHAPTER 13

The frogs and the night birds provided the music for her, although Glory did hum a few bars here and there as she practiced Mr. Beveridge's Maggot. She'd come out here to the long field by the river to practice her dancing, before tomorrow morning's lesson. She'd needed air, and a bit of freedom and the certainty that she wouldn't be interrupted.

The gentlemen in the house were rowdy tonight. They'd gathered in the billiards room—not far enough away to keep her from hearing shouts of laughter, smelling occasional wafts of cigar smoke, or worrying she'd be caught out in the ballroom.

She was practicing, because, as much as she hated to admit it, both Hope and Mr. Thorpe had been right. She was getting stronger with repetition. Not that she was exactly graceful, but she'd begun to get the particulars of the rhythm, spins and turns of this particular dance. What she needed now was stamina—she still could not make it all the way through the full dance without pain and fatigue in her weak leg.

She'd chosen the far end of the field, past the wide curve in the river, where a line of shrubs topped the bank. If she danced in front of them, she would not be so visible from the road, should someone venture past. Not that they would, so late. She felt quite safely alone, save for Poppy's comforting presence, so she hummed and carried on for as long as she could, before she sat on the bank for a rest and tried to breathe in the peace of the scene.

It was a lovely night, with a soft breeze and the murmur of the river and the stars shining so brightly overhead. She concentrated on them, instead of the place on the bank where she'd kissed Keswick. She stared hard and saw the stars had begun to fade a little across and downstream, as the moon started to rise over the trees. The dance of moonlight on the water more than made up for it.

Poppy nickered at her, then went back to cropping grass. With a sigh, Glory stood and went to begin again. Miss Munroe had been correct, too. She should arm herself with as many weapons as she could—she would need them all when she went to London next year.

She had to face facts. She was going to have to go and partake of the Season, as Hope wished. Any secret fantasy about Lord Keswick saving her from such a fate had to be rooted out, ripped from where it had been hiding, tucked away, down in her inner recesses.

He was a good man. She felt it—a truth that lived in her very bones. She knew he'd done something to help that street sweeper, just as he'd helped Tom, the stable lad, find a better life.

He was generous and kind—and he didn't want anyone to know it. He made her laugh, made her feel comfortable and safe, made her feel alive with a soaring passion—but he didn't want her to do anything about it.

She'd thought she had something to offer him in return for all of those grand feelings, but she had been wrong.

She'd thought he might need her in his life. She'd thought he'd needed a friend, a feminine point of view, a woman who could act as a confidante and sounding board.

She'd had doubts about whether he would allow her close, but now she suspected he didn't *need* her close. Clearly he didn't lack for feminine companionship. Lady Tresham was mostly bored and overdramatic and Miss Vernon was more than a little forward, but put them together with Betsy the barmaid and herself—and even here in the country's limited society, the last thing Keswick lacked was women in his life.

With resolution, she pushed on with her dance. She would master it. And perhaps another. She would let go of silly, girlish dreams and deal with the realities of her situation.

She stretched her arm out towards her imaginary partner. She made the turn and stepped forward, then back. Now to cross behind her neighbor in line, and to form a graceful arch just as Mr. Thorpe always urged . . . but in thinking too much about her arms and lines, she lost track of her feet. Her weak leg stumbled, then twisted in the wrong direction. Flailing wildly, she went down.

She lay curled in the grass for a moment, breathing deeply.

"Curse it all," she said, rolling over onto her back. But no, that wasn't nearly strong enough to voice her anger, dismay and frustration. Frowning, she searched for really good curse word.

"Damnation!" she said loudly.

It felt good.

"Hell and damnation!" she yelled at the sky while her feet pointed right toward the spot where she'd kissed Keswick.

A sudden rush of tears started to flow. They leaked from the corners of her eyes and ran back into her hairline.

"No!" Her own weakness infuriated her. "I will *not* cry!"

Yards away, Poppy's head came up. Her ears pricked toward the bridge. She snorted a warning.

Glory froze. What? What had alarmed her mare? No one would be out here now. But what else could it be? There used to be boars in the forest. But they were long gone, weren't they? A dog?

Poppy snorted again and stamped a foot. Glory braced herself. She had to get to her feet. If a wild dog—

Something dark blotted out the sky above her, just as she started to sit up. A head. A man's head, bent over from behind her.

"God in heaven, are you all right?" he asked, just before her forehead cracked into his.

* * *

"SCORCH AND BURN IT!" Keswick clutched his forehead and reeled back.

"Ow! Oh . . . Ow." Glory collapsed back onto the ground. "Keswick? What are you doing here?"

He stared at her while probing his brow. "What am I doing here? I'm going to the village. The question is—what are you doing out here?"

"I . . . Nothing." She rolled to her side and climbed carefully to her feet.

"Nothing?" he said in disbelief.

Wincing and holding her head, she gestured toward the bank. "I'm going to go and sit down a moment."

"Nothing, you say?" He followed her. "You are alone out here. At this hour. Twirling about in the dark like a demented sprite! And you say it's nothing?"

Her hand dropped and she looked back over her shoulder. "Truly?" She sounded horrified. "Did I look demented?"

"The fact that you are out here alone at all is demented. What were you doing?" A stray, unanswered question popped into his head. Something Miss Munroe had said. "Dancing lessons. Is that what you are up to? Dancing?"

"Apparently not." She sounded truly upset. "Apparently I am doing my best impression of a demented fairy, convulsing under the moon."

The moon did chase quick, shining streaks throughout her hair, which had been pulled loosely back and bound at her nape. He forced himself to look away. She started toward the bank again, her back stiff and her shoulders slumped inward. "I'm sorry. I should not have said that." He'd distressed her. "I was just surprised to find you out here." He touched his forehead. "And I was in pain."

She didn't answer, just carefully lowered herself to sit on the edge of the bank.

He stepped around her, full of remorse, and knelt before her. "I am sorry. I didn't mean to insult you. I was frightened when you fell."

His heart clenched when he caught the faint tracks of tears reflecting the moonlight. He reached out a hand to wipe them away.

She shifted, turning away. "It's fine. I am sorry, too. I am only being . . . me."

He hated the sadness, the note of defeat in her tone, but she wiped her eyes and looked at him. "'Scorch and burn it?'" she asked.

He gave an embarrassed laugh. "Yes. It's one my mother used to say. I'm pretty sure it comes from an old Irish curse—Scorching and burning upon you!"

"Bloodthirsty. Final." She nodded. "I like it. I might borrow it."

"Shocking, coming from a young lady."

"Better to be denounced for cursing than as a demented sprite."

He winced. He had struck a nerve. "Tell me about the dancing."

She sighed. "Miss Munroe calls it another arrow in my quiver. I just want to give myself as many chances as possible to appear normal."

"Normal." He snorted.

"It's nothing to snort at from the outside."

Reaching for her hand, he held it between his. "You are a thousand times better than anyone normal."

She pulled in breath and her eyes closed. "Thank you," she whispered, squeezing his hand. She met his gaze, then. "It means so much, hearing you say that, because I believe you mean it." Her hand slid out of his. "But I think we should go back—back to the place between us where you don't say such things."

He knew she was right.

"I have to make the best of my situation as it stands. There will be no escaping London, I suppose, much as I would prefer to bury my head in the sand and stay here." She sighed. "You could be right, though, and someday, some kind man might look past my differences. Maybe he will ask me to dance."

Keswick hated him already. He hated all the men in London who were to be given the chance to see her, to choose her.

"And if he does," she continued, "then I would like to be able to accept him, for at least one dance." Her shoulders slumped. "It is difficult, though. Not as difficult as learning to walk again, but still, challenging."

"You'll do it," he said roughly. He looked back toward the field. "But it's likely not wise to be hard on yourself, when you are practicing in the dark and on uneven ground."

"I didn't want to be caught at it, in the house. The gentlemen are carousing in the billiards room. They are too close to the ballroom—and I did wish to practice. At first I hated the very idea of lessons, but I've got the bit between my teeth now. I refuse to be defeated. If I can perfect this dance, I might even tackle another."

She was so endearingly brave and determined—and she was going to need those qualities if she meant to face the outside world. But for now, he reached for a bit of light-heartedness. "Perhaps you should only confess to the one—and then make the gentlemen vie for the honor of your one dance at each ball."

She laughed. "Oh, wouldn't Hope love that? It's a nice idea, but I've not had much luck with even the smoothest, most stately dance." Sighing, she leaned back to look at the stars. "I'll keep trying, though. It must be perfect, or I'll never attempt it in public."

"No one dances perfectly," he objected.

"I will. Or I won't dance at all."

"Is that your pride speaking? Or your legendary stubbornness?"

"Both. And fear, as well. And experience."

"Experience?"

Shrugging, she didn't answer.

He thought for a moment. "The speaking piece? You said it didn't go well."

"Please, don't mention it."

"It couldn't have been so bad."

"Why?" Her tone sharpened. "Because you are the only one with pain and regret in your past? I assure you, you are not."

He shifted. "You are right, of course. I apologize."

He sank down and sat with his back against the bank, next to her feet. Neither spoke. He should go. He should go on to the village, back to his carefree, libertine ways. But he couldn't leave her alone out here. Nor did he want to, really.

The breeze lifted his hair and caressed his brow. Slowly, slowly, the tension he'd been carrying all day drained away. His shoulders relaxed. He leaned over a little and rested his head on her knee. She sighed and touched the top of his head, briefly.

How did she do it? She made him feel like she'd created a refuge just for him, where he could say what he thought without guarding every moment, a place of soothing relief, free of the worry and strife that normally dogged his every step.

He wanted to give something back to her.

"Would you like for me to partner you, while you practice?"

"No, thank you. I think I'm done for the evening."

"Then, would you care to dance with me, later this week? At the ball your sister has planned to end the house party? I swear, it won't matter a whit to me if you stumble a bit."

"No, thank you," she said decisively.

"I can contrive to cover any little misstep. I promise I would never let you tumble or fall."

"I cannot." Her voice had thickened. "I'm not ready."

He tilted his head back to look up at her. A lovely halo of moonlight surrounded her profile and shadowed her expression. "It must have been very bad," he said gently.

"It was."

Grasping her hand, he peeled away her glove. He traced her fingers and along the tender skin of her wrist. Her heartbeat fluttered beneath his fingers and he cradled her hand, wishing he could protect her from harm. "Honestly? My first instinct is to tell you to keep the story to yourself. Don't make yourself vulnerable," he said softly. "But my friends are always counseling me otherwise. Sometimes when you share a hurt, it loses some of its power over you. Or so they tell me."

"Have you done so? Tried sharing your pain?"

"Yes." It had only led him to worse, but he would never let that happen to her, not with him.

She let out a shaky breath. "Keswick, we can remain friends, can we not? Separated, as you've said, but still . . . in harmony?"

"Of course."

"I wish we could keep this—this freedom and ease between us. The ability to say anything."

"I would like that," he whispered. Part of him screamed that it was not enough, would never be enough, but he shushed it.

"Then I will tell you." Her head bowed. "But first you must answer my question, or at least a bit of it."

"What question?"

"The girl. The street sweeper. She's not lost in the filthy maze of Seven Dials, is she?"

He took a long moment before deciding to answer. "No."

"You moved her. Took her somewhere safe?"

It went against all of his instincts to answer, but for her, he would bend a little. "Yes. Her and her mother."

She let out a long sigh. "I'll tell you, but you understand, it is an act of trust."

He did understand, and he would do his damndest to be worthy of it. "It will be an honor to keep your confidence."

She pulled her legs up and tucked her gown under her feet. Once, twice, he heard her draw breath as if to begin, but did not. After a moment, she tucked her forehead onto her knees, hiding her face.

"Here." Keswick drew his flask from his pocket. He nudged her. "This might help."

She took the flask. "What is it?"

"Some of Tensford's finest brandy."

She sniffed it and reared back a little.

"Go on," he urged.

Cautiously, she sipped it. "It tastes like citrus, and other fruits. And something floral." She choked suddenly. "Oh, it's gone hot. I can feel the heat spreading along my ribs."

"Have another."

She did, a longer drink this time.

"There you go," he said with approval. "It's not gin, but it will lend you a bit of Dutch courage."

She groaned. "It's foolish, really. You probably won't think it much at all."

"It's how it makes you feel that matters."

Sighing deeply, she nodded. "You'd better take this back."

He took the flask and she settled in. "All right." She squirmed a little, so that she faced away from him and towards the spot where Poppy foraged. "It was a musical evening, held at a neighbor's house near our home in Sussex. It was just past a year since my father's death. We were just out of mourning and Hope was preparing for her Season in London. She and some other girls her age got the idea for the evening, so they could practice their drawing room entertainments. I was still under the care of a governess and thrilled to be asked to participate."

"Despite not being musical?"

"Yes. I couldn't sing or play an instrument, but it was my chance to come up with something else. My governess and I perfected the idea."

"A theatrical piece."

"Yes. I chose one of Puck's speeches, from *A Midsummer Night's Dream*. I practiced endlessly. We worked out the blocking and movements so that it was lively and animated, but still within my abilities." She lifted a shoulder. "Granted, my limp likely was more pronounced then. My foot dragged more noticeably, I believe. I've grown a little stronger with time."

He nodded, encouraging her to continue.

"I was breathless with anticipation, and when my turn upon the stage came, I was full of hope and shaky confidence."

She stopped. He waited.

"It was a friend of my brother's. Mr. James Judson." Residual bitterness still accompanied his name. "He was a bully when we were children and he is a wastrel now, in my opinion. But he has money and a decent bloodline and so he goes unchecked."

"What did he do?"

"He was already the worse for drink before the entertainments began. He moved restlessly in the audience and occasionally whispered too loudly during a performance, but his behavior was ignored. He'd slumped in his chair by the time my turn came, so I had hope he'd sleep through the rest of it."

"He didn't," Keswick said flatly.

"No. He sat up when I came out and said 'Not the cripple!'"

"The wicked arse," he breathed.

"It wasn't the first time he called me thusly. I'm sure I turned beet red, but I persevered. I wasn't going to let him chase me off of the stage. Not after I had worked so hard. So, I continued on. I put my heart and soul into it, too. When I finished, I held my position and waited with bated breath, praying it would be well received."

He noticed that his fingers had ceased stroking and he had gripped her wrist tightly. Wordlessly, he loosened his hold and waited.

"The audience began to applaud. My breath came out in a whoosh and I stood. I'm sure I was grinning like an utter idiot. I made my bow and turned to step off of the stage—but Judson leapt to his feet."

"He said . . ." Her voice had begun to shake a little. Stopping, she swallowed and cleared her throat. "He said that it wasn't right that I should have been allowed to perform before an audience. I was a disgrace and he never understood why I wasn't kept at home and out of sight. I should never have been allowed to conduct myself as equal with the other young ladies." Her breath caught. "He said I ruined Shakespeare's idea of an impish sprite, free and light and airy. He said . . . that just watching me walk was an offense to the senses and ruined his picture of the ideal of womanhood."

By the end, her voice sounded tight and strained.

"I hope your brother killed him," he said savagely. If not, he would seek his own vengeance. He could happily imagine horsewhipping the bastard until he found himself with permanent wounds that could then be mocked by other bastards.

"It was all an uproar. The girls were crying. My brother was shouting. Judson and a group of other young men stormed out. My mother fainted, and that put an end to it. We were bundled out and the girls blamed me for the ruin of the evening." She sighed. "Except for Hope, of course."

"What happened afterwards? Did your brother duel with the drunken sot?"

"They quarreled, but there was no duel. I received far fewer invitations. Mother grew ill and that restricted our social lives for quite a while. Later, after her death, my brother made up his quarrel with Judson. In fact, he married the man's sister."

His jaw dropped. "Do you mean to say that that arse wipe is your brother-in-law?"

"Yes. And he runs tame in the house."

"And your brother allows it?"

"The three of them are thick as thieves." Her tone turned wry. "You can see the appeal of hiding away here with Hope, in Gloucestershire."

"Hell, yes, I can." Wild rage was coursing through him—as was the earnest desire to make her *see*. "But you must not hide away, not under any circumstances."

CHAPTER 14

Glory jumped a little, in surprise, as Keswick leapt to his feet. He paced back and forth along the water's edge in front of her.

"Your mother had a long illness, did she not?"

"She did." Bewildered, she watched him pivot and continue, back and forth.

"And that night was the start of it?"

"No. It began after my father's death, I honestly believe. But her decline became more obvious about that time." She stiffened suddenly. "I didn't cause it, if that's what you mean to insinuate."

"No! Not at all. I'm just painting the picture in my mind. Two mourning periods. A long illness between them." He stopped. "I don't imagine that your new sister-in-law included you in her social activities."

She laughed. "No. Not often."

He started moving again. "So, you've scarcely had a chance at a social life, at all. No wonder you were nervous about the house party —and it's no wonder you are reluctant to go to London."

Suddenly, he was kneeling before her. He took both of her hands in his. "You have the heart of a lioness, Glory. And the will of one, too.

And now you tackle dancing?" He squeezed her hand. "I'm proud to witness it. I would be proud to help. I am proud of *you*."

Her heart soared. She wished she could see him clearly. Her hands gripped his. "If I've had any success here, it is largely due to you."

"It that is true, then it has been my honor." He moved his grip to her elbows. "You must carry on, Glory. You have been so brave. You cannot falter now. The tyrants in your life cannot be allowed to win. Wherever we encounter them, we must push back."

Fervor lived in his statements, along with the ring of truth. "Is that what you are doing?" she asked. "Fighting tyranny?"

"Every single day." His tone softened. "You see? We have more in common than we knew."

"But you won't speak of it, will you? No one knows about that particular night. Not even Tensford knows. I asked Hope not to tell him."

"I said I would keep your secret and I will. I really do feel the need to help you in some way, though. When are your dancing lessons? Perhaps I could take part, act as your partner?"

Now she was glad the darkness hid her expression. She didn't want to think about struggling and stumbling in her lessons while Keswick watched. "No, thank you. Miss Munroe and I are getting on well together and with Mr. Thorpe, our instructor. I wouldn't want to upset the balance we've achieved."

He sighed. "And you are sure you won't allow me to help you tonight?"

She looked down. "I do appreciate the offer, but no."

He sprang away again and walked to the water's edge. Motionless and silent, he stared out over the water. Several minutes passed. Glory sat and waited, unsure what to do or say, and wondered if she had made a mistake in telling him.

"Miss Munroe was right."

She started when he spoke, it came so unexpectedly and sounded so sharp and decisive.

"You do need all the arrows you can find for your quiver. You should collect every weapon you can find to help you fight for your best outcome." He came back and knelt before her again. "I'm thinking of the bargain you proposed."

Her breath caught.

"We've already vowed to continue our friendship. Now I'm considering what you asked of me."

The air escaped her on a shaky breath and she began to fiddle with the edge of her sleeve.

"I think you were right. You should know what occurs between men and women. For one thing, I think it will give you a new confidence, to know what your body is capable of—to know the pleasure you can both give and receive."

Her face was on fire—and the heat had begun a leisurely tour of the rest of her, too.

"Also, when you do begin to entertain suitors, you are going to need to be even more careful than most girls in your situation." He leaned closer. "I cannot see you in a dynastic marriage, Glory. Not one made for the *ton's* usual advancement in titles or bank balances. You've seen what a real marriage can be—you've lived inside happy walls with one. You deserve to find the same. I hope you will someday know a man who will both cherish and defend you, whenever the need arises. And I think it would be easier to choose, knowing how a man who cares for you can make you feel."

He let go of her suddenly and sat back, running a hand through his hair. "Heaven help me, but all of that sounds like something a seducer would say, doesn't it?"

She laughed a little. "It does, rather." She reached for him. "I would be worried about it, perhaps, if I hadn't been the one to ask first."

"Thank God for that," he said fervently. "I'll agree to your bargain, if you still wish for it."

She hesitated. She'd already tried to begin the process of rooting out her hopes for Keswick. If she agreed now, she'd have to stick to the letter of their pact—and not wish for a further developing bond. Could she do it?

"I'm not talking about giddy rebellion or the naughty excitement of breaking the rules," he said. "Too many an inexperienced girl has been caught up in such feelings. I mean for you to know the touch of a man who respects and cares for you."

She shivered with longing.

"You needn't fear for your virtue, either. I would never risk your chance at making your own choices, in the future."

No. She *couldn't* do this without wanting everything from him. But by all that was holy, she was a lady, an earl's daughter. She had honor of her own, no matter what others thought. She could do this without ever letting him know how much more she ached to possess.

"Yes." It came out a whisper, without a hint of the growing hunger inside of her.

He pressed a kiss to her lips, quick and entirely unsatisfactory. "Wait a moment." He stood and cast about, his gaze ranging from the field to the shore. He looked along the edge and set out, passing Poppy and investigating the stretched out clump of bushes she'd been hobbled near. He pushed into the thicket and disappeared.

She made her way over to her mare and hugged Poppy's neck. "Have I gone mad?" she asked her friend.

Poppy's ears swiveled and she nudged Glory for a pet. After a moment, Keswick popped out of the brush.

She stared as he approached. His coat and waistcoat were gone. Clad only in breeches, boots and linen, he looked . . . primitive, some-how. In the best way. Tall, and wide and utterly masculine.

"I've cleared a spot for us. We won't be seen, there." He looked down at his plain linen. "I spread them out on the ground. I didn't want the damp to get to your gown."

"There's a blanket in my saddle bag. It's small, but it might do."

"Even better." He chuckled. "That magic saddle bag. I should have thought to ask." He fetched the woolen rug and disappeared again.

This time, she was ready when he peeked back out. He held aside a branch and beckoned her.

Holding her breath, she went to him.

It was a small space, surrounded by a fragrant mix of boxwood and yellow-berried daphne. The blanket covered the open area and he'd mounded his coat and waistcoat at one end. When he let the branch go, they were enclosed in the dim bower, with only the stars above for light.

She was glad of it. Although she'd like to see the look in his blue eyes, she would much rather not have to worry about him seeing the wreckage of her leg.

"Come and sit," he invited. "There's no hurry. We can look at the stars—"

Stepping close, she pulled him down and kissed him.

"Well, then." He returned her kiss with tender finesse and then with increasing ardor. And she relaxed into it, into his arms, and allowed her tightly strung hunger to ease and become something more languorous.

With lips and tongue, he put the question to her. She opened to him. *Yes*, she answered silently. This was what she wanted, to be surrounded by his masculine heat and spellbound by the spine-tingling exploration of his tongue.

Almost without thought, she placed her hands upon him, climbing broad shoulders and exploring the heavy muscles in his back. Suddenly, he dipped down and lifted her in his arms. "Come and lie back," he rasped. "You must tell me right away if you become frightened or do not wish to go on."

Nodding, she rested her head against him and breathed in the fresh scent of his linen. "I'll never smell bay again without thinking of you."

"Tell your sister to change out the scents in my room, when I'm gone. Or I'll be jealous of every man who stays there after me."

She didn't want to think about him leaving, so she kissed him again. He held the kiss while he laid her down with her head and shoulders resting against his piled clothing.

"Are you comfortable?" he asked.

Her only answer was to pull him down with her. She let her fingers trail along the edge of his jaw. "You have the profile of a Greek God," she murmured.

He snorted.

"It's true. Zeus sits on his throne atop Olympus and wishes for a jaw like this."

"I'd trade him for a thunder bolt, but you've already sent them racing up and down my spine."

"Don't you dare think of trading it away." Kissing her way along the edge, she let her hands wander up and into his thick, dark hair.

He groaned and she nearly did too, as he sent his lips traveling along the arch of her neck. She could feel her pulse beating against him when he paused at just the right spot. But then he moved on and kissed his way across the edge of her bodice.

"Sit up?" he asked. When she did, he reached around her. "No half measures this time," he insisted. "We are going to do this the right way."

In a shockingly quick amount of time, he had her bodice, stays and shift peeled away. She was bare from the waist up and his head bent towards her.

"I can barely see you," he complained.

"Oh, dear." She took one of his hands and placed it upon her. "Whatever shall you do about it?"

"I'll feel my way—and be thankful for it, I suppose."

She sank back as both of his hands went exploring and his lips and tongue soon followed.

"So beautiful," he murmured.

"You cannot see," she reminded him.

"I don't have to."

With one finger he teased her, blazing a slow path around one erect nipple, then the other. Her back arched.

"There's no hurry," he whispered.

She whimpered her disagreement, then gasped as he bent down and licked one nipple, then the other. For a blessed eternity she reveled in the erotic torture as he licked and sucked, switched sides and tortured her anew. Every sensation plucked a chord that sent heat and damp and pure lust spiraling through her. She was nearly shaking with it before he was through.

He came back to her mouth and she clutched at him, desperate for more—but unsure how to ask, or even what she asked for.

He knew, though. He buried his face in the nape of her neck and she shivered and stretched, giving him access. Then he reattached himself to her breast and she moaned—just as she felt his fingers at her thigh, raising her hems.

She stiffened, but he appeared to be concentrating on her breast and on making soft, teasing circles on her thigh with each rising inch of her skirts. He wasn't looking at her leg—and he likely couldn't see it, if he did.

Safe in the dark, she relaxed. He continued pulling her skirts high and she ran a hand up inside his linen, over his chest. She marveled as she roamed the hard expanse. He was so large and unyielding, even as everything he did to her was tender.

And patient. While her skirts rose, he'd begun to kiss his way lower. His lips tickled her ribs and began to move down toward the bundle of clothes bunched at her waist.

She grabbed him and held on. "Please, stay up here?"

He paused—and then understood. "You don't have to hide anything from me, Glory. I think you are incredibly lovely, just as you are."

His words warmed her, but still, something wary inside wouldn't let go. "Please. I . . . I'm not ready. I'm sorry."

"There is nothing to be sorry about," he said firmly. "This is about making you feel marvelous. I'll stay here." He kissed her breast. "It's not a hardship."

She relaxed her hold, flooded with relief—and with the increasingly familiar mix of desire, nerves and delicious frustration he always brought out in her.

His teasing fingers had moved to her inner thigh now, and she had to fight to keep from clenching her legs together.

He must have felt the tension in her. "Everything is fine, Glory." He stilled and she could practically hear the wheels turning in his head. "Would you like a turn? Touching me?"

Her breath let out quickly. "Yes." That was exactly what she needed.

He sat up. Reaching behind him, he grasped the back of his shirt and lifted it over his head. Pulling her upright, he lay back and took her place. "I'm all yours."

She could hear the grin in his voice and she responded in kind. It made it easier to bend over him and press a quick kiss onto his mouth.

"That's good, for a start."

Scooting closer, she rested on an elbow. Her index finger replaced her lips. "You said there was no hurry."

In answer, he shifted, setting himself more comfortably—and waited.

She rested her hand flat against his chest. He was so warm. His heart beat reassuringly beneath her fingers. She began to move them, investigating, searching out a path across his wide shoulders, grazing his nipples, moving over the hard planes and valleys of his muscles. At last, she followed the trail of coarse hair down to his navel.

She stopped there, nervous about going further. He lay taut before her, and she could feel his hand grasping the blanket between them.

"Go on," he urged.

Curiosity won. Her touch feather light, she moved downward. "Good heavens."

He scarcely breathed as she explored the impressive bulge. He held himself tense and motionless. She hadn't expected to find . . . so much of him—but the length and breath of the swollen ridge beneath her fingers was unmistakable. Experimentally, she placed her palm along it and explored with measuring fingers.

He groaned out loud.

She snatched her hand away. "Did I hurt you?"

"No! You've done nothing wrong." His voice sounded strained. "Everything you are doing is perfect. It's just my body wanting more of you—because you are sweet and lovely and so utterly desirable."

Pleasure flushed through her veins in an entirely new way. Confidence surged. There it was again—that feeling of feminine power. It made her bold and she placed her hand on him again and bent down to trail hot kisses along his neck and chest.

His hips raised, pressing him further into her hand. She gripped him tighter and followed the earlier path of her fingers, kissing her way down to his navel.

He surged upright then, and lifted her hand away. "Apologies, but there is only so much that a man can take."

Her lips curved. "Am I driving you mad with desire?"

"You are. Most definitely."

She glanced down. "Is it painful?" Her hand began to move. "Shall I let it out?"

"No!" In one fluid motion he stopped her and pressed her back and onto the blanket again. Looming over her, he let his weight and bulk hold her down. She could feel the hard length of him against her belly. "This evening is about you. It's all for you." He kissed her. "I've always considered myself a generous lover, but this is different." His hand caressed her temple and cupped her jaw. "It is an honor, Glory. It feels . . ." He stopped. "Thank you for trusting me."

Tears welled in her eyes. There were so many things she wanted to thank him for. She couldn't though—she couldn't speak and still keep her word, keep to their bargain. She kissed him instead.

He responded fiercely, and then pulled away. His weight shifted and gave her a clear view of the sky. "Remember this, Glory. Drink it all in. The stars overhead, the breeze rustling the leaves, the regard I feel for you, the trust we've built between us and the pleasure we are giving each other. Gather it all into your heart. In the future, when you have choices to make, pull it all back out. Don't settle for a dynastic marriage or fall prey to a passion that feels forbidden or sordid. Use this night as your measure and your shield. Promise me— and I will know that I've accomplished something worthwhile."

"I promise." She captured his face between her hands. "I will not settle."

He swooped down and took her mouth. Temptation and gentleness gave way to ruthless, zealous skill. She was swept up—and thrilled to go along where he wished to take her. This time, when his fingers lifted her skirts up, she hesitated only a moment before helping him push them up and out of the way.

His fingers teased again, lingering at the tie of her garter. "Open your legs for me, Glory."

Swallowing, she did.

He made a noise of approval. It seemed to come rumbling from his chest and she immediately wished to hear it again.

His touch climbed higher. He stroked her curls and she gasped. He ran a firm caress down the middle seam of her sex, then pressed in with a swirling stroke that made her legs drop wider.

Flames leapt, crackling higher and higher within her with each circling pass. Her heartbeat sounded loud in her ears, and desire curled, thick and heavy, in her womb.

He inched higher once more. His fingertip scraped lightly over her most tender spot. She gasped, helpless, and he nudged closer to her, paying decadent, delicate tribute to her wet, silken flesh.

Her head fell back. Her fists clenched. She was caught in his spell, in the magic he was making and the sweet pleasure that moved all through her. Her hips lifted. Her legs splayed.

"Keswick!"

"Yes, Glory. It's coming for you. Let it have its way."

The rhythm of his fingers changed, became steady and gradually more intense.

She rose up, out of herself. Desire was a string, tied to her soul, lifting her higher and higher—and then she was up and over the top of some mysterious wall—and caught up in a wave of tight, delicious shudders. Her back arched, her toes curled. She was held there, suspended in pleasure for a long, long moment, before she collapsed in on herself.

Unclear, how long she floated in a cocoon of utterly relaxed bliss, but she gradually came back to herself to find the stars still overhead, the river still murmuring and Keswick lying next to her with an arm draped over his eyes.

She drew a breath—

"Don't you dare thank me," he said starkly. He sat up, took her hand, and kissed it. "Can you get yourself and Poppy back, on your own?"

"Of course."

He pulled his shirt from the branch where it had been snagged. "Then I will leave you to it."

He stood, but paused before he slipped out. "Don't forget—and don't settle." He moved, then stopped again. "Your trust truly does mean a great deal to me."

And then he was gone. She flopped back—and discovered he'd forgotten his coat and waistcoat.

Don't forget? She nearly laughed. Not likely.

And as for trust . . . well, she did indeed trust him. But he had done just what he'd set out to do. He'd handed her a weapon.

Now she had to convince herself not to use it against him.

CHAPTER 15

Keswick went on to the village. When he entered the Crown and Cock, a great many of the tavern's patrons were gathered around a table, shouting, betting and heckling two local lads engaged in a game of dice. He veered away from the noise. He brushed off Betsy's advance and took a padded window seat where he could stare out into the murky night.

He failed to notice Betsy's affronted neglect. He never observed the swell of men who came in or felt the side-eyed glances they cast over him. He did register when Betsy finally relented and set a pint down in front of him. He drank it down and barely noticed the several times she replaced it, except to toss those back, too.

He continued to stare out the window when the taproom grew quiet and Mr. Thomkins began to scrub the tables and then the floor.

"Would ye care to take a room fer the night, milord?" the innkeeper asked at last.

"No, thank you," he replied absently. He barely heard the question over the chaotic skirmish in his head.

"Would ye be heading back to Greystone Park, then?"

"No, thank you."

He didn't know how much later it was when he looked around,

found the taproom empty, the fire banked and the chairs upside down atop the tables. Perhaps he dozed a little. He was awake when the first faint light of dawn showed in the sky and the first noises came from the kitchen.

He came back to himself sometime later when Tensford slid into the seat next to him.

"Having a bit of a brood, are we?" his friend asked.

He didn't bother to answer.

"It's been a while since you've been struck with one of these."

He blinked. Frowned. "I had my life settled. Ordered."

"Padded and numb, is more like it," Tensford muttered. He stood. "Come on. You are unsettling Thomkins and his wife. I've got a place for you."

"I don't want to go back to the house."

"No." Tensford looked him over. "Not like this." He sighed. "Come along."

He stood up.

"Kes? Where are the rest of your clothes?"

Surprised, he looked down. He'd forgotten them, forgotten the state he was in. "I . . . I'll fetch them later."

Tensford had brought the dogcart, hitched to a grey pony. Keswick crawled in and settled into a corner. The box shaped seating was lined on all four sides with benches. He laid his head back and put his feet up on one bench and watched the light grow in the morning sky as they set off.

Tensford drove back to Greystone land. Keswick shut his eyes when they crossed the bridge, so that he would not look down the long field toward the cluster of shrubs near the river. When he opened them again, the sky had been replaced with the canopy of the ancient forest and they had pulled to a stop next to a tiny hut with an attached lean-to.

"It's an old game-keeper's lodge. We're quite a ways from the house. You won't be disturbed." Tensford climbed down and untied a basket from the back of the cart. Going to the door, he held it open in invitation.

Keswick rolled over the side of the cart and went to peer in. Somehow, it appeared even smaller on the inside. There was a hearth, a low bed and a table pushed against the far wall, with two stools tucked underneath it.

"I used to come up here, when tensions with my mother, sister and aunt would thicken, or when the helpless feelings of not being able to do anything to help my tenants would grow to be too much."

He eyed the vase of dried flowers on the mantel and the copy of *Ackerman's Repository* on the table, then raised a brow at his friend.

Tensford flushed. "Hope and I do occasionally come up here, but you don't need to know about that." He set the basket on the table. "Here is food and drink. I'll be back to check on you. It's a long walk back to the house, but if you decide to come, just follow the path through the woods. It will drop you onto the road that follows the river."

Keswick started when his friend put both hands on his shoulders. Tensford looked him in the eye. "Sort it all out in your head, man. We'll support you, no matter which way you come down."

Tensford drove off and Keswick sank onto the edge of the bed. He rubbed his temples and let his head droop down. There was too much noise in there. Too many clashes of wants and needs and desperate rationales—and no resolution to be found.

Unable to sit still, he got up and went outside. A stack of shortened logs had been dumped haphazardly nearby. After a rummage in the lean-to, he found an axe. Breathing deeply, he rolled up his sleeves, fetched the first log and started in.

Hours later, the forest around him had gone dim. The logs were gone and the pile of split wood loomed high. He tossed the axe back and went inside. It was dark, but he didn't bother to search out a candle. He found the basket, fumbled inside for a bottle of cold tea and drank it all down. With difficulty, he managed to get his boots off himself and then stretched out on the bed.

When he woke, daylight showed around the door and tried to shine through the one grimy window. He had no inkling how long he'd slept, but his brood was over.

The chaos had gone quiet. Only the truth was left. He'd been indulging himself, pretending that there might be an answer to be found.

Stretching and frowning, he dug the heels of his palms into his eyes. How had he allowed things to go this far? First, Glory turned him inside out—asking for things that made his hollow places echo with loneliness. Then, somehow, that innocent slip of a girl had squeezed in past his defenses and starting busily spreading laughter, secrets and lust like plaster. Handily, she'd searched out the cracks inside of him and started filling them in.

It had to stop. There were reasons he held himself apart. Real motives for spreading himself out and indulging only in the shallowest of dealings with most people, but especially women. The recollection of the agony that followed when he abandoned his rakish role and allowed himself to need anyone—that was only part of it. He must also remember that Glory was as much at risk for grief and shame as he.

He sighed, knowing it was too late for him. It was going to hurt. He'd begun to think about her entirely too much. He'd spent—hours? days?—trying to think of a way to allow himself to feel for her.

There wasn't one. There was only one thing to do now. He had to leave her behind. He must go—back to the house and then back to London.

* * *

"THERE ISN'T enough light in here for this fine work."

The nasal complaint set Glory's teeth on edge. The sun shone bright here in Hope's parlor. Miss Vernon was only being difficult.

Again.

The other girl threw her embroidery down with disgust. "I don't have the right colors with me to finish this piece, in any case."

"Then perhaps you should have joined the countess and the others on their shopping expedition," Miss Munroe suggested.

Most of the ladies had gone down to the village. Glory had gone down herself, but only to place a special order at the mercantile. She'd returned early to join those few who had decided to stay at Greystone, where they had gathered in the parlor for a bit of sewing and gossip.

"Shopping?" Miss Vernon scoffed. "I've driven through that village. If you think there is any sort of acceptable shopping to be had there, you are sorely mistaken."

She continued on, extolling the virtues and superiority of London's shops, but Glory barely heard her. She was busy wondering where Keswick had gone. She hadn't caught so much as a glimpse of him since he'd left her side the night before last. As far as she could tell, no one had seen him since then. Except, perhaps, for Tensford. He'd had a curious look on his face when Hope had asked about his friend—and he'd answered her in a tone that no one else could hear.

Honestly, Keswick had to stop disappearing every time they had a physical encounter. He was going to make her think she'd done something wrong—except, she knew she hadn't. He might not have had the same . . . completion . . . that she had, but he had been entirely involved and pleased to be so. She knew that much, at least. He'd just escaped before she could suggest any sort of reciprocation.

In fact, she had begun to wonder if this was a new strategy he'd adopted to keep her at bay—all give and no take. He said he would agree to their bargain. He'd given her exactly what she had requested. But he had not accepted anything in return—no sort of physical or emotional connection or intimacy at all. That wasn't friendship. It wasn't partnership.

It would not do.

"How long can one afternoon last?" Miss Vernon exclaimed. "This one seems interminable. Why have we not planned more activities with the gentlemen?" She sighed. "I wish that we might have gone to watch them shoot. That would have made the time pass quickly."

"We did have their company yesterday. They might have gone

fishing or they might have chosen some other activity away from the house when their shooting was delayed," Miss Munroe reminded her.

"It does seem an odd sort of thing—to have someone try to destroy Tensford's hunting blinds," Miss Myland remarked.

"I suspect someone in the area has a sympathy for the birds," answered Miss Munroe.

"That's all very well, but they should leave Tensford's birds to him."

"I don't disagree." Miss Munroe looked to her dissatisfied cousin. "In any case, the gentlemen were very kind to picnic with us in that beautiful meadow."

"We do have cards planned for this evening," Glory told her. "We'll have a mixed crowd for that, if you care to stay." She wondered if Keswick would turn up at last—and suspected that Miss Vernon was wondering the same thing.

"She knows," Miss Munroe said wryly. "She insisted on bringing a change of clothes for dinner and the evening of cards."

"Well, what else should we do?" her cousin huffed.

Perhaps she might not automatically assume she would be invited, Glory thought uncharitably.

"In any case, what can we do *now*, to make the hours go by?" Miss Vernon asked with a sigh.

"What would you plan if it was your party?" Glory asked her.

"I'm not perfectly sure. Something lively," she said, shooting a glance toward Glory's skirts. "You've the battledore net set up, but that would be far more fun if the gentlemen took part." She frowned. "I'd get up something involving marksmanship, since the men failed to invite us. They can count pheasants, but we could keep our own score and have something to tell them." She sighed. "If only I had my bow, I could show you all something."

"Marksmanship," Glory mused. "Yes. That does sound exciting. I know there are a couple of bows fit for a lady up in the attics. Tensford's sister accounted herself an archer at one point, Hope told me." Her mouth twisted. "And if I know Fanny, then they are the best that money can buy."

"Well! That does sound the thing!" Miss Vernon wore a smile at last.

"I don't know the sport, but I should quite like to give it a try," Miss Parscate ventured.

"We'll all go," Glory said. "I'm sure the kitchens will send refreshments for those who would rather observe. Give us an hour or a little less and we'll have everything set up."

She was true to her word, thanks to Higgins', the butler's, help. The tables were still set up outside along the house. They only added a bench holding the equipment at the edge of the croquet field and a target set up several yards out. A footman and a maid trooped behind the ladies, bearing lemonade and teacake.

"This will do very nicely," Miss Vernon said. She looked as contented as Glory had yet seen her. She picked up a bow. "These are quite as fine as my own." Pulling on a leather arm guard with practiced ease, she held out her arm peremptorily for her cousin to fasten it. A pair of gloves followed and she chose a bow and stepped out.

Her first shot grazed the edge of the target and bounced off. The next hit the target, but wide of the center. "I think the string may have gone slack with age," she said critically. She shot another with the same result, then with a nod, she sent the footman to retrieve her arrows.

"I'll have a try," Miss Parscate said. "I've always wanted to learn."

"Don't nock your arrow until the footman is back," Glory warned. "Just in case."

It proved wise advice—and yet, almost not enough. The girl's first arrow went unexpectedly awry—and over the heads of several of the watching ladies. The second buried itself into the dirt at the footman's feet, as he poured lemonade nearby.

"Pull back further," Miss Vernon instructed her. "It takes effort. Hold the arrow straight and steady before you release it."

Miss Parscate's next arrow did better, making it nearly to the target. The two girls took turns, both improving as they went on, and accepting the cheers and advice of the observers.

"Will you give it a try?" Miss Vernon asked Glory at last. "Or can you not stand steady enough?"

"Steady is not an issue, if I am standing still. But the bow is not my weapon," Glory told her.

"I daresay we knew you were not proficient, or we would have had this activity already planned."

Glory stood and gave the girl an even look. "Be careful of how you judge others, Miss Vernon, lest you only reveal yourself."

Glory nodded at the footman and he set down his pitcher and went around the corner of the house. He came back carrying a long bench, with Higgins taking up the other end. They set it up at the edge of the field and placed a line of objects upon it—an odd assortment, from an earthen bottle to a sturdy teacup and on down, decreasing in size until the last—a small, shining conker.

"What's this?" Miss Vernon's tone had gone as thin and sharp as the rest of her.

"Marksmanship of a different sort." Glory took her whip from Higgins and took her place, bracing herself sturdily. With careful aim and the right amount of force, she cracked the leather. The earthenware bottle spun and dropped off of the bench. The seated ladies oohed and awed and applauded lightly, just as they had for the other two girls.

She kept her distance the same and moved down the line with narrowed eyes and a steady hand. One by one, each successively smaller object dropped, until only the small conker was left.

"My brother would envy you such a fine specimen of a conker," Miss Parscate said. "But it is awfully small. Are you sure you can hit it?"

Glory readjusted her feet and breathed deeply. She took careful aim and sent the chestnut flying with a fast flick of the whip.

The ladies burst out in applause and murmured admiration. Miss Vernon merely raised a brow and sniffed. "It's a good trick, but hardly a real skill."

"May I try it?" Miss Munroe stepped forward.

"Of course."

Glory showed her friend the correct way to grip the handle and let her try a few experimental swings. "Hold a moment, if you continue snapping at that height, you are going to hit yourself sooner, rather than later. If you like, I can show you how to get a good crack out of it."

Miss Munroe laughed. "Oh, yes. Please."

She showed her how to gently sway her elbow up and down. Bring it forward when the whip goes over your shoulder and reaches an angle . . . here."

It took her several attempts, but Miss Munroe cracked it at last and grinned in triumph. The ladies cheered. "If you think it doesn't take skill, you couldn't be more wrong," she told Miss Vernon. "I haven't even tried to hit anything yet, but my arm is already tired."

"I'm sure I would do better," Miss Vernon said loftily. "I am used to spotting and hitting a target."

"It takes quite a bit of practice before you can attempt it," Glory said. "You have to learn the qualities of your natural throw, so you can adjust for them."

"I'm sure you think so." Miss Vernon snatched the whip and gripped the handle in the middle.

Glory stepped up. "Move your grip to the—"

"I'm sure I can get the hang of it," the other girl interrupted. "Who taught you?"

"One of the grooms in my brother's stables showed me the basics, but I taught myself, mostly."

"As I thought," Miss Vernon sniffed. "I did wonder at first, why you had not contrived to show off your little trick before this. I thought perhaps it did not play well into the role of helpless waif, which I hear Lord Keswick has been responding to so well."

Glory's mouth dropped open. Several of the ladies around her gasped.

"But now I realize that you likely didn't wish for anyone to understand how very simple it is." She began to lash about her with the whip.

Furious, Glory snapped her mouth shut. If the other girl kept on like that, she was going to end up striking herself. It would be no more than the spiteful cat deserved. She sighed. But there were dangers. She could strike her own eye and seriously damage herself, or hit someone else—along with a myriad of other painful possibilities.

"Please," she began. "Raise your arm higher before you strike—"

The girl turned away.

"If you continue on like that you'll—"

Miss Vernon shrieked. She spun back, her eyes narrowed and filling with tears and a vivid red welt raised on her arm. "You churlish girl! You did that on purpose!"

Glory stepped back. "What are you saying? I tried to warn you."

"It could have struck me in the face!" the other girl cried shrilly, clapping a hand to her cheek. "You wanted this to happen all along!"

Glory was at a loss. She had no idea how to react or handle this termagant. "You are overwrought." She turned to go. "I'll ask the staff to find a room where you can rest a while before dinner." She cast an imploring look at Miss Munroe. "Unless you feel as if you must return to your cousin's home?"

"You'd like that, wouldn't you? Well, I will *not* go! You think I will just leave the field open and leave him all to you?" Her face twisted and she threw the whip at Glory.

She saw it coming, but she was already moving and had no time to react. The thing landed at her feet and curled as if it were alive, wrapping around her good ankle and catching her mid-step. She had no chance. She could not stabilize herself with her weak leg. She went down, crashing into a table, bringing it, and all the china and crockery upon it, down, too.

She lay still for a moment, breathing heavily while fury and embarrassment roared through her and tea dripped onto her neck and ran into her bodice. No one else moved or said a word for a long moment, then everyone rushed to help her up and brush her off.

Everyone except Miss Vernon, who stood and watched while an evil little smile danced about her mouth.

Glory glared at her. Stooping, she picked up the whip and was pleased at the sudden disappearance of that smile. Let the nasty girl worry. A million hurtful things swirled in her brain, waiting to be launched at that smug face. She chose the truest one—which was likely also the most terrible. "I feel sorry for you," she said quietly.

"What?" Miss Vernon looked shocked. She glanced wildly about. "What did she say?"

Glory spun around—and found Lord Keswick standing at the edge of the tables, looking on, and wearing a horrified expression.

"What's this? What's happened?" He glanced wildly from her to Miss Vernon and back again.

"Keswick!" Miss Vernon's manner changed instantly to one of smiling welcome. "You are just in time."

"Just in time? For what? To see you abuse one of our hosts?"

The girl looked wounded. "She's not our host. She's just a guest, no different than you or me." Her mouth curled. "Although perhaps she will eventually become a permanent guest. Practically another servant. Is that strange limbo not the fate of a spinster aunt?"

"Your sister has two children," Miss Munroe declared. "Perhaps you will let us know, in the future?"

Keswick looked away, at Glory. "Are you all right?" he asked.

Miss Vernon's lip wobbled. "Why are you all defending her?"

"No one is defending me," Glory said severely. "I don't require a defense. I haven't done anything wrong."

"You did this!" She thrust out her arm, where the welt marked her fair skin, looking red and painful.

"She most certainly did not!" Miss Munroe asserted. Several of the other ladies murmured agreement.

Miss Parscate laid a sympathetic hand on Miss Vernon's arm. "Let it rest, my dear. This round is over."

Miss Vernon shot her a dark look, then stalked toward Glory, glaring all the way. "Don't you dare feel sorry for me! This is merely a battle," she hissed. "The war is still to come and I have bigger weapons in reserve."

"There is no war," Glory told her coldly. "Don't be absurd. Just do me the favor of leaving me be and I will do the same for you." She turned to go and found Keswick still watching her.

She marched up to him and stopped. "And as for you," she said ferociously. "I will deal with you later." She scowled at him. "When you stop acting so afraid of me."

With as much dignity as she could muster, she continued on, into the house.

CHAPTER 16

Laughter and muted conversation drifted up from the parlor. Glory passed the main staircase and went straight for the servant's stair. She wore an old muslin gown that she normally saved for days spent helping in the stillroom or for rooting around in the attics. The last thing she wanted was to be seen.

She'd had dinner on a tray in her room and had requested apples and sugar cubes to be sent up too. Fortunately, the kitchens were used to her ways. She stuffed a small bag full and made her way to the stables.

The horses were happy for the treats and the extra attention and Glory felt some of the tension ease out of her in the warm and familiar atmosphere of the stables. When all of the equines had been seen to, she took a lantern and hung it next to the empty stall where Grumpet and her kittens lay in state. She swore the barn cat looked relieved and grateful when she entered and took a seat in the straw. The curious kittens had obviously become used to human contact. They swarmed her, climbing into her lap and up her back. Grumpet, abandoned for the moment, stretched and leapt up to the top of the stall door—and disappeared.

"Oh, you darlings," Glory crooned. "Soon, you'll be old enough and

I can bring you little treats too. A bit of kipper? A dish of cream? How does that sound, my lovelies?" She reached back and detached an adventurous grey kitten from her hair. Several locks came with him, escaping the bun at her nape. A striped tabby promptly attacked the length of hair as it fell across her shoulder. The first kitten scrambled away while the other climbed her sleeve.

"You look like you could use some help."

She looked up, but she already knew who it was. "Keswick." Her lips compressed.

"It appears all of the good company is to be had out here."

"The only company I wish to spend time with *lives* out here."

His face fell. "Does that mean I cannot come in?"

She pulled away another kitten and another strand of hair and considered.

"Will it help if I promise that I'm not afraid of you?"

She rolled her eyes and relented. "Oh, all right. Come in."

Entering, he closed the door and sat next to her, plucking the grey kitten from her back as he came. Several of the others left her to go and explore the new territory he offered.

"Did you lose at cards?" she asked.

He chuckled. "I always lose when Sterne is playing. He's a regular Card Sharper."

"I'll remember that."

He lifted a kitten that had begun digging its claws into his boots. "I heard about your demonstration."

Now it was her turn to laugh. "I'm sure you did."

"I meant, I heard about the skill you showed. Most of the ladies were impressed."

"Most," she said sourly.

"You cannot think I would pay heed to anything Miss Vernon had to say?"

She shrugged. "I wouldn't think so. But I've discovered I'm horrifically bad at predicting how you will respond to . . . most anything."

"Well, you never have to worry about her influence. Nor do you have to fear that I'm afraid of you."

"Perhaps you should be." She untangled another kitten from her hair. "I'm sure I'm beginning to resemble Medusa by now."

"I'll take Medusa over a harpy, any day," he said wryly.

"Honestly, she's the one who should be frightened of me." Bitter frustration crept into her tone. "You have no idea how close I came to showing her just what I can do with that whip. I would have loved to have snapped one of her buttons loose, or to have cracked it just next to one ear, then the other."

He bit his lip but she could tell he was trying not to smile. "Why didn't you?"

"Because she's too much of a fool. A normal person would freeze— but she'd likely do the opposite and bolt—and not where I expected her to go. Can you imagine the ruckus if I actually had given her a good, quick flick?"

He grimaced. "Yes. I can."

"So could I—and I still almost did it."

"I take it back, maybe I am a tad bit frightened of you." He stretched over, getting low to let a kitten jump from his shoulder. "Just a little."

"Keswick," she said, growing serious. "Do you pity me?"

He reared upright and the kitten squeaked. "No!" he said forcefully. "You know I don't."

"I didn't think so. I'm usually terribly good at sniffing out pity and squashing it. I hated to think I might have been so wrong about you."

"Whatever would make you even entertain the notion?"

"I asked my maid about physical matters—between a man and a woman."

"You did what?" he asked, shocked.

"I told her that Miss Vernon had a book of naughty pictures and was speaking of physical relations to the young ladies."

His eyes widened. "Well. That will spread like wildfire below stairs." He sat back. "I take it back. I am *definitely* frightened of you."

"It's nothing she doesn't deserve," Glory sniffed. "But something she said today—about gentlemen keeping score—it reminded me of a discussion I heard my maid, Lucy, having with another of the chambermaids. They were speaking of physical matters, and one of them said that when a man and woman are together, then the man always . . . finishes. And that the woman only does if she is lucky."

The light was dim, with just the light from the one lantern falling into the stall, but she could see his color rising. "The woman always finishes, if the man is skilled," he corrected her.

"Well, today I asked her what happens when the man doesn't finish —because I recalled the other maid saying it wasn't healthy for a man to be left in that state."

"And you believed that?" he asked incredulously.

She raised a brow. "Well, you did disappear, afterwards. And stayed gone."

He groaned and let his head sink into his hands.

"Lucy laughed and said not to worry—the men always finish. But when I pressed her, she said she could only wonder—if a man didn't, maybe he didn't truly like the woman—and perhaps he was only acting out of pity."

"Ah. I'm glad you knew that was only nonsense."

"I hoped it was."

"I kept to my side of our pact, Glory. You are forewarned and fore-armed about real, meaningful passion." The slow flush spreading upward from his cravat was deepening. He waved an arm as if to banish the subject. "Now, I would like to talk—"

"Have you?" she interrupted. "Truly?"

He raised a brow and waited.

"Have you kept to the bargain? We were to be friends. That implies balance between us. An even exchange. But it feels all one-sided when you don't share any bit of yourself, either physical or emotional."

Frowning, he began, "I don't think—" He stopped. "No. I don't want to argue. I want you to understand." Absently, he stroked the kitten trying to burrow into his coat.

She felt complete sympathy for the little darling. She'd like to burrow into his warmth and let him run his fingers over her, too.

"Would it help if I told you that I've been more open with you than with . . . almost anyone?"

"A little. Perhaps." Pursing her lips, she took the kitten from him and set it safely away. "Here," she ordered. "Give me your arm."

Perplexed, he did and she braced herself and carefully shifted up and swiveled around until she was sitting in his lap, facing him.

"Glory," he groaned. It sounded like an objection, but also a plea.

"Lucy said, if a lad was reluctant, one need only to sit in his lap and wiggle a bit." She tried it and he moaned again. "I just don't want you to run off again. Not quite yet. And I heard that Betsy at the Crown and Cock sat on your lap for an entire evening, so I thought you must enjoy it."

He laughed and groaned and let his head drop and lean against her breast bone. "Glory, I swear, you are enough to drive a man mad—and keep him happy all the way there."

She cocked her head. "It's not poetry, but I'll take it." She stroked his hair, making little finger paths through the soft, dark locks. "Are you leaving?" she asked on a whisper.

He nodded.

"Then you must at least bid me a proper goodbye."

He looked up and suddenly his hands were in her hair and he was holding her gently and looking into her eyes. "You mad, daft, darling girl," he whispered. "I never pitied you. I enjoy your company more than . . ." He frowned. "More than any other woman I've known. But I cannot give you what you want. I cannot give you more."

"Why not? Can't you at least explain?"

His eyes closed. "No. Just know—I don't fear you, Glory. It's more that I fear for you. Nothing good can come of getting tangled up in my life." His hands fell and he gripped her shoulders. "Miss Vernon and her nastiness? She's chased me here and subjected you to such spite and rudeness—and that's just incidental! Her hateful ways are as nothing compared to the real danger."

"Danger?" She drew back to frown down at him. "Surely you exaggerate."

"I wish I did. I know it sounds ridiculous." He shook his head. "I can't explain. Not truly. I just would never wish to expose you to the sort of trouble, the hate and vitriol—" He stopped himself. "Just . . .

please. I said the other night that your trust means something to me. It does. I've trusted you with more than most—but I cannot go further. I wish . . . I hope you can respect my request. That we'll follow our pact and this can be enough."

It wasn't. Not near enough. She wanted to push further, demand more. She'd spent all of this time thinking that his reluctance served to protect himself—now she wanted to insist that he explain what he meant when he said he also meant to protect her.

She couldn't.

He stared at her, his expression carefully blank. But she looked into his eyes and saw more. He hoped she would agree, that was clear. But so was a certain, wary resolution—as if he knew she was going to disappoint him.

She would not disappoint him. Not when he'd done so much for her. And because she might be as untidy as a gorgon, but she wasn't a harpy.

"Yes." She whispered. "Of course."

She felt a good bit of the tension drain out of him. "Thank you." His hands moved back up to frame her face and he pulled her down to press a soft kiss to her lips. "Thank you."

She let her hands slide down to his chest and then around to his back as her gaze ran over him, drinking him in. This was it, then. As far as they would go. *Please, let the passing of these moments go slowly.*

He kissed her again, and this time he didn't draw back. His tongue slid against hers, smooth as hot silk.

The bulge she perched upon shifted and grew. The sensation sent exultation and excitement and relief coursing through her. He wasn't immune to her. Lucy and her notion of pity, be damned. In this, at least, he felt something for her.

She moved upon him, opening her legs a little wider and settling more snugly against him.

He sucked in a breath and kissed her again, deeply and fiercely, as if he wished to devour her. She returned the kiss, stifling the moan of longing that was building in her chest.

As if he sensed it, he pulled back. His eyes filled with regret.

She braced herself against what he was going to say.

"Well, this is far worse than I expected."

Confused, she blinked down at him. It took her several seconds to realize that he had not spoken the words.

Tension rushed back into his frame. His head turned toward the stall door.

Her gaze followed. A stranger stood there. Older, but still tall and ramrod straight. A sneer curled his wide mouth and his eyes roamed contemptuously over her. Her own eye fell on the distinctive line of his jaw and she knew whom he must be.

"Hello, Father," Keswick said calmly. "What in blazes are you doing here?"

* * *

"I'M HERE TO ATTEND A BALL," his father replied.

Keswick held out an arm to steady Glory as she scrambled off of his lap. He climbed to his feet, then helped her to stand up next to him. Only then did he roll a scornful glance his father's way. "Not in a thousand years will you convince me that Tensford invited you here."

His tone bit out, sharp as ice, as it always did when he addressed the earl. He reached for the calm impassivity that was the only face he ever showed the old man, but Glory had had him on fire a moment ago and her presence—bloody hell, within feet of his father—blocked his grasp of that utterly necessary mask of indifference.

"He did not. I had business in Birmingham. On the way south, I heard that you were staying here. Naturally, I stopped over to see you. It has been some time since we last met." He narrowed his eyes at Glory.

Keswick set his hand at the small of her back and gave her the smallest nudge, a motion that his father would not see. "Run on back to the house," he murmured.

His father's brow cleared.

"Ah. She's a servant? That is a relief. I'd heard that you were in danger of a serious *mésalliance* out here, and for a moment, I feared it was worse even than I expected." He raised a brow in Glory's direction. "Run along and tell your mistress that I will require a room. I came in a hired carriage and it has already headed back."

"Go. Now." Keswick said it under his breath and prayed she would let it go.

He should have known better.

Her shoulders straightened. "I am no servant, sir." Glory took a brace of steps toward the door and his father's sharp gaze focused right in on her limp. She turned to look back at him. "Won't you do the honors?"

He sighed. "Father, may I present Lady Glory Brightley? Glory, my father, the Earl of Braunton." He cleared his throat. "Lady Glory was just leaving."

She curtsied and his father raised a brow. "*Lady* Glory?" he said doubtfully. "Well. You will forgive my mistake, of course." He glanced around at the stall, the piled straw where they'd sat and the jumble of sleeping kittens.

Glory's chin went up. "The house is full, sir, but I'm sure my sister will . . ." she glanced over as Keswick shook his head. " . . . be glad to find you a respectable room in the village."

"Will she, indeed? Perhaps you will go along and inform her of my arrival, while I have a moment alone with my son?"

She cast an uncertain glance his way, but Keswick nodded and she took her leave, murmuring her thanks as his father swung open the stall door.

Keswick followed her, and then they both waited as her slow footsteps faded away. After a moment, his father whirled on him.

"What do you think you are doing, boy?"

He rubbed his brow. "Who told you I was here, Father?" he asked on a sigh.

"Someone who worried that you were making a tragic mistake— and very rightly so, it would seem! What were you thinking, allowing yourself be caught alone in the stables with a girl like that? Anyone could have seen you. And then you'd be good and trapped, wouldn't you? Even now, if she tells anyone what you were up to out here, Tensford would be within his rights to demand a betrothal."

"She won't tell anyone."

The earl scoffed. "What makes you think so?"

"It is not who she is."

"Who she is?" His father gave a sharp bark of laughter. "She is a cripple, with no other prospects, that's who she is. I've asked around. She has a dowry of two thousand pounds, if she is lucky. And I saw her leg dragging behind her. If she possessed a fortune, it could be overlooked, I suppose. By some. But who is going to take her for that paltry amount? She's a fool if she doesn't force you to the altar."

"She's not a fool. Nor will she force my hand."

"I hope to the heavens that you are right. You should never have been so careless. You have responsibilities. One day you are going to have to begin caring for them. I've let you run amuck. Many young men must run wild and free before they take up the yoke of their birthright, but you must *think*. Use caution. You will ruin us all if you let yourself be caught in such a disastrous match."

"Disastrous?" Keswick's mouth twisted. "I think you exaggerate, Father. Have you become old womanish in your later years? Lady Glory is a fine girl and a perfectly acceptable match, should I wish one. She knows I will not marry her, but if I wished to, there would be no hindrance. Her birth and bloodline are excellent."

"She is neither fine nor acceptable. She is *weak*," he declared flatly.

"Well, we know there is no more damning word in your vocabulary, sir," Keswick interrupted. "But you could not be more wrong."

"I am certain I am correct," his father countered. "She clearly has a weak moral sense—as witnessed by my own eyes. You insist she's not smart enough to trap you, though you've given her every chance. And she couldn't even walk a straight line out of here with that . . . physical impairment," he spat.

"As is usual, you are utterly wrong about everything."

"You know the efforts I have gone to, all in pursuit of shoring up and strengthening the bloodline—"

"Oh, yes! Of course, I know! Your great sacrifice. You passed by all the pretty English flowers in London and sought out a girl of Irish descent, all to bring a bit of strong peasant stock to the ailing Newland blood."

"Your mother was the granddaughter of a duke. She only insisted on *acting* like a peasant."

Keswick shook his head in disgust. "You were as wrong then as you are now. My mother was a lady in heart and deed—and that lame girl is likely the strongest you will ever meet."

"I've come in the nick of time, it's clear."

"I don't need saving from Lady Glory," he repeated. "Or any damn thing from you."

"I pray you don't need saving, but I've clearly got work to do—making you see what's in front of your nose." His father shook his head. "How could you make such a colossal mistake?" he asked in disbelief. "How could you turn away from a girl like Miss Vernon in favor of a crippled recluse?"

"Wait. Miss Vernon?" Alarms rang sharply in his head. "What do you know of her?"

"I know she is a strong, determined young woman—"

"*Miss Vernon* called you here?" He could not keep the disgust from his tone. He should have known. If ever there were two more unscrupulous, manipulative peas in a pod . . .

"She is a young woman who knows what she wants—and goes after it. Strength! Tenacity! She is exactly what the Newland line needs."

"Then you marry her! For I certainly never shall." He shuddered at the mere thought of it.

"You are not to be so contrary. It is beyond foolish to ignore a good match, just to spite me."

"I'm not going to enter in any match, but if I were, that is the worst one I could conceive of!"

"Her dowry is twice that of the Brightley girl's."

"And her character is many times deficient. The girl is a schemer."
He snorted. "Hardly a fault in your eyes, I know. But I heard the girl
myself, plotting to take a lover after we were married—and we've
never had more than one dance!"

That did give his father a second's pause. "She's not a fool. She
knows the rules. She'll do nothing of the sort until she's secured you
an heir."

He gave a disdainful laugh. "Oh, as if you'd have been so accepting,
had my mother made you a cuckold?" He took a deep breath and
reached for reason. "Listen, Father. I am not marrying anyone. But
your thinking is clouded."

He should stop now. Just go. But he found he could not leave
without defending Glory.

"You are not making sense. Lady Glory is a virtuous girl. But even
if their moral characters did cancel each other out, it still doesn't
wash. You'll trade Lady Glory's title and connections for a couple of
thousand pounds? It doesn't sound like you—or like a man so keenly
interested in the heartiness of his bloodline."

"Yes, well, that's the main point, isn't it? The family says that her
withered leg resulted from an accident, but how do we know the truth
of it? If she was born with that . . . anomaly . . . then they wouldn't
admit it, would they?"

Keswick's temper roared to new heights. "That is utter nonsense.
Her injury is nothing, but now you insult her honor and that of her
entire family! I forbid you to spread such a vile rumor or speak so
again! There has never been a hint of deception from Glory or her
family."

"Oh, truly? I don't recall her sister being so forthcoming about the
size of her inheritance, when she came out."

"What heiress does crow about her fortune? Would you have her
driving about in a coach of gold, tossing largesse to the crowds? I do
not understand your thinking. Who could have put such a thing in
your head?"

Oh, but he knew the answer already, and he saw it confirmed in
his father's shifting gaze. "She does have you spellbound, doesn't she?

You cannot listen to the Vernon chit. That virago will say anything to get what she wants."

"Perhaps, but she could pass that spirit and determination on to your sons."

Spirit and determination—he should have been talking about Glory. She had all that—and caring and a lovely, sweet nature that any man should be glad to have in his life. But it wouldn't be him, so it didn't bear thinking about.

"I'll not be marrying either girl. If you admire the Vernon harpy, then have at her."

"Nonsense. I've already been in talks with her father."

Of course he had. Keswick's eyes closed in despair.

"Believe me, I had to dance about a bit, explaining your reputation,"

"I wish I might have seen it, but you've wasted your time. I've already told you—I'll never marry while you live. Did you believe I didn't mean it? I won't marry a woman I can't respect and care for—and if I found such a creature, I assure you, I would never expose her to you."

"Your responsibilities—"

"Yes! Let me at my responsibilities, why do you not, Father? Turn over the home estate, one of the farms in Ireland, or one of the shipping ventures you've invested in, why don't you?"

His father's face remained impassive and blank.

"That's what I thought. You harp on about my responsibilities, but I cannot touch a parcel without your permission—and you won't give it. You complain about my wild ways, but what else am I to do with myself? You set me on this road and I'm performing beautifully, am I not?"

"When you are ready—"

"Oh, I am ready! But I don't want your damned earldom. You can hold it hostage until the end of time, as far as I'm concerned."

His father's eyes narrowed. "You think I don't know what you are up to? I know. Your worn down little estate in Berkshire? *Solas Ag Crithlonrú*," he snorted. "Sentimental twaddle."

"Thriving and profitable," Keswick corrected with extreme satisfaction. "And that is only the first of my blissfully lucrative projects."

That caught the old man by surprise and Keswick happily turned the knife. "Oh, yes, Father. You can drive the earldom into the ground, if you wish. I'm well on my way to having an empire that will dwarf it." He shook his head. "I don't know why you would think I would ever do a single thing at your bidding. You've made my life a misery, stolen or destroyed everything or everyone I cared for."

"It was all to toughen you up," his father said roughly. "God, you were a sniveling little thing when you were small. But you learned, didn't you? My lessons made you strong."

"Oh, yes," he answered. "I did learn." The words sounded soft and deadly even to his own ears. "It worked. I'm tough. I'm independent. And now, I don't need anyone, Father. Least of all you."

His father's fury coiled tightly behind his eyes. He looked like a snake, all tensed up with nowhere to strike. Well, it wouldn't be at him. Keswick had cut the head off of this serpent—and now he knew it.

Mean as a snake, but stubborn as a badger. Even as he watched, his father collected himself. "This isn't over," he said, and walked out of the stable.

It was, for now. But there would be more battles, Keswick knew it. He paced, fuming. Unless he left. Now. This minute. He should draw the old bastard away from Glory and her family. He waited long enough to be sure his father would have made it to the house, then turned to follow.

And found Glory standing near the doorway, waiting.

CHAPTER 17

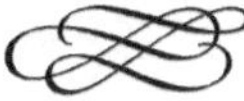

Once again, Keswick did not look pleased to see her.

She didn't let it deter her. She just waited while he stomped up, a belligerent look on his face.

"You've been here the whole time?"

She nodded.

He cursed.

"What does it mean?" she asked gently. "*Solas Ag Crithlonrú*"

He was going to balk again. She saw it in the shuttering of his gaze.

"You might as well tell me. The secret is out."

Alarm lit up his expression. "You cannot mean to tell anyone else?"

"Not if you don't wish me to."

"I don't. Of course I don't."

"I admit, I understand your hesitations better, now that I see what you are up against."

He gave a bitter laugh. "You don't know but a portion of it. But you know more than most, and I would ask you to keep my secret, just as I promised to keep yours."

"You know I will," she soothed. "But were you not the one who said it might help, to speak of your pain?"

He started to answer, then stopped. Running a hand over his face,

203

he spun around, walked to the empty stall door and back again. He stared at her for a long moment, then crossed to another wall of the stable and emptied a crate of its tack bits and implements. "Sit down," he said, upending the crate and sitting it at her feet. "I'll tell you, but only because you don't know what I am up against. What you are up against. Not truly."

She sat. And waited quietly.

"Shimmering light," he said after a few moment's of silence.

She frowned. "I'm sorry?"

"Shimmering light. *Solas Ag Crithlonrú.* That's what it means. I named the place for my mother. She always brought light and laughter with her, everywhere she went."

"She shielded you from the worst of it?" she asked softly. "While she lived."

"She tried, although at times it only seemed to make him worse. And after she died . . ."

Grumpet came sauntering back into the stable just then, and Keswick swooped down to pick her up and tuck her into the crook of his arm. Absently, he stroked her, and it seemed to make the words come easier.

"He's always been caught up with the idea of shoring up the family, strengthening the blood line. The heir after me is my second cousin. He's a nice enough chap, but my father despises him, as he also hated his father. For what reason? I don't know. But he's horrified at the thought of the title passing to that branch of the family tree.

"And you've no idea what caused the enmity?"

"No." He grimaced and shook his head. "They were at school together. Perhaps something that happened there? But it might not have been a specific incident." He frowned. "I learned, after I was grown, that my grandmother lost several children, both before my father and after him. One other boy was born, but he was sickly and died while still a babe. My father was young at the time, perhaps four or five years of age, but he was old enough to see and remember. Maybe that is what started it?" His lips compressed. "All I know is that he is convinced of his own superiority."

"Over the dreaded cousins?"

"Over nearly everyone. He regards himself as smarter and stronger in almost every way. And he lives in fear of frailty. He has always watched me closely. My earliest memory of him is the weight of his stare. His measuring gaze. He could not abide any sign of anything he considered weakness—and he would go to great lengths to do away with it."

His gaze sharpened as it landed on her. "That's what you need to understand. It's why I don't want him to think you mean anything to me at all. He will hurt you, Glory. He'll stop at nothing to run you off."

Her mouth twisted. "What will he do? Mock me? Call me a cripple? That's going to happen in any case. It's happened here, in my own family's home."

"Yes, he will mock you. To your face. To his friends. To the entire *ton*. He'll have broadsheets drawn up. He'll publically call you a cripple, a hoyden, an adventuress. He'll hire someone to write a song about it. He'll print up pamphlets shaming you."

She stared at him. "Don't be absurd. Of course he would not do all of that."

"He will. It's what he does." He set the cat down and started pacing again. "My mother kept a dog as a pet, a great, shaggy beast of an Irish Wolfhound. I adored that dog, and she returned my affections. She slept with me in the nursery and followed me about all day. Fern, the nursemaid, used to complain she was trying to steal her position. We were inseparable. Until one day, when the dog ate something bad for her. She grew very ill and my mother thought she would die. She tried to prepare me and I was inconsolable. My father was furious about the fuss. Eventually the dog did recover, to our relief. But he had it drowned—to teach me not to become so attached."

She gasped and tears filled her eyes.

"That was just the beginning," he said hoarsely. "After my mother died, the only person who would talk of her was Fern. She kept her memory alive. She tried to look after me, just as my mother would have wished. She sang me to sleep when I awoke in nightmares and tears. She told me the old tales my mother loved. She bandaged my cuts and scrapes. You asked about birthdays—she was the only person ever, after my mother died, to remember the day. My father, however, decided she was making me soft."

"What did he do?" she asked fearfully.

"Bribed her away. He didn't just fire her. He bought a boarding house and gave it over to her, just so I could see that she was choosing it over me."

She shivered at the cruelty of it. "I'm so sorry," she whispered. The memory of her brother in law's story came back to her. "And Saoirse?" she asked.

Startled, he raised a brow at her.

She blushed a little. "Tensford told me about her. I did push him a bit. He said you bought the horse yourself."

"Yes. I wanted something of my own. Something he couldn't take away or destroy. Lord, how we did ride! I went everywhere, anywhere, to escape the house and my father." He scowled. "It didn't matter that I owned her outright. He sold her the day after I left for school."

It all made perfect sense. His reluctance to form connections. His trust in only his proven friends. "Keswick, I've asked to be your friend, practically forced it upon you. I want you to know, he won't change that."

"No. I've told him you mean nothing to me. He must believe that."

"He cannot bribe me, or sell me, or shame me into abandoning you."

"You don't know what you are saying."

"I do."

'You think so. You believe so. But you wouldn't be the first woman he decided to drive away."

She stilled.

"I won't see it happen to you."

"*What* happened?"

He heaved a great sigh.

"Tell me, Keswick."

He leaned against the stall door. "I rode all over the estate, all over the countryside, really, in those days with Saoirse. I began to see the strengths of our estate, and some of the weaknesses, too. Places where a change in tenancy would do good, others where an application of modern methods might yield much better results. But the land agent, the game warden, even most of the tenants, they turned away from me. He had denied me a place in the running of the estate and they all knew it. None of them wished to bring down his wrath by encouraging or engaging with me."

He slid down to sit on the dirt floor and his head dropped back against the door. "So, I began to ride farther afield. I spoke to other land managers, saw how other estates and villages were run, and noted which were thriving, and why. I was up near the old Heddon Mill when I met a man, a squire, in a pub. We struck up a conversation, and though he was older, he was interested in my ideas and willing to share his. We met up several times and talked and talked. One day, he invited me back to his house."

He gave her a bleak smile and she stood up and went to sit beside him, their backs against the stall door. "His home wasn't anywhere near as grand as ours, but it was so much better. It *was* a home, warm and comfortable and full of a real family—and all of the love and squabbles that went with it. I was enchanted—and I certainly liked the look of his eldest daughter."

Glory swallowed, but said nothing. She'd wanted to know.

"She was small and blonde and quiet-mannered. So normal. She seemed pleased with my attentions and her parents seemed so, too."

"But not your father?"

"She was a squire's daughter. Solid gentry. Perfectly respectable. I wanted nothing more than to become part of their family. But my father would not have it. She wasn't lofty enough to suit him. They had no connections in the *ton*. He told me to end it."

"But you didn't?" She couldn't help but feel a bit jealous. Angry, too, because no matter what had happened, she knew he'd been hurt by it.

"No. But Father cornered her somewhere. He was typically rough in his address and it frightened her. I think she would have ended it right then, but her father had got his back up. He felt for me, for my situation, I know he did. But I think he also liked the idea of his daughter becoming a countess one day. He decided to speak to my father himself. He told him to stop interfering and to allow us to be happy."

She grimaced. "I don't imagine that went over well."

"About as well as you'd expect," he sighed.

"What did your father do?"

"What he usually does. He won. I don't know what the information was, but he dug up something embarrassing or incriminating, and he used it. It must have been bad enough, for it silenced her father instantly. And my father, who likes to do things thoroughly, combined the stick with a carrot—he offered not to expose his dirty information, if the family took his generous offer of a stay in Bath, where their daughter could be sure to find another suitor, more appropriate for her station."

"Good heavens," she said faintly. "He is diabolical."

"He is—and he will aim it all at you, if he thinks you are a threat. And if you persevere, he will turn on your family. Is that what you want?"

"Of course not, but it is better than the alternative. You told me I must fight tyranny. And so I shall."

"You shall not. I won't have you hurt."

She was awash with emotion, each a wave crashing against her. Defiance. Both a thrill and a sense of tender gratitude for his fierce protectiveness. Pain, thinking of all that he'd suffered. And utter determination that there would be no more.

Hope.

She felt hope. Truly. For the first time.

She knew what she faced now. Both Keswick's father and his own fears. She wouldn't fail him, not even if it meant giving up her own dream.

"I'll go. Immediately," he continued. "Back to London."

"But won't that prove to your father that you do care for me? He'll expect you to do just that—as a gambit to draw his attention away. He'll see it for a protective move."

"That's what it is. I don't want him near you."

"But if you want to convince him of your disinterest, you should stay. Spend time with Tensford and pay no attention to me or to Miss Vernon."

He groaned and knocked his head against the stall door. "Damn. Why are you so often right? You likely are, in this case, too."

"I'm afraid you are just going to have to get used to it." She rolled her head against the door and looked over at him. "Besides which, Tensford will have a fit if you go. He has that man from the British Museum coming tomorrow, to see the fossil and attend the ball. Apparently he's already requested to speak to you, me, and Miss Munroe. He wants to ask questions about how we found it."

His head fell in his hands. "It sounds dreadful. I'll have to avoid you, and keep myself occupied while doubtless both my father and Miss Vernon try to plague me." He peeked at her. "And the worst part? I'll have to endure the damned ball, without a dance with you."

"Well, that was always going to be the case." She grinned at him while an idea bloomed in her head. He'd suffered enough. He'd fought alone, long enough. He deserved a bit of support. He deserved a bit of a win.

And it was going to start with her.

CHAPTER 18

Keswick came down carly to breakfast the next morning, determined to be done with it and in hiding before his father could show up from the village.

He sat down with a plate from the sideboard and nodded a good morning to Hope.

"Good morning, Kes," she said warmly. "Here's fresh tea for you."

He smiled his thanks as a footman entered with a fresh pot—but the expression died away as Miss Vernon followed on the servant's heels.

"Miss Vernon!" The countess appeared to be surprised. "Were we expecting you so early, today?"

"Is Miss Parscate not down yet?" the girl asked innocently. She carried a stack of ladies magazines in her arm. "We were going to go over new hairstyles for the ball this evening."

"She retired a bit late last evening," Mr. Sommers said. "A group of us spent too long discussing the pleasures to be had in London's Season."

Miss Vernon cast a glance at Keswick, but he had picked up an abandoned newspaper and pretended not to notice.

"I have not seen her this morning," Hope answered, "but do come in and sit down. Have you breakfasted yet?" She waved for the footman to bring the girl a cup of tea.

"I wouldn't refuse a bit of tea and toast, thank you."

"Well, we haven't any amusements planned for today. Most of the guests expect to spend a quiet day in preparation for dinner and the ball this evening, but I'm sure Miss Parscate will be down directly."

"What of your sister, my lady? I daresay she must be interested in learning some of the newest, fashionable hairstyles. Is she available to spend the morning with us?"

Hope blinked at the girl a moment. Keswick felt sure she was trying to decide if Miss Vernon meant to be insulting. He could have told her that the girl absolutely did.

"How kind." The countess had clearly decided not to waste time arguing with her uninvited guest. "Glory is not available, I'm afraid. She left early this morning. She's riding to Brockweir to visit the saddler."

Again, Keswick pretended not to be attending. But he was.

"The saddler?" Miss Vernon sounded incredulous. "On the day of your ball?"

"That's our Glory," Tensford chuckled. "She is a serious rider. She takes exceptional care of her mount and her equipment. Her saddles are specially designed."

"How . . . unusual."

"It doesn't seem so, when you see her ride. I've never seen anyone with a better seat." Keswick knew better than to speak up, but he could not bear to let the nasty creature get the last word on Glory.

"It's true," Tensford said cheerfully.

"She will be back this afternoon, in plenty of time to prepare for the evening." The countess stood and the men did as well. "My preparations for the day begin now, however. I'll bid you all a good morning."

Miss Vernon turned a calculating smile in his direction.

"I will try to stay out of your way, my lady, and perhaps take a walk in the gardens while I await Miss Parscate. That is, if you will accompany me, Lord Keswick?"

Tensford set down his coffee. "I'm sorry to disappoint you, Miss Vernon, but I've already claimed Kes for the day."

Keswick nodded and tried to look like he knew what his friend was talking about.

"There's a good bit of work to be done on my specimen before Mr. Simon, from the British Museum, arrives later today. I'll need Keswick's help to finish in time."

"I've rearranged the seating for dinner, so be sure to ask Mr. Simon to join us," Hope told him.

Tensford kissed her, right there in front of everyone. "Thank you, my dear."

Keswick took a last sip of tea. "I'm ready when you are," he told Tensford. He nodded to the rest of the table. "Until dinner and the ball, then."

"What?" Miss Vernon stiffened in her chair. "Surely you'll return for nuncheon?"

Hope looked at her, somewhat exasperated, but Tensford merely shook his head. "Very sorry. We'll be working through, to get done in time."

"I'll have cook send out a tray of sandwiches." Hope cast a cool look at Miss Vernon and departed.

Keswick and Tensford followed her out and set out for the workshop.

"She's persistent, that one," Tensford said over the crunch of gravel.

"You see why I imposed myself upon you, days early," Keswick said. "She ran me right out of London."

"Who would have thought she'd follow you out here?" Tensford opened the workshop door and nodded to the footman sitting inside. "Thank you, James. We'll be here for the rest of the day. And I'm sure my wife will have a list of duties for you to help her with."

The footman bowed and left while Keswick stared at his friend. "You've set a guard?"

His friend shrugged. "Perhaps it's foolish. I just can't get that fish-tail out of my head. It's bothered me for years, and I can't bear the thought of this one disappearing."

"I had no idea naturalists were such a nasty bunch."

"Yes, well, I had no idea debutantes were such an incessantly persistent breed." Tensford sent a warning look his way. "You might have to do something drastic to dislodge this one, at this point."

"If you have any good notions on how to accomplish it, I'd love to hear them. I need to get rid of her quickly—especially as she's somehow convinced my father to push her cause."

Tensford looked truly horrified. "If your father likes her, she must be worse than I already thought."

"My sentiments exactly."

"No wonder you wished to bolt back to London. I do appreciate your staying, all the more. Mr. Simon seems very interested in hearing just how you three found this lovely piece." He ran a hand along the large fossil. "I suspect he is thrilled at the prospect of attaching your name to it."

"A bit of notoriety to sell tickets?" Keswick rolled his eyes. "*See the fossil accidentally exposed by London's famous rakehell!* Does he really think that will work?"

"Evidently. I hope you won't mind. I also suspect it has something to do with the surprisingly high price he's willing to pay—and I admit, it's a bit of a sop to my pride, getting it."

"Tired of spending Hope's money, are you?" He tossed his friend a grin to ease the sting of the question.

"Not precisely. I'm not too proud to spend it, in order to restore Greystone and help our people, but well . . ."

"I understand. It will be nice to get a bit of your own back. And in support of such a cause, I'm happy to let my name be bandied about with this old thing."

"Good." Tensford picked up a brush. "Will you check the varnish on the framing pieces, to be sure they have dried? And I think we'll need some shim pieces, if you wouldn't mind cutting a few varied sizes from those strips of thin wood?"

They got to work and had been at it thirty minutes or so before the workshop door opened. Miss Vernon stuck her head in. "Oh!" she said. "Here you both are."

Keswick just stared at her, but Tensford gave her knowing smile. "Indeed. Just where I said we would be." He waved a hand over the large stone piece. "Are you interested in fossils? I would be glad to tell you all about—"

"No, thank you," she interrupted. "I thought I would check to see if you might be done early, but I can see that . . . you won't." She started to withdraw. "Good day!"

"That's one," Tensford said, after going to the door and checking to see that she'd hurried away.

"One what?" Keswick asked with a shudder. "Don't tell me there are more to follow?"

"Just wait."

An hour later, they were maneuvering the first corner of the frame into place, coming at it from different directions, when the door opened again. Keswick started when his father stepped in.

Tensford repeated the same offer, but this time his father took him up on it. Keswick kept working while his friend showed the older earl around, telling him about all the different sorts of fossils that had been found on the estate and why the newest find was special.

Keswick felt his father's gaze fall on him more than once as they spoke, but the old man never spoke to him. When Tensford had talked himself out, the earl stood, staring at his son.

"And you say the museum's man will be at dinner this evening? And at the ball?" Braunton asked.

"He will. He wishes particularly to speak to Kes and the young ladies who were responsible for the find."

His father nodded. Keswick kept working.

"I do thank you for my own invitation."

"Of course." Tensford glanced at Keswick as he answered.

"I shall speak with you this evening, then." His father spoke to him directly. "We have matters to attend to."

Keswick glanced up and managed a small nod.

His father gave him another long look, then took his leave.

"And that is two." Tensford shook his head. "Damned if she wasn't right."

"She?"

"Glory. She said that those two would come in to check up on you. And now that they have, I am to give you your instructions."

He said nothing. He felt odd at the mention of her. Raw. She knew. She'd peeled away his armor and seen the ugly truth inside. No one else knew the full story, not Tensford or Sterne or Chester or Whiddon. He didn't know how to act with his secrets abroad in the world instead of tucked safely away.

"Kes?"

"Instructions?" he asked hoarsely.

"She wants you to saddle up your horse and ride out to meet her—at the height. She seemed to think you would know what that meant."

He did. And his heart pounded in anticipation and trepidation.

"She has something for you. She wanted to give it to you before this evening, and before you left to return to London with the rest of the party."

He thought about it. He'd spent years shaping his life so that he didn't feel vulnerable, would never feel that way again. She did that to him. But she also made him feel connected and strong and *whole*. He thought about seeing her tonight at the ball, surrounded by strangers and foes. He thought about saying goodbye to her as a mere acquaintance, practically a stranger, and never seeing her alone again, in a place where they could laugh and he could tease and share real conversation and feel utterly safe just being himself.

He eyed the half-finished framing. But he knew.

"I can finish this up." Tensford drew close and put a hand on his shoulder. "But Kes? I ask you to be . . . gentle with her. She sees the spot you are in."

If only he knew how true that was.

"She's exactly the sort to offer to help with drastic measures. If you allow it, I fear she won't escape unscathed. She's fragile, you see."

Keswick drew a deep breath and looked his friend in the eye. "I've been honest with her from the start, I vow it. The last thing I want is to hurt her. But Tensford? You all need to blink and step back and really look at Glory. Perhaps bits of her are fragile. But for the most part? She's brave and loyal and *strong* and she's got a core of steel. It's time you all saw it."

And with a nod and a smile and a reassuring clap on the back, Keswick walked out, heading for the stable.

* * *

HE'D JUST LEFT the thinning trail and turned onto the fern-thick track when he saw the first one. The bright red bow caught his attention. Dismounting, he plucked a carved, wooden horse from a fork in a tree. It was painted a sorrel color and sported a tag, along with the ribbon.

I hope this brings only good memories of Saoirse.

He felt a twang in his chest and knew suddenly why people spoke of heartstrings. Glory had surely just plucked one of his.

He became suspicious when he found the second parcel—a small picnic basket—sitting in the bottom of the dip before the steep climb. It contained a dish of sausages, another of colcannon and—

"Brown bread," he said out loud in amazement, and wondered how she'd remembered—and how she'd convinced cook to make it.

He knew for sure what she was up to when he reached the top of the first rise and found a small basket full of India rubber balls—and it made him laugh out loud. He was still chuckling when he crested the second hill and looked down into the glen—and saw her waiting, standing on the fairy stage.

His grin faded. He tethered his job horse next to Poppy and walked slowly down the slope. She stood in the middle of the makeshift stage, dressed in a light and gauzy gown of green and wearing a garland cleverly woven of branches and vines. She gave him a tight-lipped grin and he could see her nerves in the twisting of her fingers.

He took a step forward, concerned, but she held up a hand. "I sincerely hope you don't mind my presumption. I mean only to try to make up for a few of those missed birthdays."

"It does. It was a kind notion."

She gestured around the stage. "This is the last present—but I ask that you do not say anything, not yet. Not another word. Just sit." She nodded toward the logs sitting in the appropriate, audience position. "I mean to do this, but you cannot speak until it is done."

He held silent and took a seat. She watched, her anxiety clear, and he only gave her an encouraging nod.

Their eyes held for a long moment. Suddenly, her back straightened and she nodded back. She took a couple of steps to the right, then stood for a second, head bowed toward the center of the stage. She looked up—and transformed into . . . something else.

It was Puck's verse, from *A Midsummer Night's Dream*. The one where he calls himself the merry wanderer of the night and talks of the nonsense he gets up to for Oberon. She gave it her all. She held nothing back while she forgot herself and became the mischievous sprite, bragging of her misdeeds and pretending to be a horse and then a crab, and falling off of a stool and laughing until her sides split.

He couldn't look away. She was magic, come to life in this fairy glen. And when it was over, he stood up. He gazed at her in wonder, still silent for a time, before he began clapping and nodding like a fool. "That was—" He couldn't find the words. "No one has ever . . . That was the finest gift I've ever received. I feel so honored."

He wished he could say what was truly in his heart and mind. She'd trusted him, as he'd trusted her. She'd given him a piece of herself. She had understood how vulnerable he felt and had again moved to even the balance between them. To ensure their equality and their mutual ease and comfort.

"Thank you," he finished simply.

She came forward and held out her hands. He moved to the edge of the stage and lifted her down. Unwisely, he didn't step away, but held her close and looked down into her cognac gaze.

"I should thank you," she whispered. "You've changed me, Keswick."

That sent his shoulders up, but she reached up and ran both hands over them, as if soothing all of his misgivings.

"You made me see things differently," she continued. "You've made me want things I refused to consider before." She shrugged up at him. "You inspire me, Keswick."

His skepticism must have shown.

"It's true." Her grin grew a bit twisted. "I should be dizzy with the transformation you've wrought upon me, in so little time. When you arrived, I was closed and wary. Then I was . . . hopeful. Then you made me laugh, you made me think, you listened and you made it easy to talk—both to you and to others. I began to see that I am not the only one with burdens. It seems everyone has them, but the heft and shape of them vary. And now . . ."

She paused and his gut twisted in anticipation of what she must think, now that she knew the darkest bits of his life—and of his soul.

Both of her hands came to rest against his chest. "I see that despite the terrible weights that your father continues to lay upon you, it's your mother's legacy that continues on in you."

His heart stopped beating. He wondered, vaguely, if she could hear instead, the surely audible sound of all of his internal armor cracking.

"*You* are a shining light, Keswick, despite your efforts to hide it from your father and the rest of the world. I see it. I want to be like you. I want to start by shining my light upon the person I find most deserving. You."

Reaching up, she trailed a finger along his jaw. "I'm using the courage that you helped me to find, to ask for what I want—to give us both the present we need. Each other. Even if is it only for today."

Everything inside of him reeled. He reached for strength, for balance. But he was tired. So very tired of convincing himself that he didn't need anyone. Tired of clutching his armor close and moving through the world alone. Tired of knowing he shouldn't want her, though he did, so damned much.

Her sweet, kindly meant words tore up his innards because he was tired of not being known.

And her earnest, hopeful smile told him he wasn't, not any longer.

So, he let go.

He let go of caution and guardedness and suspicion—and all the strings that held his armor together—and it shattered, fell to pieces at his feet.

And, metaphorically naked, he leaned down and kissed her.

With soft, but scorching kisses, they plundered each other's mouths. After a moment, she pulled back to drag in a long, shuddering breath. He used the moment to savor the shock of pleasure coursing though him, and to rejoice that he did not have to push it away.

Feeling almost joyful, he kissed her again. She was everything hot and sweet. A drug that called to him, that demanded his tongue to dance with hers, that each stroke and twining should send desire cascading through his veins, that each should set his cock to stirring and reaching for her.

As in all things, she was his equal. Her lips clung to his, demanded more, sent his passion soaring higher.

But she pulled back again, and she gave a low moan when he transferred his kisses, moving along her jaw and down her throat.

"Keswick," she whispered. "Come. I've prepared a place for us."

He straightened, struggling to focus. And found a stray doubt, still lingering. "Glory, are you sure?"

"Yes," she said firmly. "Perhaps we are not meant to spend our lives together, but now, at this moment, we have the ability to make each other happy. It's a gift, one we both need at present. We are not going to squander it."

She led him through the bracken to the ledge that hovered over that spectacular view. He drank it in once more, then realized that she'd spread several layers of thick blankets in front of the rock outcropping, where they'd sat once before.

"Here," she said with determination. "In the open. In the light."

He deliberately kept his focus on her face. "Are you sure?" he asked again. He recalled her shyness regarding her leg, that night by the river.

"I am. Today is my day for being brave and true to myself. The first of many, I hope. I'm finally going to listen to Hope, and to you, and even to Miss Myland." She gave him a nudge. "Go and sit on the rocks, please."

Pursing his lips, he obeyed, but when she moved to stand in front of him, and paused to gather herself, he surged back up and took her in his arms. "You've already given a performance today." He trailed a finger along her brow. "Why don't we do this together?"

Breathing in, she nodded.

He gathered her close and bent to press a kiss behind her ear. She shivered and clutched him tighter. Murmuring sweet words and tender noises of appreciation, he made his way down over her bodice, then lower, shifting positions until he knelt before her, his hands on her hips.

She steadied herself with one hand on his shoulder and took her skirts in her other hand.

Sitting back on his haunches, he ran a hand behind her leg and urged her to rest the foot of her injured leg on his thigh. "Take your time," he said quietly.

She nodded, paused, then began to hike her skirts up on that side.

He watched the determination and the resolve on her face until her hems reached her knee, then he looked down.

Even through her stocking, and without comparing this leg to her sturdy one, he could see that this limb was thin. The first sign of damage began beneath her knee, where the shinbone extended outward at an awkward angle before turning sharply inward. Her walking boot had a sole that was several inches thick.

"This leg is slightly shorter," she explained. "The boot helps keep my gait even. Will you remove it?"

He did, and revealed an ankle that looked slightly tilted and uneven and a small, slender foot.

He looked frankly up at her. "Honestly, it's not half so bad as I feared. Does it pain you, still?"

"Occasionally. Most often when the weather is going to turn bad. It aches, then." She sighed. "Or in all the dreaded turns in the cursed dancing."

"I resent every moment of pain or distress it's ever caused you. I wish I could ensure that you never have another."

"You cannot." She raised a brow at him. "But you can ensure that my next few moments are filled with pleasure."

"Few moments?" he repeated in mock indignation. "Give me some credit, please!" And he stood suddenly, and swept her up into his arms and laid her down upon the waiting pallet.

She was still laughing when he kissed her, and it filled him with . . . something beyond joy. She grabbed two fistfuls of his shirt and waistcoat and pulled him closer.

The desire came quickly this time and hit them both hard. Their mouths and tongues dueled, their kisses surging deep and frantic. They broke apart again and again as they removed clothes from each other, and came back together again.

Finally, he was bare and she was too, save for her stockings. He let them be and filled his hands with her breasts and gave a happy sigh. Her head went back and he settled in to lick and tease her taut nipples. Several minutes of that highly pleasurable activity left her panting, but she eventually put her hands on his chest and pushed him back.

"We're in the light. You've seen me. Now, I want to see you." He held himself above her while her fingers roamed his chest and explored up and over his shoulders. "You look like you could hold the weight of the world alone, Keswick, but I want you to know, you never have to."

She wriggled then, sitting up and urging him to lie back beneath her. He shifted carefully, taking care to support her and they ended with her straddling his thighs, while his cock bobbed happily before hers.

She bit her lip and eyed it.

"Touch it, if you like." He tried to keep any hint of order—or begging—from his tone.

"Would you mind?"

'No," he said on a strangled laugh. "I would love it if you put your hands on me, Glory."

She did and her cool, little fingertips drifted softly over him, like dandelion fluff in the wind, touching him up and down his shaft, exploring ridges and smoothing over the head, before reaching down to cup his scrotum.

"Harder," he asked in a whisper, and took her hand in his to show her how to stroke him. Then he leaned back and groaned while his cock grew as tall and hard as a post.

"Would you like me to put my mouth on it?"

He stilled. "What do you know about that? *How* do you know about it?"

"Lucy showed me where the naughty books are hidden in the library."

He lifted his head. "Tensford has naughty books in the library?"

"I don't think he knows about them. They have been there a long time, it seems. But the servants know they are there." She paused. "At least the lower servants. I doubt the housekeeper would sanction them staying."

He gave a heartfelt groan. "Please do not discuss the housekeeper while you . . ." He gave a nod to her hand still wrapped around him.

She shrugged. "In any case, Lucy showed me, since I'd already seen one, or so she believed. She said I might find answers to my questions." She moved her hand again. "It only gave me more questions, though. Do men really like that? The thing with mouths?"

"Yes." Heroically, he managed not to sound over-eager.

"And women enjoy doing it?"

"Some do."

"And woman enjoy . . . when the favor is returned?"

He raised a brow at her. "The women I'm with, do so."

Her grip tightened, and he winced, laughing. "Or at least, I believe they do."

She let go of him, braced her hands on his thighs, and started to move back.

"Glory," he began.

"I want to try it." She paused and looked up at him. "Do you object?"

He stared at her, naked and beautiful and eager to please and be pleased, and he sent silent thanks up to anyone who might be listening. He shook his head and watched avidly while she leaned over him. Experimentally, she moved closer and ran her tongue up the length of him. He clutched his fists in the blankets below and cursed right out loud.

She grinned, clearly heady with her own power and hold over him, then she leaned in and took him in her mouth.

His head dropped back and his hips thrust up. Her soft, sweet tongue explored and her mouth was so warm and wet. She showed every sign of enjoyment at his moans and he braced himself, letting her have her way while every muscle in him went tight and he fought not to lace his fingers in her hair.

Hell and damnation, nothing had ever looked or felt so good as her mouth moving over him, while stray locks of her hair fell forward to caress his skin.

She sat up suddenly and wiped her lip in a delicate motion. "I think I should like to—"

She never finished the sentence. He surged up and clasped her against him, spinning her around and beneath him in one smooth move. He moved between her thighs and reached down to stroke her wet sex.

"Oh, yes," she said on a groan. "That will do, as well."

He stroked harder, allowing her whimpers and movements to set the pace. Gradually he increased both, until her pleasure was climbing and she began to make small sounds of urgency.

He took his hand away and poised at her entrance. "Yes," she said, wild and fervently.

He eased his way in, clenching his teeth against the feel of her tight, hot embrace. Her eyes had gone wide. "Oh, heavens. Yes. Keswick . . . I didn't . . . I want . . ."

He would celebrate the sheer triumph of making her next to speechless, if he weren't so caught up in the incredible feel of her.

He moved carefully, but she didn't wince or pause even a beat in her encouragement. And then he was in, slid all the way home, and it was like nothing he'd ever experienced.

She made several unintelligible sounds, then let out a long sigh. "Oh, yes."

He thrust hard, then, and she moaned her approval. And he was lost in the rhythm, moving with quick purpose. She tossed and twisted beneath him, rising up to meet his every stroke. He could feel her reaching, reaching, so he put a hand between them and touched her slick nub and in just a moment the wave broke over her.

"Yes, Keswick." Her body arched against him and she gripped him hard. He gritted his teeth and held on while she shattered around him and then he was thrusting again, hard and deep, while she held on with her arms around his shoulders. Their bodies rocked and his hips drove faster. When he couldn't hold back a moment longer, he twisted away and with a groan of agony and ecstasy, he spilled his release onto the blanket.

And then he rolled back and collapsed onto her, his head resting on her breast.

He came back to himself minutes later, when her fingers began to run lightly through his hair. "Well," she said faintly. "No wonder they won't let the young ladies get a taste of that."

He chuckled against her soft skin.

"Was I . . . Was it . . .?" For the first time, she sounded hesitant.

"It was utterly amazing."

"Oh, good." Now she sounded a bit smug. "It felt so, to me, but I have no basis for comparison."

He tilted his head slightly so he could look at her with one eye. "Neither do I."

She flushed with pleasure.

He closed his eyes again and turned them both to their sides so he could nestle around her. She sighed with satisfaction and relaxed into his embrace.

He had no idea how long they lay there before she stirred. "We are going to be sun-browned in some very hard to explain places if we don't get up and get dressed."

"If Lucy dares question you, lay the blame right at her door," he said, yawning. But he sat up and they helped each other to dress and he obligingly crawled about, searching for lost hairpins.

He was ready first, so he scurried back for the picnic basket and he perched next to her and ate brown bread while she sat, her arms stretched up and over her head, tucking her hair back into order. He leaned in and gave her a bite and a quick kiss—and it was such an intimate thing, almost more so than what they had just done to each other. It felt so right. So much like what he'd longed for his entire life. She felt like home. He closed his eyes against the rise of emotion.

"Keswick?" She'd sensed his change in mood.

"You said I changed you," he said, low. "But you did the same to me. I fought the good fight. I tried to keep my distance. Told myself we could be calm, platonic, friendly." He gave a wry laugh. "Foolish. Now it's here. Everything I feared."

"Surely there's nothing to fear," she said quickly. "I haven't asked for anything beyond today. It can be enough."

He shook his head. "This wanting is not going to go away."

"I know your father is an obstacle. Perhaps we could hide our attachment from him—"

"Secret lovers?" he asked acidly.

She gave a shiver. "It does sound thrilling," she said hopefully.

He kissed her hand. "I doubt we'd be able to hide how we feel."

"Likely not," she said on a sigh. She folded her arms, the picture of belligerence. "I refuse to regret this."

"I won't regret it either, just the fact that we cannot repeat it."

"I don't want to lose you," she said quietly.

She still didn't understand that they had never really belonged to each other. Because no matter how much she might affect him, one thing would never change. He would never allow her to pay the high price of caring for him.

"I will see you this evening. We can talk and laugh, perhaps. But this is our true goodbye." He kissed her hand. "And it has been lovely."

She heaved a sigh and nodded.

"Let's go back. And try not to get caught."

She climbed to her feet. "We won't be caught. I'm not giving any one of those scoundrels an ounce more of triumph or satisfaction."

CHAPTER 19

Mr. Simon escorted Glory down the hall and toward the ballroom, lending his arm as they moved in the wave of guests leaving dinner. They had been seated next to each other, where she answered his questions about how she and Miss Munroe and Keswick had literally fallen into the discovery of the new fossil specimen. He had many questions about the size of the boulder, and how far it had been from the cliff face and what sort of rocks had been collected around it. She answered them all as best as she could, and then found that she barely had to speak again at all.

First, because Mr. Simon had a great many amusing stories about his travels for the British Museum and he clearly enjoyed telling them. And second, because he didn't seem to have been fed well on any of them. He tucked into each course of Hope's dinner with enthusiasm. Glory didn't mind. It allowed her to blame his slow and careful ambulation on overindulgence instead of over-concern for her lameness.

"Have you spoken with Miss Munroe or Lord Keswick yet, sir?" she asked as they passed through the flower-flanked doors.

"Not yet. I have spoken with Lord Tensford and Mr. Sterne, and I've seen the specimen. It will make a wonderful addition to our collection. The guests should be quite impressed with the presentation tonight."

"Tensford will make sure of it," she said wryly. "His enthusiasm is contagious."

"Yes. Mr. Stillwater has certainly caught the fossil bug. He had as many questions for me as I had for you. He lives in the county, nearby?"

"Yes. His estate lies about ten miles away, I believe. I did see him speaking to you quite seriously in the parlor, before dinner."

"I didn't mind. It's always a pleasure to talk with someone with shared interests. Mr. Stillwater meant to go straight to the room where Sterne is watching over the fossil after dinner. He said he wants to examine it thoroughly before he has to fight the crowd. He certainly seems quite knowledgeable." He grinned and gave her a gallant bow. "Although, of course, the conversation was not nearly so enjoyable as talking with a lovely lady like you."

She smiled her thanks. She and Lucy had made a real effort tonight, and she knew she looked well. Her under gown was one of simple elegance, with detailed white-on-white embroidery, while her over gown was of shot-silk in her favorite color of bluish green. The colors changed with every shift of the light and perfectly set off her skin and hair.

Nearly everyone smiled and nodded as she passed, which felt remarkably gratifying. At least, it would if she didn't know it was all due to Keswick.

He had not been present at dinner. Clearly Hope had known that he would not attend, as there was no embarrassingly empty place at the table.

Glory did not crane her neck to look for him, although she was sorely tempted. She kept her attention on Mr. Simon, and tried not to debate whether finding Keswick here would be worse than not.

On the one hand, she ached to think that this afternoon had been their final goodbye. On the other, she knew she would also ache to see him tonight, to act calm and collected as he smiled, perhaps flirted, and definitely danced with other women—or any woman who was not her.

She was destined for misery either way, it seemed.

They passed by Miss Vernon, who stared, but did not speak. Glory thought the sour look she cast her way made her pale yellow silk resemble curdled milk instead of springtime blossoms. She walked past, then stopped and looked over her shoulder. "What a shame, Miss Vernon, that you did not bring a pair of long gloves on your journey north."

The other girl gasped and clapped a hand over the unsightly welt on her arm. "Well, I told you the shopping would be highly inadequate in your tiny excuse for a village," she sneered. "There was not a pair to be found anywhere."

Glory merely smiled. She knew there had been none available. She'd sent Lucy down last evening to buy up every single pair.

She gave the girl a sympathetic look and walked on.

"There is my spot, Mr. Simon." Hope had made sure that there were chairs scattered throughout the ballroom, but Glory knew this one had the best view of the room. "You may leave me here, but I urge you to go over and speak to Miss Munroe. She will likely be very busy dancing, soon."

"Which is she?" he asked, looking around.

"There, the very pretty girl in pink. I know she is looking forward to speaking with you. She is very interested in the natural sciences, you see."

"Is that so?" He held the chair for her and bowed over her hand. "Thank you for you company at dinner, my lady. I have greatly enjoyed it."

He turned to go, but found his path suddenly blocked.

"Good evening, Lady Glory." Lady Tresham smiled at Mr. Simon like a cat that had just scented prey. "Won't you introduce me to your friend?"

Glory made the introductions.

"If you know of someone available for the opening dance, Lady Glory, please let me know. I've somehow failed to engage a partner for that one." She smiled at Glory, looked at poor Mr. Simon through her lashes, and turned to go.

"Oh, I say, I'm free for the first set, should you care to dance it with me." Mr. Simon looked slightly dazzled.

"Oh, how lovely. Thank you." Lady Tresham took his arm and began to lead him away. "Tell me, please, about your position. It must be fascinating." She grinned over her shoulder as they left and Glory laughed and gave her a nod and a wave for good luck.

Sitting back, she gazed around, and froze. Keswick stood near the double doors, watching her. He inclined his head to his left, toward the buffet table at the far corner of the room, where Hope had made sure to feature plenty of lobster patties. Glory gave a nod and stood, and began to casually make her way around the perimeter of the dance floor, to meet him there.

She was greeted often as she went, and paused to exchange pleasantries several times. A glance or two showed Keswick making the same, slow progress. Mr. Sommers waved at her and stopped to tell of the news he'd received from home—the birth of a colt with a distinguished pedigree and the hope of a great future on the racing circuit. She offered warm congratulations, then moved on, her gaze seeking out Keswick.

She began to move with purpose when she saw him. He was laughing with Miss Rutledge and Sir Blackwell in the opposite corner, but his father was fast approaching behind him, his expression grim.

She started to hurry.

By the time she grew near, his father had engaged him. Miss Vernon stood nearby, a satisfied smirk on her face. Glory eased into the crowd and moved along the wall to hide her approach. She came upon the group from behind.

" . . . childish behavior." She caught only the end of this particular scathing remark. "You cannot avoid me forever," the earl continued.

"No, but I can rejoice in every moment not spent in your company, sir. And I believe I'd like to add a few more to the balance." Keswick bowed. "Good evening."

His father reached out and seized his arm to stop him. "No. I've let the leash play out long enough. It's time I pulled you back in. This nonsense about refusing to marry ends now. I've arranged perfectly satisfactory terms with the Vernon girl's father. He's agreed to increase her dowry, included shares in his chemical manufactory, and has offered a bonus to be paid out to you both on the birth of an heir."

"Stud fees?" Keswick said in disgust. "No, Father. I'm not marrying the chit."

"You will."

Keswick had turned to go, but he looked back in exasperation. "Just stop. There is no need for this endless, horrifying dance. Just, please, let me be. I've already told you, you don't have any leverage over me. Not anymore."

"I do, though."

Keswick started to walk away.

The earl took a step after him. "Your good name," he said, more loudly than he perhaps should have. "Stop, Keswick, and listen." He gave his son a terrifying smile. "I am announcing your betrothal. Tonight. Now. You will smile and agree and dance with the girl when they open the ball."

Keswick glanced over to where Miss Vernon waited. He shook his head.

"Don't even consider not cooperating. I will swear to all and sundry that you have known of the negotiations, courted the girl, and agreed to the settlements. If you disavow my words, then I, and the girl, and her father will all name you a liar and a jilt. The world will know you as a man who has broken his vow. A man without honor."

Keswick, suddenly pale, looked at the man in horror. "You wouldn't," he breathed.

"I will. And you will become a pariah. We'll sue for breach of promise. You will be cut by your friends, turned away from your clubs. Shunned by all of good society. Your little empire?" he said with disdain. "Finished. For who will risk doing business with a man who does not honor his commitments?"

Glory watched all of the color drain from Keswick's face. Her heart fell—but fury and determination rose like the fiery ascent of the sun inside of her.

The musicians were tuning their instruments. She didn't have much time. She caught sight of Miss Munroe passing and slipped out to grab her. She whispered frantically in her ear.

Her friend pulled back to stare in amazement. "You don't mean . . .?"

"Now, please!" Glory urged. "It is *vital.*"

Miss Munroe glanced over to see Keswick and his father arguing face to face. She raised her brows at Glory and turned to hurry away.

Glory threw her shoulders back. She stepped over to join the group in the corner.

"Good evening, my lords. Has my sister not created a magical atmosphere for us this evening?" She turned to Keswick. "Sir, I hear the musicians preparing themselves. Are you ready for our dance?" Not waiting for his answer, she turned to his father. "If you do not care to dance, Lord Braunton, then may I suggest you try the lobster patties? They are one of Hope's specialties."

She took Keswick's arm, but Miss Vernon had joined them, wearing a ferocious frown on her face. "What is this foolery? You do not dance. We have all heard it said so."

Glory have her a haughty look. "Then you have heard wrong. I dance *one* dance in particular. And with *one* gentleman only." She cast a dazzling smile up at Keswick. "And he has promised me the opening set."

She gave them a nod, then tugged on Keswick's arm. Looking stunned, he led her away. But when she actually stepped out onto the empty dance floor, he stopped abruptly. Frowning, he shook his head.

Raising a brow, she nodded.

"Glory, what are you doing?"

"I'm fighting tyranny, just as you told me I should." The musicians were settling in. She tugged his arm again, and still looking confounded, he accompanied her to the middle of the floor and stood ready, across from her.

The music began. She curtsied. He bowed. Where in heaven's

name were the other dancers? Why were they the only ones on the dance floor? She risked a glance around—and froze in her tracks.

Everyone stared at her. Every person in the room. Ladies whispered behind their fans. She could see Miss Parscate talking low and fast to the group around her. Gentlemen watched with the same morbid fascination she suspected they must trot out at a bear baiting or a cockfight—in anticipation of blood.

She started to shake. It was her worst nightmare, come to ugly, soul-chilling life.

"No." Keswick looked directly into her eyes. "It's too late to panic. You got me out of there," he nodded toward the corner. "I will get you through this."

She blinked at him, unable to respond.

"*Move,*" he ordered.

He was right. She lifted her chin. Extended her arm. Took his. And began to step in a circle with him, in time to the music.

They made the first revolution. Faced each other again. Took each other's opposite hand and began to circle in the opposite direction.

She stumbled. Tripped. Nearly went down.

An audible gasp came from the crowd.

A shiver of icy shame ran down her spine.

But Keswick was there, supporting her, setting her back on balance, and guiding her smoothly through the turning.

And at last, others came. Hope and Tensford pushed through the crowd and hurried onto the dance floor. Miss Rutledge and Sir Blackwell followed, then Lady Tresham and Mr. Simon.

Glory and Keswick carried on, able to meet in the middle and advance down the line. They joined hands with Hope and Tensford and she successfully managed the steps forward and back again.

Then she was facing Keswick again. He grinned triumph at her and all of the tension abruptly drained out of her. She relaxed into his grip and gazed into his eyes while they circled again.

At first he looked at her hungrily, like a man enjoying his last meal before execution. But she knew better. She smiled at him in relief and exultation as she continued to navigate the dance and in the complete joy of doing it with him. Her leg was forgotten. Any thought of strife abandoned. The rest of the ballroom faded and only the two of them existed, and for several, long, wonderful moments she reveled in his gentle touch, in the pride in his expression and in the ever-present pull between them.

Eventually, the music ended. She gradually came awake, back to the reality of his hand in hers, of Hope hugging her with tears in her eyes, of Tensford shaking Keswick's hand.

She came awake to the truth—there was still more fighting to be done.

"I need to speak with Tensford," she began. But the pain in her ankle and the ache in her leg were vying for attention, too. "I need to sit down."

Keswick immediately lent her his arm and she leaned heavily upon it, while trying to seem as if she was not. He acted utterly casually too, understanding without words her wish not to appear fatigued.

He escorted her to the side of the dance floor and claimed her a seat as the guests lined up for the second dance of the set. Glory took her sister's hand. "I need to speak to Tensford, right away."

"He's right here," Hope said and pulled her husband forward.

Tensford knelt down beside her and she reached out and squeezed her brother in law's hand. "Listen, Tensford. As soon as this dance finishes, you must call for the attention of the crowd." She met Keswick's gaze. "You must announce our engagement."

Keswick choked. "What? Glory, no!"

Hope's breath caught.

Tensford's gaze moved gravely between them. "Drastic measures, Kes?"

"No. Do not listen to her," Keswick ordered.

"You must! His father means to announce his betrothal to Miss Vernon, despite his refusal of the idea. The earl is scheming with her and her rich father. They mean to force Keswick's hand. He'll have to marry the girl or they will see him shunned. He's threatened to sue for breach of promise and blacken his name with everyone in the *ton* and in the business world."

"I don't care," Keswick insisted. "Either way, I am defeated. I will not carry you down into the muck with me."

"I've already pulled you from the muck once, damn you." She laughed weakly. "I'll do it now, as well, for it's more than your precious boots that are in danger this time."

He shook his head.

"You listen to me, Keswick. I will not see them win—not when your destruction is their aim. Either way, married to her, or with reputation and opportunity destroyed—they will make you miserable. And do you think they will stop at this? No. They will never stop trying to destroy you. I'm forging us a different path. All you have to do is take it. And finally, this ends here and now."

"I cannot let you—"

"You cannot stop me." She reached up and pulled him down so that she could place a hand on that magnificent jaw line. "I've seen how your father's manipulations have convinced you that you do not deserve love or caring, or that, once given, it will be snatched away." She blinked back tears. "I'm telling you, Keswick, that *it is not so*. I admire you, so greatly. I love you, so dearly. I will never abandon you. I will always be your friend, or your lover, or whatever it is that you need and choose. I will be proud to be your betrothed for a time. For a short time, if that is all you wish." She gave a shrug. "We will ensure your freedom today, and then, in a few weeks, I can cry off. We can decide that we do not suit. I am sure I will be considered eccentric amongst the *ton*, so this will only add to my reputation. As long as we part amicably, no one need be destroyed."

She looked at Tensford. "Do it."

He looked at Hope, who was still fighting tears. Her sister took her hand and nodded.

Tensford let out a long sigh. He glanced back to the dance floor where the set was ending. He strode out in the middle and called for attention.

Glory let go of her sister and held both of Keswick's hands tightly. His brow was furrowed as if he was weighing steps and consequences. He still had not responded to her declaration.

It took a moment for everyone to quiet down, but Tensford beckoned a footman to bring him a flute of champagne and stood with his glass raised. "I know many of you are expecting to hear me expound upon the very great discovery made here at Greystone days ago. The specimen found near our cliffs is indeed a fascinating object. But I have only just made an even more wonderful discovery—"

There was a murmur and a growing wave of consternation by the door. A lady shrieked. The crowd parted and Mr. Sterne stumbled into the open space around Tensford, supported by Miss Munroe.

Glory gasped. Blood ran down Sterne's face and he held his sleeve pressed to his temple. "It's gone," he said, clearly distraught. "The fossil is gone."

CHAPTER 20

Chaos erupted in the ballroom. Hope rushed to Sterne and began to give quiet, effective orders, calling for water and bandages and footmen to help him to a chair. Tensford checked to be sure Sterne was in no immediate danger, exchanged a few words with him, then rushed out.

Nearly half of the guests followed on his heels, eager to witness more of the spectacle. The other half scurried about the ballroom, fussing over Sterne, questioning Miss Munroe, gossiping, or just generally contributing to the pandemonium.

It all seemed utterly appropriate to Keswick. It all mirrored the turmoil in his heart so very well.

Glory. She clutched his hands, still, and he gazed down at her in wonder and consternation. Another gift. She'd given him her heart in a way that no one had ever done for him.

He rather felt as if the giving of her heart had set his own free.

They moved Sterne off to a more comfortable location and Keswick turned to find his father behind him, staring with narrowed eyes. "I know what you are trying to do," he spat. "It will not work. You will marry—"

People were starting to look.

"Lord Braunton." Glory let go of him and rose from the chair. She stepped up to his father. The old man glared down at her. Keswick moved beside her while she smiled sweetly up at him. "It was such a lucky chance that led you north, so that you could be here for the announcement of our engagement." She transferred her smile to the guests around them. "Don't you all agree?"

"You . . . you . . ."

"Indeed." Lady Tresham was in the group. She eyed the earl closely and moved in. "Is that the announcement Tensford was trying to make before he was so unfortunately interrupted? Betrothed! Let me be the very first to congratulate you, then!" She transferred her gaze to his father. "And you, my lord. I congratulate you on your good fortune. You are welcoming a special young lady into your family." She gave Glory a laughing nod. "In fact, I think you'll find you have more in common than you might expect."

His father turned a mottled red.

Keswick tightened his arm around Glory.

His father nearly spit anger when he spoke. "It won't—"

"I know, Father. It won't be the same." Keswick cast a wry look at the crowd beginning to form around them. "Certainly, I will never be the same. I suspect I will be happy—in a way that I never thought to achieve."

His father glared daggers at him, then turned to stalk away.

Keswick turned to face her. His instinct was to whisk her away to tell her all that was in his heart, but they needed this to be seen and heard—and she deserved a public declaration. "Honestly, I never thought my heart would open this way. I've been a fool for so long, I almost missed what was right before me. I liked Lady Glory. I laughed at her quick wit and enjoyed her sprightly conversation. I admired her beauty—and her seat on a horse."

Someone laughed and he raised a brow. "In all seriousness—have you ever *seen* her ride?" Now everyone laughed, even Glory.

"The bit that scares me most is that I almost didn't recognize what a treasure she is. Fortunately, my addled brain cleared enough, and my skeptical heart grew brave enough to realize that in her care is the only place for me. I humbly ask her to take my hand, even though she never meant to marry and I am nothing but a rakehell—and sure to be a bother."

"It must be you," he said directly to her. "And it must be forever. You are the only one I could ever trust to see inside of me—and still want to stay."

Now there were tears in her eyes. "It must be you," she whispered. "Because you are the only one who looks at me and sees more, instead of less."

Someone applauded. Lady Tresham loudly called for a toast to the happy couple. People surrounded them to shake hands and offer hugs and kisses and slaps on the back. Miss Myland herded in a pair of footmen with trays of champagne and Hope and Tensford arrived back just in time to take up a glass.

"Let us raise our glasses," Tensford called. "Sterne will recover quickly, thank goodness. And while it seems I have lost a fossil, I have gained a brother-in-law—who also happens to be one of my best friends." He smiled down at his wife. "I am the most fortunate of men."

"I beg to differ," Keswick objected. And with a wicked grin, he bent to kiss his betrothed.

EPILOGUE

"Here, my darling. I've made a copy of the young *lavandula angustifolia* for Lady Tensford. Will you give it to her, the next time you visit at Greystone?"

"Yes, Mama." Penelope Munroe knew better than to compliment the artistry of the botanical drawing her mother handed her, even though it was quite beautifully done. She'd suffered enough lectures on the importance of technique, exacting detail and scientific documentation over beauty. Still, privately, she marveled over her mother's talent.

"And will you remind her, please, that I would like a mature specimen in bloom when she has one, so that I may capture the complete record of the plant?"

"I will, Mama."

"I suppose she's had too much on her mind to remember," her mother sighed. "She must be so glad to be done with the fuss and bother of the wedding."

Fuss and bother described anything that drew her mother's attention away from her work.

"Although, to be fair, I find myself glad that you and your father convinced me to attend the affair," her mother conceded.

Penelope blinked in surprise.

"The crowd was horrid, of course, but even my scientific fellows have heard the gossip surrounding the event. Several have included questions about it in their latest letters. I've answered and assured them that the rumors are true. The couple did wed under a flower-bedecked bower in a field by a river." She shook her hand and stretched her fingers. "I've included descriptions and images of the local flora used, in each of my responses."

"That was kind of you."

"What is the scientific name of the autumn gentian?" her mother asked suddenly.

"*Gentianella amarella.*" Penelope was used to her mother springing random test questions at her.

"Very good. They were attractive, I admit." She sighed. "Most of the questions, however, were about the horse. None of them could fathom a bride arriving alone on horseback and *riding* down the aisle, makeshift though it was."

"I thought it was lovely—and very fitting for Glory, of course. She was practically glowing, all through the day."

"Yes, well, thank goodness you are not horse-mad or prone to other such peculiarities."

"I don't think my interest in the natural sciences is considered normal, Mama."

"Poppycock," her mother declared. "It is the modern age and you have a fine mind. It would be unnatural to waste it. It should not be considered strange to take advantage of it. It is time women gave their intellects the same attention as they do their wardrobes. We have a duty to show them how to do so."

"Yes, Mama." She was very familiar with her mother's views.

"In any case, doubtless Lady Tensford is happy to get back to her own duties, now that all of her guests have departed at last. Heaven knows I was relieved when your cousins all went home."

"I do believe she is looking forward to Glory and her new husband returning to the neighborhood, at least," Penelope replied. "I had a letter from Glory, and she is vastly enjoying their bridal journey. Ireland is beautiful, she says, and there are plenty of horses and stud farms for them to visit, but they will be coming back to Roudley Farm before too long. They mean to stay here for some time, at least for part of the year, to get their own horse breeding program started." She took a breath, reaching for a relaxed tone. "Also, I did hear that at least one guest has returned to Greystone."

"So soon?" her mother said with disapproval.

"Yes. Mr. Sterne is back." And it took all of her considerable willpower not to let show the fluttering of her heart or the anticipatory shiver of her spine. But the very last thing she wanted was for her mother to get a hint of her interest in the gentleman. "I believe he feels it is his duty to discover who it was who struck him down and how they disappeared so quickly with that very large fossil."

"Why should he?"

"It was under his care when it disappeared." Penelope swallowed. She suspected it was partially her fault—and that she had distracted Mr. Sterne from his vigilance. "He feels responsible."

"It is good of him to help, then, I suppose. I do know Tensford is distraught at the loss of it."

"I thought I would offer to help them in their investigation—at least while they are looking at things locally."

"Why?" her mother asked in surprise.

"I do like Lord Tensford. He and his family have been so kind to me. And Mr. Sterne is good company—and he is well known in some naturalist circles."

"Not in the botanical community."

"No."

"Is he published?"

"Of course. And his uncle is Mr. John Sterne."

"Oh, yes." Her mother thought a moment. "That is a well known name. Well, then. Perhaps you should pursue the connection. You never know when it might come in handy."

"Very true. I will, then, Mama."

Penelope watched her mother turn and head back to her studio. Then, being her mother's child, she turned to pick up a pen and began to organize her plan of attack.

246

ABOUT THE AUTHOR

USA Today Bestselling author Deb Marlowe adores History, England and Men in Boots. Clearly she was destined to write Historical Romance.

A Golden Heart winner and Rita nominee, Deb writes Regency Romance and Young Adult Fantasy Adventure.

A proud geek, history buff and story addict, she loves to talk with readers! Find her discussing books, movies, TV, recipes from Deb Marlowe's Regency Kitchen and her infamous Men in Boots on Facebook, Twitter, Instagram, and Pinterest.

Connect with Deb
www.DebMarlowe.com
Deb@DebMarlowe.com

ALSO BY DEB MARLOWE

A Series of Unconventional Courtships

Love Me, Lord Tender

Nothing But a Rakehell

Kiss Me, Lady, One More Time

A Cup of Cheer

Why Do Earls Fall in Love

The Half Moon House Series

The Novels

The Love List

The Leading Lady

The Lady's Legacy

The Lady's Lover

The Novellas

An Unexpected Encounter

A Slight Miscalculation

A Waltz in the Park

Liberty and the Pursuit of Happiness

Beyond a Reasonable Duke

Lady, It's Cold Outside

The Earl's Hired Bride

The Castle Keyvnor Pixies

Lady Tamsyn and the Pixie's Curse

Lord Locryn and the Pixie's Kiss

Writing as D.M. Marlowe:
The Eye of the Ninja Chronicles
Eye of the Ninja
Obsidian's Eye
The Fire in the Ice

www.ingramcontent.com/pod-product-compliance
Lightning Source LLC
Chambersburg PA
CBHW021247200726
48288CB00015B/2549